➤ 11,000
YEARS LOST

Other books by Peni R. Griffin

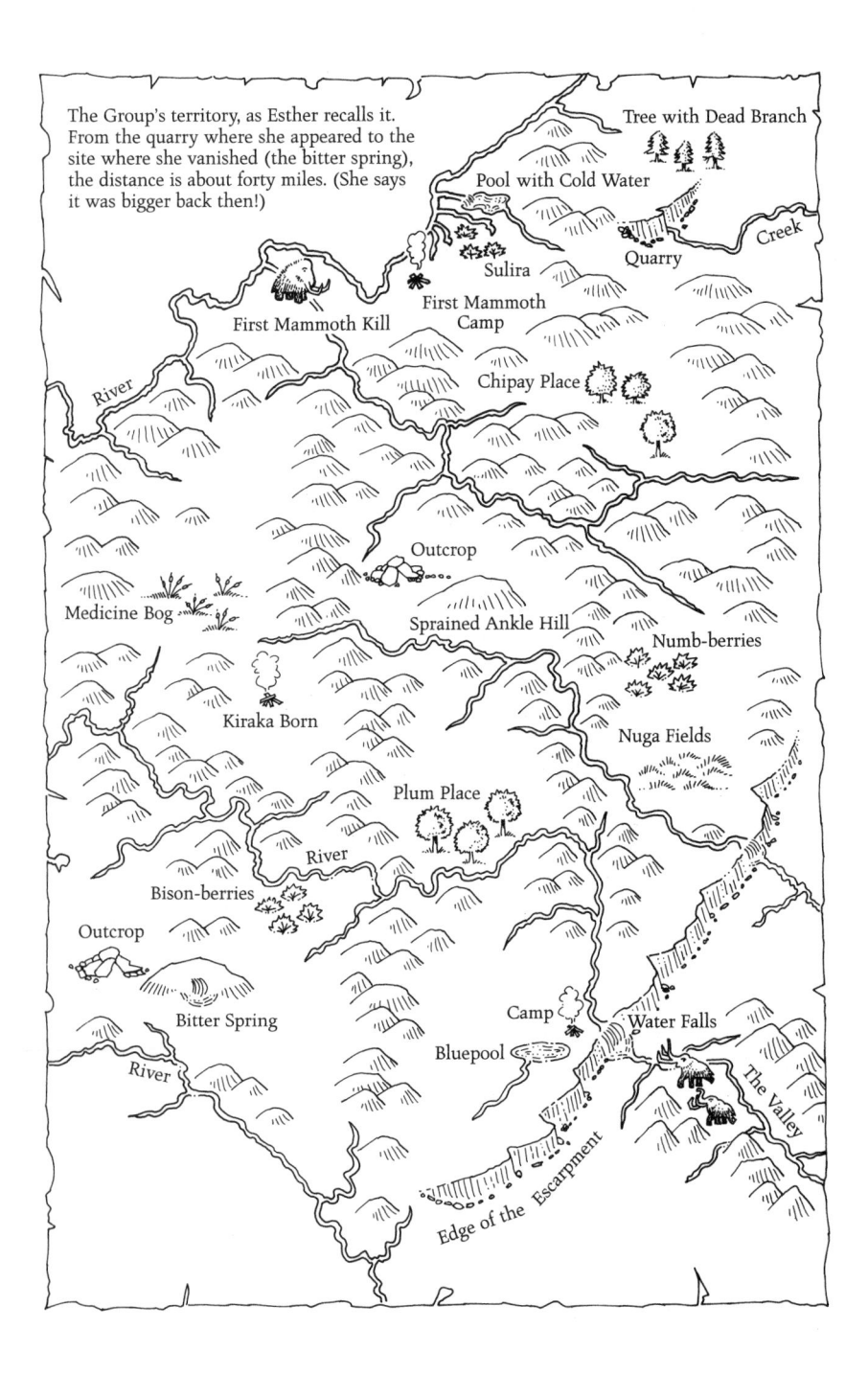

The Group's territory, as Esther recalls it. From the quarry where she appeared to the site where she vanished (the bitter spring), the distance is about forty miles. (She says it was bigger back then!)

Tree with Dead Branch

Pool with Cold Water

Creek

Quarry

Sulira

First Mammoth Camp

First Mammoth Kill

Chipay Place

River

Outcrop

Medicine Bog

Sprained Ankle Hill

Numb-berries

Kiraka Born

Nuga Fields

Plum Place

River

Bison-berries

Outcrop

Bitter Spring

Camp

Water Falls

Bluepool

The Valley

River

Edge of the Escarpment

11,000 YEARS LOST

PENI R. GRIFFIN

AMULET BOOKS
NEW YORK

The Library of Congress has cataloged the hardcover edition as follows:
Griffin, Peni R.
11,000 years lost / Peni R. Griffin.
p. cm.
Summary: Fascinated with the archaeological dig that is going on near her Texas home, eleven-year-old Esther magically travels back in time to the Pleistocene era and discovers first-hand how people lived at that time. Includes a list of sources and author's notes.
ISBN 0-8109-4822-2
[1. Time travel—Fiction. 2. Prehistoric peoples—Fiction. 3. Glacial epoch—Fiction.] I. Title: Eleven thousand years lost. II. Title.
PZ7.G881353Aae 2004
[Fic]—dc22
2004011184

Paperback ISBN 978-0-8109-9251-1

Originally published in hardcover by Amulet Books in 2004
Text copyright © 2007 Peni R. Griffin
Design by Interrobang Design Studio
Map by Rick Britton

Printed and bound in U.S.A.
10 9 8 7 6 5 4 3

HNA
harry n. abrams, inc.
a subsidiary of La Martinière Groupe
115 West 18th Street
New York, NY 10011
www.hnabooks.com

For Gramma, in one direction through time,
and Hannah, in the other

THE GROUP'S FAMILY TREE

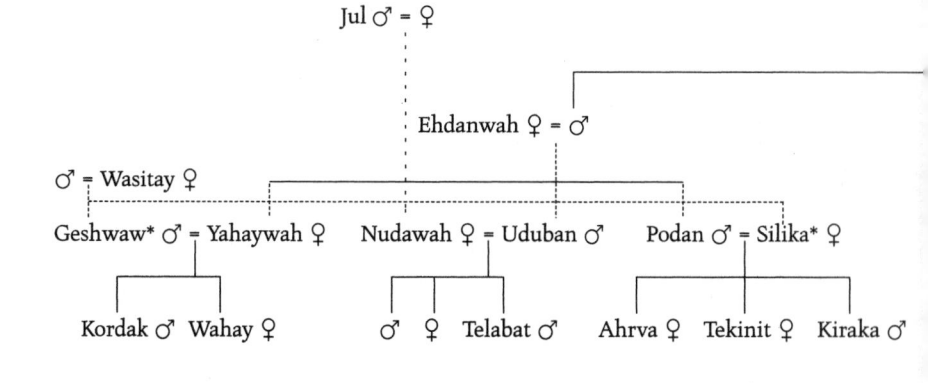

*siblings

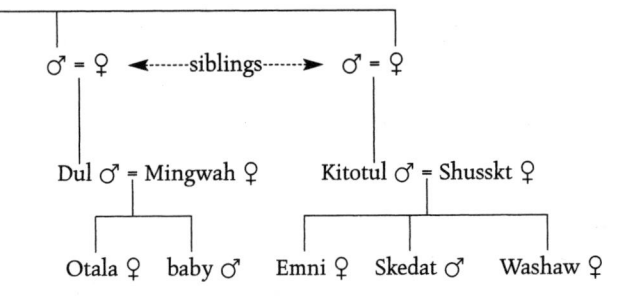

► CONTENTS

►11,000
YEARS LOST

ONE

➤ DR. DURHAM

Well—if you're sure she won't be in the way," said Esther's mother.

The archaeologist—a scrawny woman with blue eyes younger than her skin—shook her head. "She'd be doing me a favor, Ms. Aragones. I need her to show me where she found the artifacts."

Esther tried not to fidget too hard. *"Please, Mama?"*

Mama frowned at the card in her hand. It was embossed with the logo of the University of Texas and printed with the archaeologist's name—Dr. B. A. Durham—as well as a mobile phone number, an office phone number, a fax number, and an e-mail address. The card made Dr. Durham not a stranger, and the place where Esther had found the stone point was close enough to walk to, and Dr. Durham had *said* she needed Esther to show it to her, so what was the problem? Esther crossed both sets of fingers and held herself still, until Mama said: "All right. But if she gets to be a nuisance, you send her right back."

"Mama!" *I'm not a little kid,* Esther wanted to say; *I'm eleven, I know how to act*—but Dr. Durham had opened the door, saying: "I'm sure she'll be very helpful."

Esther skipped ahead and then walked backward to slow herself down. But she didn't have to slow down much. Dr. Durham was a little woman, but she took long strides, and unlike other grown-ups Esther had tried to show the place to, she was dressed to climb the hill—hiking boots, jeans, and a gimme cap with a multicolored world map on it. "The kids are always picking up arrowheads off the playground," Esther said. "But these were different. Mr. Morales didn't know what they were, exactly."

"The unbroken one's a preform," said Dr. Durham. "That means it was all ready to be made into a tool, but somebody lost it before he had a chance to finish. And the broken one is a Clovis point. That means it was made about eleven thousand years ago, give or take a thousand years."

Eleven thousand years. The back of Esther's head crawled at the idea: a thousand times as long as she'd been alive. "I didn't think people'd been in Texas that long."

"Possibly longer," said Dr. Durham. "The people that made Clovis points are the first ones we're sure of. They lived at the same time as a bunch of other animals that died out. Big animals—megafauna."

"Is that why my, uh, Clovis point is so much bigger than the arrowheads? Because they had to hunt big animals with it?"

"Those little arrowheads killed big animals, like bison," Dr. Durham pointed out. "Arrowheads are small because the arrow has to be light in order to shoot it out of the bow. When Clovis points were made, bows and arrows hadn't been invented yet. People think they were fastened to spears."

"People think," said Esther. "What do *you* think?"

"I think if you think too much, you see your ideas instead of the facts." She looked straight at Esther, as if she were a grown-up—or a fact. "But spears are a good bet. We have reasonably good evidence that Clovis people used atlatls."

"Whichl whichls?"

"Spear-throwers. It's a stick with a notch on one end." Dr. Durham gestured. "You put the end of the spear in the notch, and then you wind up like this and throw the spear. It makes your arm about a foot longer, and the longer your arm, the harder you can hurl the spear, which means it can go farther and hit harder, which is important if you're hunting mammoths."

"Mammoths!" Esther's brain quickly shuffled through what she knew about mammoths. She didn't want Dr. Durham to think she was stupid. "They lived in the Arctic. So it must've been a lot colder back then. Was that the, um, Ice Age?"

"It was, but Texas didn't have glaciers and woolly mammoths. We had Columbian mammoths, which were bigger and probably not very hairy. And we know people ate them. We've found the points in among the bones. Some people think that's why there're no mammoths now. But Clovis people hunted bison, too, and bison are still here. They've changed, but they're here." Far from finding Esther's questions a nuisance, she seemed eager to talk. "The Ice Age was ending, so there was global warming. Other animals moved in from Asia, like elk and grizzly bears. Maybe they brought diseases. Maybe humans killed off some megafauna and diseases killed off others and others couldn't adapt to the climate change. In the archaeological record, the extinction looks sudden, but it took at least five hundred years, plenty of time for multiple things to go wrong."

"That's a long time!"

"In human terms, yes. Especially if, as is possible, people only lived to be forty years old or so."

"Can't you tell how long they lived from their bones?"

"We could, if we could find their bones. Mostly all we find are Clovis points. It's exciting to find a new point, because you start to hope: *If there's a point here, maybe there's something else, too.*" Dr. Durham was grinning. "Is that the playground where you found it?"

"It wasn't in the playground," said Esther. "Come on."

She sprinted past the elementary school up the hill, her sneakers slipping where spring rains had washed worn soil away. "See—the playground fence is at the foot of the hill. That's where we find the arrowheads."

Dr. Durham pulled a much-folded, worn piece of paper out of the breast pocket of her vest. It was a photocopy of a map Mr. Morales had put on the bulletin board, showing the school, the play equipment, the course of the creek, the planned computer center on the hill, and the arrowheads marked with lots of Xs. Dr. Durham looked at the map and the landscape and back at the map. "I see. That line of trees is the creek."

"It's not even a creek unless it rains," said Esther. "About once a year it floods, and then you find new arrowheads."

"Showing that the surface scatter is eroding from a site farther up the creek, yes," said Dr. Durham. "And it was here you found the preform and the point?" She held her finger to a spot on the map, and scanned the ground.

"Here's where I found the preform." Esther knelt by the pile of rocks she'd made, and started unbuilding it. "I tried to stick my pencil in the ground, but it wouldn't stand up, so I covered it. You can see where I took the rock out."

Dr. Durham pulled a camera out of her side vest pocket and took a picture before she knelt down. "How did you know to mark it?"

"Mr. Morales had been talking about the arrowheads and the computer center," Esther explained. "He said we're almost all of us Indians, more or less—we're mostly Mexican in our school, you know, and even a lot of the Anglo kids say they're part Cherokee or something. Anyway, he said the arrowheads were our history and the school board was going to wipe that out. The principal got mad. He says Mr. Morales is supposed to teach math and science, not history."

"Science is the only way to learn this history," said Dr. Durham. "It's not as though the Clovis folks knew how to write. So anyway, you listened to Mr. Morales, and you went looking."

"Yes, ma'am. Mr. Morales said the washed-down arrowheads were useless and it was important to find things in the place where they'd been for umpteen thousand years. I found the . . . the Clovis point over there. I'll show you—it's easier to get at from the top. What are you doing?"

"Checking out your other rocks," said Dr. Durham, turning over the pieces of her pile one by one. "See this one? And this one? They've been worked, too. Somebody broke this one off a larger piece, and decided it wasn't good enough—see that flaw in the flint surface? If you made a point out of it, it'd probably break the first time you used it."

It looked like a rock, a smooth gray flint core with a rough white layer around it. "How do you know a person broke it?" Esther asked, feeling very grown-up and scientific. "Mr. Morales says rock expands when it gets hot, and shrinks when it gets cold, and breaks itself."

"It does, but those fractures look different." Dr. Durham picked over the rocks and selected a smaller piece. Holding them up side by side, she touched each surface. "See here—and here? This is a man-made break, and this one is natural. We'd have to put it under a microscope to be one-hundred-percent positive, but I'd bet money on it. Were there any flint chips lying around?"

"Lots," said Esther. "Just a minute, I'll find you some." *What could you tell from chips?* she wondered, so excited she could hardly see.

"Yes, here's some," said Dr. Durham, also scanning the ground. She touched one next to Esther's hand. "See that shape? Flint that's been chipped off on purpose has different shapes than flint that's flaked off from normal geological processes. Sometimes you can rebuild the original rock from the flakes, and you get a mold of the tool that was finished and carried away. And if a chip hasn't been disturbed, you'd be surprised at what you can find out about it, with enough expensive equipment."

Esther's heart sank. "And I shoved a bunch of chips around to get them out of my way! I'm sorry!"

"Hey, if you hadn't been smart enough to spot the preform, I wouldn't know the site was here at all, much less be able to learn anything from it," said Dr. Durham. "Let's see where you found the Clovis point."

Esther led her downslope, through Queen Anne's lace, tufts of bear grass, and baby hackberry trees. "Careful," she said. "You'll have to crawl. And there's snakes."

"What kind?"

"I don't know—snakes."

"If it doesn't rattle, it doesn't scare me." Dr. Durham crawled after Esther underneath the ledge to the little hackberry with the hole by its roots, to which Esther had tied her shoelace. Mama had been mad, but it was a neon pink shoelace and made a great marker. Esther pointed at the hole without touching it. "I saw the end, and pulled, and it came out. I couldn't believe how big it was." And how smooth, and how sharp! She could still feel the shape in her palm, the curving base and the regular irregularities where someone had chipped it into shape; notably a smooth hollow on either side, extending from the base to about a third of the way up. The fingers she'd cut on the edges were still sore, but she didn't care.

"Clovis points are—amazing," said Dr. Durham, lying on her stomach to take a picture of the hole. "Beautiful. Clovis people liked pretty stone. Agate from the Panhandle was traded as far away as the Rocky Mountains."

She put the camera back into her pocket and examined the ground, spiraling out from the hackberry. Esther crawled backward, scanning, remembering the moment she had spotted the peculiar shape jutting out of the ground below the root. Could she do it again? With Dr. Durham to tell her how to do it right?

"And you can find them lying on the ground," Dr. Durham went on, dreamily. "Perfect and sharp, after eleven millennia.

When someone finds one, it's like a little miracle; but it's also frustrating, because most of the time, that's all you find. One point. No animal bones, no human bones, no spear shafts, nothing to tell us who used them or how or why they went to so much trouble to make them . . . so . . . perfect."

She stopped, staring at the slope above the ledge. Esther stared, too, at dirt, chunks of rock, and a barkless, splintering, knobby-ended log. Dr. Durham took out her camera again.

"What is it?" asked Esther.

"Animal bone," said Dr. Durham. "Something biggish, but not huge. It reminds me of a camel leg."

"A camel? Here?"

"Oh, yes. Camels, horses, lions—they were all part of the megafauna that died out."

Esther's heart thumped. "Did people eat them?"

"They could have." Dr. Durham wound the camera. "Don't get too excited. It might have nothing to do with people. Or it might have the broken tip of your Clovis point in it."

Esther sank back on her heels, head whirling. "That would be—so cool."

Dr. Durham grinned. "Oh, it would," she said. "Thank you."

*C*hain-link fence went up around the site almost at once, but it was late May before Dr. Durham and her two assistants began marking out the hillside in grids of string and wooden stakes.

All the kids peered through the chain link; but Esther would sneak out of the playground to watch. She got detention a couple of times, but was the first to know that the site was a rock quarry, that Dr. Durham had found flint from this quarry—flint which she could prove came from *this* quarry—far to the east. She also knew all about the builder trying to rush the dig because he was impatient to start the computer center. For once, she had news at dinner, to go with Danny's news about high school, Dad's stories about customers, and Mama's office gossip.

She checked out all the books on the Ice Age in the school and neighborhood public libraries. None mentioned Texas. Only Dr. Durham could tell her what had happened right here.

When summer vacation started, Esther and her best friend, Oralia, would go to the dig in the cool mornings, and then go home to watch TV, play Nintendo, or catch a bus to the mall in the hot afternoon. Only TV, Nintendo, and the mall weren't as interesting as they'd used to be. After Oralia left for camp, Esther started staying at the site all day. Danny was supposed to look after her while Mama and Dad worked, but he slept late, and as long as she showed up by the time Mama got home, he didn't care what she did. Sometimes Mama would say: "Now, don't you be a nuisance up there" or "Isn't there anything else you could be doing?" Esther would answer: "I'm not" and "No."

Esther never touched anything she wasn't told to, not even the labeled plastic bags full of evidence that accumulated every day. Instead she passed tools, fetched drinks from the cooler, and turned the tap in the water drum to wash dirt through fine mesh that caught impossibly tiny things—like petrified pollen, which could be analyzed to learn that places that were now desert had once been lakes, or swamps, or pine forests. Dr. Durham and her graduate students, Mike and Delia, thanked her and explained everything they found, expecting her to understand.

Esther got up every morning before Mama and Dad did, so she could be at the site as soon as Dr. Durham arrived. She stayed till they packed up. She got her clothes and skin and hair filthy. She sweated till Dr. Durham made her take salt pills. Her legs got covered in bug bites and scratches. She'd never had a better time in her whole entire life.

June flew by. Dr. Durham said they would wrap up on the first of July. "Not a bad haul for such a small site," she said, taking out a cucumber sandwich. "But dating's going to be a pain. I wish we could find a hearth."

Delia had explained to Esther, and every single book she'd read about archaeology had explained again, that charcoal from a campfire could be run through an expensive scientific machine to find out how old it was. "If they spent so much time here, they had to have cooked sometime," Esther said.

"All we've found is quarry stuff," said Mike. "This is where they worked. The hearths will be where they lived."

"There *must* be campsites nearby," said Dr. Durham. "On top of the hill, maybe. Clovis people liked a view."

"So why don't you dig there?" asked Esther.

"Because the state pays me to salvage sites *they* pick, not to wander off digging on a guess."

"What if you found something accidentally? Would they pay you to dig it up then?"

"Sure," said Dr. Durham, "but I don't have time to look."

On the last night of June, Esther had trouble going to sleep; and when she did, she dreamed that she saw smoke at the hilltop. Dr. Durham said: "I can't go, but if you don't look, you'll never learn." So she climbed a hill covered with strange trees and bluebonnets. Children played with a ball made of leather strips tied around and around. Most wore skins, or were naked; but one had a knee-length, belted T-shirt. When Esther walked toward them, the little girl in the T-shirt waved. "It's too late, star-child," said a voice behind Esther; deep, and slurring, like a man with his mouth full. Esther understood him with her brain, not her ears. "You can't save her."

Esther turned, and saw the lighted numbers of her clock

radio. Three o'clock in the morning. *Save who from what?* The little girl had looked happy. She puzzled for a few minutes, uncertain why it seemed important; then fell asleep again until almost seven.

Dressing hurriedly, she ate cornflakes while examining the pictures in a book on Ice Age animals. The artist showed dire wolves, scimitar cats killing a baby mammoth, lions, improbably long-legged bears, and, in the last pages, men stabbing a mammoth mired in a bog. Esther was drinking off her milk when Mama shuffled in. "Good morning, sunshine. You're up early."

"Good morning. I'm always up by now."

"I guess so, lately." Mama got bake mix out of the cupboard. "I was going to make blueberry pancakes."

"You can still make them for Dad and Danny," said Esther. "I've got to go."

"Hang on," said Mama. "I figured we could have a nice family breakfast, and then go get you a new swimsuit."

"We can do that tomorrow," said Esther.

"But if we do it today, you won't hang out of your suit when we go swimming this afternoon. Don't you want to go swimming?"

"Sure. Tomorrow. Today's the day we pack up the site."

Mama frowned, getting milk, eggs, and blueberries out of the refrigerator. "Tomorrow we're going to the waterfall pool."

Esther saw the point. The waterfall pool was the best place anywhere for a picnic and a swim, if you went in the morning before the crowds arrived. Waiting till the malls opened and buying a suit would mean starting too late. But this was a matter of priorities. "The swimsuit I've got is good enough for one or two swims. This is the *last day* of the dig."

"And the *first day* of my vacation." Mama sounded impatient. "I'd like to spend it with my kids that I've barely seen yet this summer. You, me, and Danny—we'll get new suits, eat lunch at McDonald's, then go swimming."

Esther rinsed her bowl. Dr. Durham would have the site unlocked by now. "I bet we could be done at the site by lunch."

"I bet they'd be done by lunch whether you're there or not."

"No, they wouldn't. I save them lots of steps. We can't do your stuff till after lunch, anyway. Danny gets up at noon."

"He'll be earlier today," said Mama. "Now get dressed."

"I am dressed."

"Dressed fit to be seen. Good shorts and your new sneakers, and what about that bracelet Oralia got you?" Mama didn't think you were dressed properly unless you had on jewelry.

Esther plotted as she tied her hair with a new scrunch and put on her Fiesta Texas T-shirt and the hollow plastic bracelet with the stars floating in liquid inside, which Oralia had given her because "Esther" meant "star." She'd go up to the dig till Mama and Danny were ready. Danny would take forever to get up, then he'd eat pancakes, then he'd argue about the mall, then they'd come for her; and Dr. Durham would tell Mama that she wanted Esther around for the last day.

But Mama said no. "Find something else to do for once. You've been eating and sleeping and dreaming about this dig ever since you found those arrowheads."

"They weren't arrowheads, they were—"

"It's time to do *something else*. Pretend you're interested in the present instead of the past."

"But I'm supposed to help pack! Dr. Durham's expecting me!"

Mama reached for the phone with one hand while dropping batter onto the griddle with the other. "I'll tell her not to."

"But Mama—!"

"No buts. They've been really patient with you, but they don't need a kid underfoot when they're putting things away."

Esther turned and ran out the kitchen door, slamming the screen behind her. "Where do you think you're going?" Mama yelled.

"The playground!" Esther screamed. "Unless you think I'm going to bother the swing set!"

Fueled by anger, Esther ran hard for two blocks, till the weight of morning heat slowed her. Her long shadow pointed at the hill, where Dr. Durham's multicolored gimme cap was in the trench next to Delia's blue one. Mike stood at the screens, washing the last of the dirt, hoping for one or two more jigsaw pieces of the past.

Esther's soles slapped the sidewalk. Come tomorrow, no one would be here to show Esther how the pieces fit together.

Come tomorrow, no one but Esther would care.

She paused, panting, at the ruts leading to the site. Mike waved. She waved back. She could go up. She'd be grounded—but who cared?

They've been really patient with you, but they don't need a kid underfoot when they're putting things away.

She shoved the playground gate open so hard it hit the fence and bounced back, rattling. If she went up, Mama would say she was a nuisance, but if someone came after her and invited her, even Mama would say that was all right.

Tense with waiting, Esther walked up a seesaw to the middle, where she balanced, arms extended, trying to keep the board level as she listened for her name. Eleven thousand years from now, would archaeologists dig here and know it was a playground? Or would it be gone except for bits of rusted pipe? What would be left of *her* in eleven thousand years?

Esther leaped off of the seesaw, jarring loose the lump in her throat. Up in the quarry, Delia dug in the cooler for a drink. Had Mama called them? Was that why they weren't inviting her up? She'd *never* been underfoot. She could fetch things. She could spot bones. She could—

She could find the campsite.

The one Dr. Durham didn't have time to hunt for.

And if she happened to find a Clovis point—or another bone—or the dark signs of an old, old campfire—

She'd better move fast. Mama would probably come after her as soon as she could leave the pancakes. Esther climbed the fence separating the playground from the creek bottom and crashed through the tangled floodplain growth. Rye grass scratched her legs and branches of huisache and mesquite snagged her shirt and hair till she got into the nearly dry creek bed.

What if the most complete Clovis campsite in the world were upstream? What if Esther found it? She leaped from gravel patch to gravel patch, easily clearing the trickle of water. The rhythm of her body changed from anger to anticipation. Sparrows whistled; distant cars cruised the highway; the music of Delia's Melissa Etheridge CD drifted from the site. Mama would come looking for her, would tell Dr. Durham how bad Esther was, and Dr. Durham would say they'd missed her help, and then—in she'd walk, with her wonderful find!

Soon she was above the music, out of sight of the quarry, scanning the stony ground. If you wanted to find traces of people, you had to find where they'd been, and to do that, you had to see things from their point of view. Facing west, Esther saw the highway, the new housing development, the open sky and distant hills of the Edwards Plateau. All the books said that Ice Age people moved around a lot, looking for food. How would a Clovis girl have felt, facing west? Would the thought of all those wide, high miles have made her tired? Would she have been excited, thinking, *There are mammoths out there?*

To the east, the sun glared off shingle roofs, windshields, asphalt streets. Esther's brain went to work overlaying the view with an open prairie. For an instant, she almost had it— wide sky, camels grazing, lions stalking them.

The birds out-sang both Melissa Etheridge and the highway. A cloud passed, creating odd shadows, as if trees crowded the creek bed. Kids laughed. Esther looked around.

She saw long grass, weeds, and the familiar contour of the hill; but directly in front of her, the trunks of two evergreens that didn't exist rippled, framing bluebonnets, trees, and hill contours that didn't match. Two girls romped waist-high in flowers, gathering pinecones. The older girl wore a loose dress. The smaller girl, who had worn a T-shirt in Esther's dream, wore nothing.

Esther rubbed her eyes. Voices faded in and out, not English, not Spanish. A cool breeze blew between the trees onto her face, smelling of grass, flowers, and barbecue. A hot wind from one side smelled of gasoline and dust. She could see two different colors of sky, two different shapes of hilltops, overlapping, solid, simultaneous.

This was too weird. Could she still be dreaming?

You can't feel the ground pressing against your sneakers in dreams. You can't smell gasoline and barbecue.

In real life, no one let kids run around naked.

She glanced downhill toward the hidden quarry. What would Dr. Durham do, if she were here?

If you don't look, you'll never learn.

The evergreens held open a slice of spring. Three steps would take her there. Three steps would bring her back.

Esther held her breath as she walked between the trees, ducking under a dead branch.

THREE

➤ AHRVA AND TEKINIT

*T*he girls saw her, and fell silent. Birds sang. Trees rustled. The smell of barbecue mixed with those of flowers, water, and grass. She stared at the girls, who dropped armfuls of pinecones, snatched up sticks with pointed ends, and stared back. The small one didn't exactly hide, but the big one stepped in front of her.

"Um—hi," said Esther.

The big girl answered; but her words fell off of Esther's ears. Not English, not Spanish, though the girl looked Hispanic, with her dark tan skin and straight black ponytail. The girl spoke more loudly, stepping closer and waving the stick. The end closest to Esther had a stone point.

Esther ducked her head humbly, but looked the girl in the face. "I'm Esther," she said, resisting the impulse to hold her nose at the smell coming off the girl. That would get her beat up for sure! Esther was taller, but the stranger had visible muscles, plus the stick. Spear? The point would be sharp, whatever you called it.

The girl lowered the point as she talked, plucking at the Fiesta Texas logo on Esther's T-shirt, then at the shorts. "If you can do it, I can do it," Esther said, taking hold of the girl's dress, which was leather, with short reddish-brown hairs on the outside. It was basically a poncho, with the sides sewn up about three-quarters of the way.

The big girl let go of Esther's shorts and touched her bracelet. The little girl pointed, speaking shrilly. The big girl replied, and reached for Esther's scrunch.

Esther jerked her head away and pulled the cloth-covered elastic off, letting her hair fall loose. "You can look," she said, "but you better give it back!"

The big girl's eyebrows rose as she pulled on it. *She's never seen anything stretchy before*, Esther realized. She did not touch the spear, but she saw that both ends were sharp, one carved wood, one tied-on stone. Toward the wooden end, a twig protruded from the side. At the other end was a Clovis point—definitely, impossibly, a Clovis point!—wedged into a split and bound with something like translucent strips of plastic.

Esther felt giddy. This didn't make any sense!

She looked back between the evergreens. No roofs, no windshields, no playground—just broad expanses of grass and flowers and trees, rippling in the wind, under the noonday sun.

Noonday. Not morning.

The older girl spoke, a question—*what's your name*, maybe? *Where'd you come from?*

This was a dream with smells and hair tickling her face and the feel of solid earth under her feet.

This was terrifying.

This was impossible.

This was way better than finding an old campsite!

Esther squatted to smile into the little girl's face, holding out her hand. "Hi," she said. "I'm Esther."

The little girl smiled back, but continued to clutch her spear across her body. It was shorter than the big girl's, but the Clovis point was just as wickedly sharp. Esther laid her hand on her chest. "I'm Esther. Esther."

The big girl handed back the scrunch. "Ess-ta. Ess-ta."

"Esther."

The little girl giggled. "Ess*ter*! Ess*ter*!"

The big girl touched her own chest and made a sound. Esther took a stab at repeating it. "Arba? Arva? Aaahrva? *Ahr*va!"

The little girl struck herself on the chest and rattled out syllables that at first sounded like birds twittering. After some practice and laughing, Esther managed to say "Tekinit."

Ahrva bent down and touched one sneaker, raising her eyebrows as she picked at the Velcro fastener. "Shoe," said Esther, kicking off first one, then the other. "That's a shoe."

Ahrva was distracted by the socks, which Esther put into her pocket to keep clean; but Tekinit grabbed the sneakers, rubbing the soles and playing with the Velcro before sticking them on the wrong feet and walking with them flopping at the ends of her skinny legs. When Esther and Ahrva laughed, she talked back, ran a few steps, tripped, and caught herself. Recovering her dignity, she walked again; but the turned-out toe of one shoe caught in a runner of grass, and down she went.

Ahrva pulled the shoes off Tekinit's feet with calm authority. "There's a trick to putting them on," Esther said, reaching for them.

Ahrva, grinning, held them out of reach.

"Aw, c'mon," said Esther. "I'll show you." She sat down and patted the ground beside her.

Ahrva sat cross-legged and handed over the shoes. "Okay, now," said Esther, tugging at Ahrva's leg, "give me your foot."

Ahrva held her leg out straight across Esther's lap. Esther slipped the correct shoe onto the callused foot and fastened the Velcro as tightly as she could. It was only slightly too big. Ahrva put her other foot into Esther's lap, watching the fastening alertly. In a moment she was up, raising her knees high and setting her feet down well apart from each other.

Tekinit crowed and danced after her for a minute, then hurled herself to the ground beside Esther. "Ess*ter* gibberish gibberish gibberish." She tugged at the bracelet.

"Hey," said Esther, jerking her arm back. "That's mine!" She didn't mind sharing her shoes, but this was a present. "Here, you can play with my scrunch, instead." She slipped it over Tekinit's wrist, twisting it to fit. Tekinit held up her arm and chattered proudly as she pranced through the bluebonnets. If only whatever magic had sent her here had enabled her to speak the language, too! She could find out all sorts of things— biodegradable things—if she could talk to them! Esther touched a bluebonnet. "What's this? What's your word for it?"

Ahrva raised her eyebrows.

Esther waved it. "Flower. I call this a flower."

"Flar," said Ahrva.

"No. Flow-er. Flow-er."

"Floura," Ahrva said; then made a sound so alien Esther could barely hear it. She repeated it until Ahrva flicked her hands and smiled. Tekinit pulled up a grass blade and held it out, making an explosive sound, like blowing a raspberry. Esther tried to imitate her. All that came out of her mouth was spit.

Tekinit and Ahrva laughed. When Esther's second and third tries fared no better, Ahrva patted her chest and demonstrated, slowly, how the sound came out of the top of her lungs, instead of being made in the mouth. Esther tried again, forming the air into a ball in her chest before letting it out through her lips.

Ahrva laughed and flicked her hands. "Weh, weh," she said.

"Weh," said Esther, wondering if that meant "good" or "right" or "yes." "Now you try. Grass. This is grass."

Hair, tree, water, dress, sky—they swapped words and laughed. The word for "sky," confusingly, was "ahrva." The short, two-ended spear was a "stran" and the plastic-looking stuff that fastened the point on was "wesk." When Tekinit got restless, they started exchanging verbs—run, jump, walk, throw, climb. Esther's mouth felt warped from making new sounds.

Everything was so normal, and so weird at the same time! These girls must have a campsite somewhere. Esther wondered how to go about seeing it without meeting any more people. Kids were one thing; but did she want to get mixed up with grown-ups?

Tekinit tugged at Esther's shirt, talking a mile a minute, then picked up a pinecone. Ahrva nodded, collecting cones in her skirt. Esther picked up as many as she could hold, and followed Tekinit downhill, wondering what the game was. Unless she was completely confused, they were heading for the site she knew so well—the quarry. Her dig.

As they walked, angling away from the creek bed, Esther gazed out over the alien landscape, trying to match it up with familiar landmarks. The creek twisted through what should have been the playground, cypresses soaring higher than the unbuilt school's roof. The subdivision was open plain, dotted with clumps of unfamiliar trees. Some had needles; others seemed to be in new leaf. Large animals grazed, too far away to identify; some bunched, some scattered; too small to be cows, too big to be deer. Camels? But they didn't have humps.

Ahrva walked holding the skirt full of cones with one hand and making "be quiet" gestures with the stran in the other. Tekinit covered her giggles with her hand. Esther, wondering what was so funny, tiptoed behind. The sound of rock striking rock and men talking rose to meet them.

Ahrva led the way to one of several clumps of juniper where the hill fell away sharply. Tekinit dropped to her belly and wiggled beneath the branches. Ahrva motioned to Esther, who tried to do the same, dropping half her cones, conscious of shaking the bushes and of getting her clothes filthy. Lining her head up with Tekinit's gave her a good view down.

It *was* the quarry, though smaller than she'd expected, and the hill was so steep no truck could have climbed it. Instead of raw, dug-up dirt staked out in a grid by Dr. Durham, there was a grassy floor and a shelf of rock, where four men and two boys dug flint nodules out of the cliff. She couldn't see the tools clearly, but Dr. Durham had said that they would be pieces of bone, antler, and rock. At first she thought the men were naked—gross!—and then she saw that they wore leather aprons. Their long hair was tied back, and a couple had scraggly beards.

One of the bearded ones said something forceful as a lump of flint split in his hands. A beardless man laughed as the first man hurled the flint down the hillside.

Ahrva, crouching, eased between Esther and Tekinit, holding her skirt with one hand and laying down her stran to pick up a cone between two fingers of the other. With a motion so fast Esther could barely see it, she flipped it out and up. Silently, it arced into the sky, then plummeted, to bounce off the head of the man who had thrown the lump of flint. He jumped.

Ahrva threw again, hitting the man who had laughed. Esther sat up and gave it a try. Her cone caught in the juniper branches and dropped straight down. Tekinit threw one, which bounced harmlessly on the ground. Ahrva, throwing with ease and elegance, hit each boy and the biggest man.

By now, the flint thrower was scrambling up the rock shelf. Esther threw, avoiding the branches but getting no lift, and Tekinit got a lucky shot at someone's nose. The flint thrower shouted: "Ahrva! Tekinit! Gibberish!"

Ahrva jerked her skirt, sending a rain of cones arcing beautifully out, and shoved Tekinit backward. The little girl retreated nimbly on her knees and elbows, followed by Esther. The flint thrower was halfway up the cliff.

Tekinit vanished stran-first into a clump of bushes beside a rocky outcrop. Esther followed. Her face was full of branches; then she broke through into dark space, squashing Tekinit, who "oomphed" and pushed back. Esther banged her head on rock, but managed not to cry out. Ahrva climbed in on top of them.

"Ahrva!" roared the flint thrower. The girls held their breath as the voice passed their hiding place.

Throwing cones at people wasn't that bad, was it?

And what would he think of *her*?

Other voices joined the first, laughing. Esther gritted her teeth, wishing she could move her leg.

The voices retreated. The quarry sounds resumed. A dove cooed, and was answered by another. Tekinit's stomach grumbled. Esther's leg cramped.

Ahrva eased forward on her elbows, peering through the branches. Eventually she made a "stay put" motion with her hand. Tekinit's stomach growled again as Ahrva crawled out. Her legs looked skinny and absurd in Esther's sneakers.

"Aha!" The voice roared. The sneakers vanished. "Tekinit!" called the man, in a tone that convinced Esther that this was Ahrva and Tekinit's dad, and they were busted.

Tekinit crawled to the front of the burrow, pausing to look back at Esther. Esther shrank back to indicate that she didn't want to be seen, and shooed her.

"Tekinit!" The voice added a string of syllables—probably, *Come on out or I'll come in after you!* Tekinit left Esther's field of vision.

Esther didn't need to know the language to understand what followed. Dad was reading them the riot act, but trying not to laugh. Occasionally Ahrva said, "Yes, sir." A couple of times she made longer answers, maybe explaining where the sneakers and scrunch had come from. Lying, because he didn't call for Esther.

The voices retreated along with the sound of feet swishing through grass. Esther planned her next move. She'd go home, mark the magic place in her own time, and come back with a camera and tape deck. Mama would ground her for running off and being gone so long, but she'd find a way around that. This was important!

She crept into the open, looked around, and headed uphill. No one was in sight as she picked out what she thought was the right pair of trees. They looked ordinary, but she remembered that dead branch. She walked between them.

Into the same birdsong, trees, the smell of barbecue, cool air.

Maybe to go forward in time, you had to go through in the other direction.

The blue jay that flashed between the trees remained solid and loud. But it might not work for birds.

Esther walked through again, and still smelled barbecue.

FOUR

➤ STRANDED

*E*sther ran between the trees, turned, and ran through again. And again. Her eyes prickled. She pictured her own time. Air hot, grass dry; highway there, school down there. She squinted, she concentrated, she tried different trees.

Nothing.

Esther twisted her bracelet, watching the plastic stars drift as her mind and heart raced. She mustn't panic. Maybe you couldn't travel back to your original time if you didn't have everything you'd had to begin with.

Or maybe time travel only worked in one direction.

No! She'd get her stuff back. Everything would be fine.

Esther walked toward the barbecue smell and soon heard voices. Peering around a tree, she saw piles of brush, a fire, movement, laughter, conversation. Women and children passed the shoes and scrunch from hand to hand. Ahrva sat poking holes in leather with a piece of antler, Tekinit beside her, looking subdued.

A tall woman with multicolored feathers fluttering on her

dress fastened and unfastened the Velcro strap of one sneaker, and spoke to an old woman. A pregnant woman with squirrel tails waving from her shoulders pulled the scrunch and called to Ahrva, who answered without looking up.

Eventually, the old woman collected all three items, made an announcement, and tossed them upward. Kids raced to catch them in midair. A teenage girl got the scrunch and put it around her wrist. The shoes became the targets in a game of keep-away.

The women went back to work, or helped themselves to a heap of roots piled by the fire. The pregnant woman got some and sat beside Ahrva, handing her one.

Esther counted. Five women, one teenage girl, two big girls besides Ahrva, Tekinit, and a baby. Everyone but the baby had at least one stran, either like Ahrva's, or shorter and carried in a belt of twisted leather. A woman in a plain hide dress sat near Ahrva's family and started cutting a bone with one of these knife-like strans. As she drew the sharp edge along the bone, she began to sing.

The tall woman, scraping a hide, joined in. The old woman, sharpening the Clovis point on her stran, raised a high, wavering voice in counterpoint. The kids, tossing sneakers from hand to hand, fell into the tune. High, wavery notes bridged short, punchy ones from other mouths, tying them all together.

Ahrva laid aside her work, picked up her stran, and walked downhill, singing.

Esther marked her direction with her eyes, and moved to intercept her. She stopped at a trampled area of weeds with big leaves, which Esther's nose warned her must be the camp latrine, though it was well within sight of everybody. Eeuw. But she might not get another chance. Hiding behind the nearest tree, a tall, pale sycamore, Esther stuck her head out and whispered: "Ahrva? Ahrva? Over here!"

Ahrva, not pausing in her singing, made eye contact and gestured—*wait*. Esther obeyed, and soon they crouched, knee to knee, behind a sycamore. Esther touched her feet, then her hair. "Shoes. Scrunch. I need them."

"Shuss," said Ahrva, nodding. "Scrunsh." She pantomimed carrying them; then put her palms together and leaned her cheek against the back of her hand, imitating sleep. "Nepi."

"Um—okay," said Esther. Would she have to be here all *day*? Mama would be past furious—she'd think Esther was dead!

"Ahrva!" Someone sounded cross. Ahrva patted Esther's knee and left, calling out: "Nuaah, nuaah!"

Esther belly-crawled through the long grass to better shelter. The barbecue smell made her hungry. Mosquitoes a half-inch long, fat gnats, monster butterflies, horseflies, a spider with a body as big as a quarter—were these all extinct, or had they just shrunk over time? Blue jays, goldfinches, mockingbirds, and cardinals flashed in the trees. Duller-colored birds scratched, fought, sang, and strutted. Sometimes a blur quivered above the flowers—a large bee or a small hummingbird. The grackles and sparrows that would be everywhere in the twenty-first century didn't appear, but when Esther rolled over on her back, the familiar shapes of turkey buzzards soared against the blue sky.

She hadn't crossed eleven thousand years to go bird-watching. Esther sneaked closer to camp. Ahrva worked. She must be in the doghouse, because the other kids played, the scrunch passing from hand to hand, the shoes used as bases in a ball-dribbling game. The ball was like the one in her dream the night before, made of leather strips. She thought she could tell how the camp was organized—kitchen over here, sewing over here, sharpening tools over there. But what were the piles of brush for?

The bird songs changed their tone and rhythm as the day progressed. Frogs began to sing in the creek. When shadows lay long upon the ground, and Esther was certain that she was within an inch of starvation, the men returned, carrying bags bulging with rocks. They dropped their burdens, greeted children, stretched. Ahrva ran to her father. He listened to her, then put his fingers into his mouth and whistled.

The camp fell mostly silent. He spoke, making broad gestures, ending with his eyes leveled at the girl wearing the scrunch. She took it off, walked over to Ahrva, and held it out. Another returned the shoes.

The women levered something large, black, and smoking from a bed of coals hidden under a layer of dirt. Dinner. The tall woman cut the meat into chunks and served the old woman, then the pregnant lady, who seemed to be Ahrva and Tekinit's mother, then the woman holding the baby, then the biggest man, then Esther lost track.

The group had a strange way of eating meat, putting it into their mouths, then cutting it off. Tekinit sat on her mother's lap and ate shreds torn off the end. Esther closed her eyes. At home, was dinner cold on the table? Mama making phone calls? Dad leading a search party?

People went back for seconds and thirds. Tekinit slumped against her mother. Someone started a song.

The frog chorus lay underneath the human one like a rhythm track. Men, women, and children sang different parts, blending into a sound as big as the sky. In time, a fifth part moaned around the melody. Esther looked downhill and saw a dozen dogs, their heads thrown back, their music weaving in and out of the human tune.

Not dogs. Coyotes. Big ones. Maybe even wolves.

Suddenly her hiding place didn't seem like a good one. The song, human and canine, died away. So did the sunset. The frogs continued. The pregnant lady carried Tekinit into a brush pile. Kids and grown-ups clustered, talked, broke up, visited the latrine area, and vanished into brush piles—oh. They were shelters. Two women wrapped the remaining food in a hide and hoisted the bundle into a tree. *Oong-KA-choonk*, shouted something out in the darkness, and *oong-KA-choonk*, something replied. Esther made her way back to where Ahrva had left her.

Stars bright as candle flames bloomed across the sky. A coyote yipped. She heard voices. A man's. Ahrva's. Esther held her breath. An owl hooted. Bats zipped around, snatching mosquitoes out of the air. Something touched her head.

She jumped. Ahrva clapped a hand over her mouth. Face to face they crouched, until Esther relaxed. Ahrva took her hand away. "Pfft," she whispered, pulling something out from under her dress. "Scrunsh. Shuss."

"Thanks," whispered Esther, fishing a greasy hunk of meat out of one shoe and a root out of the other. Gross—but it'd be rude to refuse. How did you say good-bye in this language?

"Khenupadna," said Ahrva, and slipped away.

Socks and shoes and scrunch in place, food in her pockets, Esther hurried away. Something swooped past, black against the stars, looking as big as she was. Could there be killer birds that even Dr. Durham didn't know about?

These were the right trees. She was sure of it.

I want to go home, I want to go home!

But she walked between the trees, and was not home.

Something trampled through the grass, grunting and snuffling. Esther jumped for the lowest branch. Missed!

Grunt, snuffle, an abbreviated squeal. A smell like skunk.

Bracing against a knob on the trunk, she vaulted up and snatched the tree limb, which scraped as, pushing with her legs, pulling with her arms, she hooked her body across the branch. A herd of low-backed, flat-headed animals surged below. One raised its snout above the mass. Javelinas.

The stink of the javelinas nauseated her, but her stomach growled as they trotted down to the creek to slurp water. *I've got to get home,* she thought; but what hadn't she tried? *Please, God,* she thought, *please, God—*

A sound like giant fingernails on an enormous blackboard sliced the night. Hooves pounded; grunts and squeals; javelinas scattered; and a complicated dark shape crouched in the creek bottom. Its movements coincided with slurping, smacking noises, like a cat at a food bowl. Something had killed a javelina.

A mountain lion, she thought. *Or maybe—were there saber-toothed tigers in Texas?* It would be too full of javelina to bother with her. But what if it wasn't the only one around? Her skin felt shuddery and her throat tight. *You'll feel better after you eat,* she told herself.

Ahrva's root was like a potato, but different. The meat was stringy. Her brain kept trying to run in circles and she kept trying to calm it down. What would Dr. Durham do?

She'd freak, that's what she'd do! This isn't science!

Then what was it?

First she'd dreamed of Clovis people; then she'd seen them in the hot light of day, and walked into their world as easily as walking through a door.

Maybe she had to dream her own world to get back to it?

How was she supposed to sleep in a tree?

Well, she sure wasn't going to sleep on the ground surrounded by saber-toothed tigers! She lay down cautiously with her feet folded behind her, her hands under her cheek, and her legs and elbows straddling the branch, and closed her stinging eyes. She didn't dare cry. What might hear her?

The only way that she knew she'd slept was when she jerked awake, startled by an *oong-KA-choonk*, or by slipping sideways, or by a sound like some prehistoric predator sniffing for her blood.

Eventually, the light turned gray and the bluebonnets regained color. Esther's mouth felt dry and wrinkled. Mockingbirds, redbirds, and jays sang, above a crunching, cracking sound.

In the creek bottom, barely visible in the dawn-dim shade, two wolflike creatures held the javelina's leg bones between massive paws, gnawing with jaws as big as the vise on Dad's workbench. Even lying down, they were nearly as tall as Esther at the shoulder.

Esther had seen a picture like that in her library book. *Canis diris*—the dire wolf. Supposedly, they scavenged because, though they were strong enough to break up bones, they were too slow to catch most prey. But if they found slow prey—like, say, a human who always came in last in races—why wouldn't they try to catch her?

Her limbs cramped. The creek bottom was almost ten feet below the level of the surface. Once out of the tree, she wouldn't be able to see the dire wolves, and they wouldn't see her. They were full of javelina anyway. Esther shifted, moving so slowly she thought her arms and legs would fall off before she relieved the pain. One of the dire wolves approached the other, wagging its tail. With whiny yips, they washed each other.

Now. While they're not thinking about food. Esther closed her eyes. Imagining the twenty-first century as hard as she could, she swung down, walked between the magic trees, and opened her eyes.

FIVE

➤ CAUGHT!

Esther knew at once that she'd failed, by the smell and feel of the air. She tried to swallow the tears in her throat, and found she was too dry to swallow.

Trying to see all around her at once, holding her breath, sprinting from climbable tree to climbable tree, she tiptoed past the playfully wrestling dire wolves and proceeded downstream until she found a low-ceilinged tunnel of shrubs that led down the bank to the water. She couldn't see what awaited her below, but evidently nothing huge used this trail, or the ceiling would have been higher. A wet smell blew softly up to meet her as she crawled down to a large, flat rock at the edge of the water.

She peered left, right, up, down, behind her, and across the creek, before crawling onto the rock. The birds and frogs were so noisy she wouldn't have heard a freight train. A mother duck led a string of ducklings nosing along the opposite bank, where moss grew thick under a nearly horizontal live oak. An egret, its white feathers tinged pink by the dawn light, stood in reeds, watching the shadowed water.

As Esther dipped her sticky hands, a frog plopped in, and she nearly jumped out of her skin. *Frogs can't hurt you.* She rubbed her hands together to get off most of the dirt and made them into a cup. Leaning over as far as she dared, Esther slurped cold water from her bent palms, until her mouth felt normal, and then one more slurp for good measure.

A bird cried, three times, and silence fell. A breeze cut through Esther's T-shirt to her skin, making her shudder as she raised her eyes—

To those of the cat opposite.

It stood black against the sky, above her and to the left, on the trunk of the horizontal live oak. Its tail, as thick and long as Esther's arm, twitched. Its head lowered, its shoulders hunched, like a cat stalking a pigeon, its round eyes flaming gold straight at her.

Esther heard her own voice, screaming, as she scrambled backward, fighting the branches, rocks, and slope that barred her way. Birds exploded upward, but all her attention was directed back, toward the shadow leaping in her wake.

She stumbled out of the tunnel of brush into the open, directly into the path of something huge and tan and bellowing that crashed into her and kept going, knocking her flat. Trying to move, to breathe, to crawl if she couldn't run, she heard the bushes behind her making way for the jaguar.

A man appeared in front of her, stopping short as the cat hesitated, its paws now on either side of Esther's legs. She managed to roll over, and saw it look at her, then at the man, who held a spear ready to throw. The jaguar faded into the brush, like a special effect in a movie.

Esther closed her eyes, and breathed at last, only it was more like crying. A hand touched her head. She opened her eyes. "Hi," she said, in a small voice. "You're Ahrva's dad, right?"

Ahrva's dad felt her over, not rudely, but like the playground monitor the time she'd fallen from the top of the jungle gym, checking whether anything was broken. Esther stood, testing each muscle. She hurt from her fall, but everything seemed to be working okay. "Weh," she said. "I'm weh."

He smiled, touched her scrunch, and asked a question. The only word she recognized was "Ahrva."

Esther nodded, swallowing. "I was playing with Ahrva. Tekinit, too." She touched her chest. "Esther. I'm Esther."

"Esster?" He touched his own chest. "Podan."

"Podan gibberish gibberish," called another man, standing over a dead camel and beaming at Esther as if greeting his best friend. Podan held up Esther's hand, and said: "Esster gibberish," as she put things together in her head. She'd run right into a camel these men had been hunting. Ahrva's dad had scared off the jaguar and the other man had killed the camel, which seemed to make him happy. Good. Somebody should be happy.

"Aiee!" said the other man, bounding toward her. His bloody hand left a red mark as he touched his chest. "Kitotul," he said, and kept talking, grinning broadly out of a round, big-jawed face. Esther smiled back, feeling sick.

She stood around awkwardly as Podan helped Kitotul skin and cut up the camel, tying the meat inside the hide so they could carry it between them on a spear shaft. The spears came in two parts, long wooden shafts that slotted into short bone pieces, with Clovis points in the ends. They also had notched sticks like the atlatls—spear-throwers—Dr. Durham had described. Noticing all these details was easier than thinking about her situation. She touched a bone foreshaft and said: "Stran?"

"Stran gibberish," Kitotul said, flourishing the one he was cutting with.

She touched a long shaft. "Stran?"

Kitotul laughed and made another sound, something like "thune." Pausing in his work, he took a spear shaft and fit a foreshaft into it. "Stran," he said, shaking the whole thing, then taking them apart again: "Thune. Stran."

So. If it had a Clovis point in it, it was a stran. She hoped she wouldn't be here long enough for the distinction to be important to her.

When the meat was all bundled together, Podan motioned to Esther, and said her name, as Kitotul beckoned with broad movements of his arms. Esther walked up the hill beside Podan.

As they approached the sleepy-looking camp, Kitotul whooped. People tumbled out of the brush shelters, some rubbing their eyes, some grabbing strans. The tall woman put her hands on her hips, wrinkled her long nose, and called out a question. Podan answered. Everyone stared.

Why were they looking from her, to the meat, and back?

The biggest man, who looked like Podan but had gray in his hair and whiskers, spoke in an annoyed voice as he looked her over. She stood up straight and looked him over back. Podan talked, gesturing at Kitotul. The crowd fell silent.

Starting softly, Kitotul's voice became loud, slow, and rhythmic, almost like singing. His gestures were large, sweeping, and startlingly clear.

The camp was sleeping, he said. He and Podan were both up early. They decided to go down the creek. Esther couldn't follow the next bit. Suddenly, he screamed—a thin, pathetic sound that made her face hot with embarrassment.

His body became a flurry of movement, for a number of things happened at once, and Podan joined in to act out some of the parts. Esther's scream had scared the camel into charging at the hunters—this bit made the group laugh, except for the biggest man, who didn't seem to be enjoying the story, and the tall woman beside him, who didn't look as if she ever smiled.

Kitotul killed the camel. Podan took over talking at that point, about scaring the big cat away. He pulled Esther in front of him, touching her scrunch, pointing at her feet. Esther obligingly picked them up so everyone could see her shoes.

At this point, Ahrva ran up. She talked rapidly, mostly addressing Podan. In the end, she pointed to the camel meat, to Esther, and back again.

The tall woman, looking down her long nose, spoke. The group laughed. Ahrva and Podan looked mad. The pregnant woman spoke, and got a bigger laugh. The tall woman tossed her head and sniffed. Then the old woman walked toward Esther.

People made way as if the old woman took up more space than could be accounted for by her body. Her gray hair was short, her face collapsed and wrinkly. Red hand-prints decorated her buckskin dress, and a scaly choker—red, yellow, and black—encircled her throat. *Red and yellow, kill a fellow*—a poisonous coral snake's skin!

Ahrva ducked her head, clasping her hands. Esther copied her. The old woman spoke, all vowels and breath until the last word—"Ess-*ter?*"

"I'm sorry, ma'am," Esther said. "I don't understand you." At a loss, she knelt, as if to a queen.

The old woman made an emphatic sound, helped her to her feet, and looked at the biggest man, who looked less big next to her. He spoke, sourly. The crowd relaxed and split up. The teenage girl and a plain woman dragged the meat to the cooking pit, visibly trying not to grin. Ahrva's mother touched her own chest. "Si-li-ka," she said.

"Silika," repeated Esther.

"Gibberish pfft?" Tekinit tugged at her T-shirt.

Pfft meant food. "Weh pfft," Esther said. Tekinit giggled and fetched Esther a root, crying: "Zulotul!"

"Zulotul," agreed Esther, biting off a yawn by biting into the root. The starchy, cold mass would have been better hot, with butter and salt. She ate neatly, aware of the eyes watching her, as the other children squatted to eat, not too close, but not too far away. When they gave her meat and a stran, she carefully copied what she'd seen yesterday, though it made her nervous to have the blade so close to her face.

The men ate, gathered their spears, and left. *Were they looking for her tribe?* Esther wondered.

Whatever. Until she got home (Esther refused to pay attention to the fear nibbling her brain), she had to get along with these people.

So when one of the boys hung by his knees off a branch, then called, pointing to her, she picked a higher branch on a taller tree, climbed up, and (with a whispered "Hail Mary") hung upside down till the blood filled her head.

She didn't know how to dribble the ball, but she gave it her best shot.

Whatever anybody gave her to eat, she ate.

When a boy who acted like he owned the world addressed her with a word that sounded like "tookam," everyone looked at her expectantly, and Ahrva scowled. Realizing that he had insulted her, Esther touched his head, and said: "Oh, you zulo-tul!" The kids laughed.

So she seemed to do all right, but if she didn't pay attention every minute, she did something stupid, like pass to the wrong team in a game she hadn't realized had teams. Or get some-one's name wrong.

And every time (followed by every child in camp) she went back to the tree with the dead branch and tried to get home, she failed.

In the evening, the men straggled in and went to the old woman, talking and gesturing, finding Esther with their eyes. What would they have done if they had found a gate like the one she'd walked through? Would they realize it was con-nected to her? Why should they? The big man, whose name was Uduban, had caught something (a javelina, judging by the bristly skin), and it was buried in the earth oven when Kitotul's camel came out.

At supper, Esther slumped between Silika and Ahrva, eat-ing camel meat and hot roots, her eyes burning with smoke, tiredness, and tears she didn't want to shed in front of all these people. Tekinit chattered. Silika and Podan talked with the plain-dressed woman. What was her name? Shusskt. She had a pointy chin. Esther tried to run through the name of everyone in camp; but there were too many. Her head hurt.

First the grown-ups, then Tekinit, fell silent as the old woman sat down in front of Esther. Esther clasped her hands and ducked her head. A scrawny hand patted her knee. "Ess-*ter.*"

"That's me," agreed Esther. Wait, she knew this woman's name. "Um—Ehdanwah."

The old woman's smile revealed brown, crooked teeth. "Ess-ter," she said, pointing to the sky. Words poured past. The first stars shone, too bright to be real. "Esster?"

"Weh! Esther means star! How did you know?"

The grown-ups murmured. Ehdanwah grinned. The kids stared.

"Wait. You couldn't know. It's from Hebrew. Did I just tell you I came from the stars?"

Apparently so; but what could it hurt? Esther was too tired to think; too tired to try to sing when the others started. She was almost too tired to crawl into the shelter with Ahrva.

The shelter contained bags and gourds, two piles of grass and furs, and a smell of hay and animals. Silika and Podan crawled under the furs on one pile of grass, and Ahrva and Tekinit crawled into the other. Esther lay down beside Tekinit. *When in Rome, do as the Romans do*, her mother said.

If she were in mammoth times . . .

Esther fell asleep.

If I'm in mammoth times, Rome isn't built yet, she thought, as she woke. It was still dark, and no birds sang. Podan crawled out past the girls' bed. Meeting Esther's eyes, he smiled, and motioned for her to go back to sleep. Esther snuggled back between Ahrva and Tekinit. *Please, God, let me go home today!*

She'd better say her prayers. She'd forgotten them two nights in a row. Except for that "Hail Mary" yesterday—

But the Virgin Mary wasn't born yet.

Jesus wasn't born yet.

Crowded into a space as small as a closet with three people, Esther felt hopelessly alone.

SIX

➤ SETTING OUT

The next morning the camp bustled. Ahrva showed Esther how to fold animals skins inside a sleeping fur and lace it up with plastic-looking string, wesk, through holes punched around the edges. The sleeping furs had mysterious purplish stains on the skin sides. What else were they used for? Esther wondered.

While the women packed, the men huddled, pointing, talking—especially Podan and the big man, Uduban. Esther remembered what Dr. Durham had said about ancient peoples moving as plants ripened in different places and game animals migrated. If they stayed put too long, they'd starve.

If Esther left, would she ever see home again?

Would she if she stayed?

She thought of the coyotes, the jaguar, the dire wolves, the big cat in the dark—things she hadn't seen yet. She didn't know how to find food or build a fire.

Big-jawed Kitotul, who wasn't taking part in the discussion, grinned and gestured at her. Esther came over, wondering what was up. He spoke, much too fast, then rubbed her head, nodding and smiling. Esther wanted to jerk away, but his children were watching. "You have a good day, too," she said.

As soon as everyone finished eating javelina for breakfast, the men and boys set off. The men carried one spear and one gourd each, along with several short strans at their belts, and loaded the boys with spare shafts and more gourds. The bossy boy immediately dumped part of his load onto Kitotul's son, who trailed the rest with an I-don't-care face. The women and girls attacked the burned-down fire with their strans, gourds of water, and leafy branches, dousing sparks, stamping on them, scattering charcoal. No wonder Dr. Durham had a hard time finding hearths! The women sang a song that was half whoops.

Under cover of the noise, Esther slipped away. Thigh-deep in flowers, she stood as near as she could tell to the spot from which she had first seen Ahrva and Tekinit three days ago. She imagined the hot sun, the highway, the music.

A bug buzzed in her ear.

Esther swatted it and took a deep breath around the tightness in her throat.

The bug came back, with a friend. The women's song pulsed in the background, nearly drowned out by birdsong. Esther squinted at the sky, pink in the east, dark blue in the west. "Please, God. Show me how to get home."

A new bug landed on her.

"I know you're not into answering people directly, God," said Esther. "But I *can't* stay here! I need to get home!"

Smoke puffed across the sky and blew apart, seeming to take

the stars with it. She walked between the trees. No good. She walked back. Sinking to her knees, she searched in the grass for rocks.

"Ess-*ter!*" Ahrva's voice. "Ess-*ter?*"

Esther fished in her brain for words to say: "I'm coming," as she arranged the rocks in an E. If they ever came back, she wanted to be able to find these trees again.

The shelters were broken down and strewn across the landscape. The women and older girls carried packs, bags, gourds, the baby, and strans. Tekinit darted around shouting and waving her stran. It was a wonder she didn't put an eye out.

When Esther arrived, Ahrva held out a funny-shaped pack of soft pale leather. Though small, it was heavy, and clanked. "Rocks," said Esther. "You want me to carry rocks." She had some trouble with the straps till Ahrva showed her that she was trying to put it on upside down. Ahrva carried four bags and a gourd, but no one seemed to think Esther was up to such a burden. They were probably right.

Silika handed her a yard-long stran. Imitating the others, Esther held it loosely under the protrusion on the wooden end, stone point down. Together, the women and girls went to the creek, drank, and filled gourds. Esther copied them, sucking down cool, mineral-tasting water until it sloshed in her stomach. At last Ehdanwah, the old woman, started walking west. Silika held Tekinit's hand. Ahrva and Esther walked shoulder to shoulder, down the hill, up the next.

Esther looked back once; but the glare of the rising sun made her squint and pull her eyes away.

Already, the men had ranged so far that Esther couldn't see

them among the tree-spotted humps of the Hill Country. The women and girls strolled in clusters, talking, singing, scanning the ground. No one was in a hurry. When the baby cried, his mother—Mingwah—shifted him around to nurse without interrupting her conversation or altering her pace.

After a while, they came to a cattail bog. Women and girls waded in mud over their ankles, digging up cattails with the wooden ends of the strans, peeling the stalks to get at the crisp cores—eskway—and chopping off roots—zulotul. They dumped the zulotuls into carrying bags, but ate the eskway on the spot. They laughed when the zulotuls Esther dug up were too small, so she laughed, too, and watched to learn the difference between cattails with big roots and ones that would be too small.

The tall woman with the long nose, Nudawah, robbed a bobwhite's nest, replacing all but four eggs with smooth white stones. She ate two, raw, then looked over the rest of the women with a critical eye. She presented Silika with one and Mingwah, the nursing mother, with another, and old Ehdanwah with three. Silika and Mingwah ate theirs right down, but Ehdanwah casually passed two of her three to Kitotul's wife, Shusskt, and one of the girls.

At noon, they stopped by a shady spring and had a picnic, resting their feet in the water and talking. Esther was too tired to eat much, but gladly took off her sneakers to soak her feet. Tekinit and Mingwah napped. The rest competed to see who could hit the most squirrels with rocks, old Ehdanwah keeping score. *Rats, I'll have to learn to kill things,* Esther thought; but she wasn't in any danger of hitting

anything today. After a while, Ehdanwah slung the
squirrels, strung on a piece of wesk, over her shoulder and
headed out, leaving the rest to follow as they could.

Trying to understand the conversations around her made
Esther's brain as tired as her legs. Her back and side ached. The
high, round sky, the scattered trees, the grass switching her
calves, the butterflies wandering drunkenly from blossom to
blossom, never changed. Only the flowers transformed gradually, pink ground-hugging primroses giving way to spider
lilies, bluebonnets to Indian blanket.

As the group's shadows shifted behind them, Esther noticed
that they were drifting toward a cedar-lined ridge. Tekinit,
holding hands between Ahrva and Esther, began to hang on
them. Esther's mouth was dry, her stomach aching with the
thought of cookies and milk, when they topped the ridge.

Below ran an unexpected creek. Ehdanwah sat, her string of
dead animals beside her. Everyone dumped packs and
stretched. Esther dropped her rocks, sure she had a bruise
where they had bumped against her back all day. Tekinit threw
herself down beside Ehdanwah, but the others scattered, gathering fallen branches and old logs. Esther wanted to lie down
with Tekinit, but stuck to Ahrva's side. She kept dropping the
sticks she had when she went to pick up a new one. Who
would have thought gathering dead wood could be hard?

Tekinit made a circle of rocks, and Ehdanwah built a tent of
wood inside. From one of her bags, she produced fluffy bits of
stuff—dried moss?—flat pieces of wood, and a contraption
made of sticks, wesk, and a turtle shell. Crooning a yearning
song, she placed the end of a stick against one of the flat pieces,

braced her hand against the turtle shell on the top, and pulled on the wesk until the stick spun in place. *She's making fire by rubbing sticks together!* Esther thought. The women sang in harmony with Ehdanwah as she spun, spun, spun the stick. Mingwah cut and sharpened a piece of wood and set it across two forked sticks over the place where the fire would be, and Silika skinned the squirrels. Just when Esther was afraid she'd have to eat raw squirrel, she smelled smoke, and the song changed to one of triumph.

After adding a couple of loads to the woodpile, Ahrva pointed toward the creek and asked her mother something. Silika gestured with her hands. Ehdanwah spoke. All the girls snatched up empty bags and stampeded to the creek.

Water tumbled under trees draped with vines heavy with— were those grapes, where the late afternoon sun lit the bank? Birds burst out of the trees, scolding with fifty separate voices. The girls laughed as they picked fruit. Esther was cheered by the sight of something that resembled food she was used to, though only a dozen pea-sized grapes were in each bunch. The girls bit them off the stems, spitting out skins and seeds. Esther's first taste scraped her tastebuds. Then the pulp slipped out of the bitter skin, and sugar hit her tongue. Ahrva grinned at her stickily, popping two bunches into her bag. "Mingwah!"

"Mingwah?" So the lady with the baby was named "Grapes"? Well, there were worse names.

They ate and collected grapes till none were left. Esther knelt to wash. Ick—she'd gotten juice all over her bracelet.

What were Mama and Dad and Danny doing now? What did she mean by "now"?

They'd have talked to the police and made posters. Maybe they were sitting around the table staring at their food and not talking. Maybe Mama and Dad were out searching while Danny waited by the phone for someone to call with a ransom demand.

If she were home, they'd be eating dinner and she'd be fighting with Danny over something stupid and Mama would be planning what to do with the next day of her vacation and maybe she'd better not think about this.

Fish flashed in Esther's shadow. Tekinit played with rocks on the slope opposite. Ahrva waded, poking her stran into a backwater. A jay called. A buzz went off, and Esther wondered who would have an alarm watch out here.

Then she realized how stupid that was, as she spotted the coiled, buzzing snake in front of Tekinit.

If Esther had thought, she would have frozen. Instead, she cried out, snatched up her stran, and jumped, knocking Tekinit aside as the rattler struck.

SEVEN

*E*sther's stran wounded the ground beside the snake, which recoiled, rattles buzzing like a power tool. Tekinit snatched up a stone and crashed it down. The snake snapped out to its full length, rattles stuttering, as Tekinit pounded its head one, two, three times, yelling with each blow. The body writhed noisily all over the slope. Esther grabbed Tekinit, jerking the stone away and hugging her. "Stop! That's enough!"

The girls gathered round, shouting. Esther watched the twitching remains of the snake, sick and embarrassed. Tekinit wiggled out of her grasp and threw herself on Ahrva, words pouring out of her mouth, pointing at Esther, at the snake, at the stran stuck in the ground.

Emni, the teenage girl, inspected Esther as Ahrva checked Tekinit. Esther held out her arms. "See, I'm fine. Weh. Weh."

When the snake stopped flopping, Tekinit, chattering proudly, picked it up in both hands. The crushed head dangled, fangs sticking out at odd angles. The girls made a circle, holding hands—Esther included. Ahrva led a chant, cutting the head off with her stran, and Tekinit piled stones over it. Then she draped the body around her shoulders and climbed the bank. The other girls followed.

"Was that a snake funeral?" Esther asked, but she had to ask in English, and got no answer.

Silika made a fuss over Tekinit and Esther, then skinned the snake and put it with the other small animals over the fire, which hissed as fat dripped into it. The women and girls avoided the billowing smoke as they worked—scraping skins, stacking grapes, cutting sweet-smelling grass, and singing as they did. Ahrva was showing Esther how to lay one armload one way and one armload another to make a bed when a sound between a howl and a shout made Esther jump. The women howled in reply.

The men, shadows stretching for acres in the last rays of the sun, waded through grass and flowers up the ridge. Children ran to meet them. Everyone talked at once. Tekinit hung onto her father's leg, pointing at Esther as she jabbered.

Kitotul put his arm around his youngest daughter, Washaw, and started telling her about something. She squealed and grabbed his hand, looking over his arm as though she were surprised to see it. Kitotul's son Skedat shook his stran and added some detail; then they all looked over at Esther, and fell silent. Had they noticed she was staring? Esther looked away.

They all helped themselves to the stacked fruit, meats, and cooked zulotuls raked out of the fire with strans. The smell of the food overcame Esther's weariness, and she went for seconds, then thirds, then—to her surprise—fourths. Each hunter got up and talked, starting with big Uduban and ending with Kitotul.

Mostly they seemed to be saying *I looked, and I didn't see any-thing;* or *I saw something, and it got away.* Kitotul, weirdly, started off by pointing to Esther and indicating how he'd rubbed her head, which made everyone look at her. She wished they wouldn't. What came next involved roaring and slashing. Apparently he had met something big and scary—a bear?—that had almost gotten him, but he escaped without a scratch. Uduban grunted something that made his grumpy wife Nudawah laugh loudly. Kitotul pressed his lips together—Uduban must have put him down. Podan spoke. Kitotul looked grateful, and sat.

Esther's legs and side ached, her feet hurt, and her mouth felt icky. People kept staring at her and talking to Podan and Silika. When Ahrva led her off to bed, she lay on her back under the open sky, still feeling her body walking, walking, walking.

In the morning, Esther could barely move. She choked down grapes and zulotul while the sun came up in pink splendor and the grown-ups—mostly Uduban and Podan again—argued. Kitotul and his son Skedat came by, spoke to Ahrva, and rubbed Esther's head. She jerked away, and Ahrva stepped in front of her protectively.

Kitotul held up his hands. "Kru," he said—Sorry? He added something else that made Ahrva smile. *What the heck,* Esther thought, and shook hands with him. That didn't seem to be what he was expecting, but as soon as he got the idea he pumped her hand up and down, smiling broadly.

The men and boys went down to the creek to drink. The women demolished the fire and grass beds, got their drinks, and started walking. Esther limped in the rear, longing for Ben-Gay, for orange juice and toast, for her mother.

How bad had it hurt Mama's feelings that Esther would rather go to the dig than to the mall with her? *If—no, when—I see her, I'll tell her I'm sorry.*

This day was like the one before, as was the one after, and the one after that. Ahrva made a belt from the rattlesnake skin, and a hair ornament from the rattle. Tekinit wore the belt; but she tied the rattle into Esther's hair, where it buzzed gently with every movement.

Kitotul and his son Skedat made a habit of shaking her hand every morning. *I'm a good luck charm,* Esther realized. The big man, Uduban, ignored her. His son Telabat jeered at her occasionally. Podan didn't shake hands, but said good-bye to her along with his daughters, and Esther suspected that this meant he got luck automatically. The remaining man sometimes pumped her hand when Uduban wasn't looking. What if someone got eaten by a mountain lion after shaking her hand? Would they ditch her?

Uduban, she could tell, didn't like her, which was worrisome, since he usually acted as if he was in charge. But the really important person was his mother, old Ehdanwah. She started the fires. She carried the group's only bag of salt and decided what food to put it on. No matter how the morning argument went, everyone looked at Ehdanwah before they split up. Some mornings, she would flick her hands in a gesture Esther had learned meant "yes," and would point in one direction or another.

On those days, the argument was short and the day ended with a bounty that kept them in one place longer than overnight. Once they camped above a slope so thick with tiny, red, gloriously sweet strawberries that it was nearly impossible to move without crushing them; once they dug up bags full of a root and dried it over the fire; once they spent three days eating crisp, sweet wild plums. Small animals came for these plants—raccoons, possums, rabbits—and the women set traps.

Sometimes the men brought deer or javelinas, which also kept the group in the same place for a couple of days, cooking, eating, and curing hides. No one wanted hungry predators coming into camp, so the men butchered the animals where they were killed and brought home only skins, usable bones, and meat. If tall trees were handy, they made a grass rope and hung the meat up; otherwise, it was buried. The wife of the hunter who made the kill distributed the meat as she saw fit, generally giving the best parts to Silika (because she was pregnant) and Mingwah (because she was nursing).

Esther learned to throw a rock straight and to use her stran as a knife, a shovel, or whatever. She learned to skin and gut small animals, though she always missed when she tried to hit one. She learned to do without privacy—even using the latrine meant being in an open space where you could see predators coming . . . and everyone could see you, which Esther hated. She could comb nits out of Tekinit's hair with a coneflower blossom, sort people into families, howl a welcome when the men approached, sing and, more or less, talk. Soon she could almost follow the morning arguments.

"There aren't enough trees," said Podan.

"Telapa don't eat trees," said Uduban. Esther didn't know what telapa were, but everyone wanted to find one.

"But they eat grass, and the grass is wrong, too," said Podan. "It gets harder to find telapa here every year. Just because we killed ten long ago—"

"Our father and I killed ten," interrupted Uduban. "You were still throwing stones at raccoons."

Podan made a noise that Esther translated as "Whatever." Every time the ten telapa got mentioned, everyone who wasn't Podan or Uduban shut up. Since Uduban seemed to be Podan's big brother, Esther figured it must be one of those family things, but she wondered about the rest of the argument. It seemed to her there were lots of trees, and grass was grass. How could you tell what had been eating it? She asked Ahrva during the day.

"Oh, that's men's knowledge," said Ahrva. She explained with gestures as well as words. That fallen tree over there had been pushed over by a telapa. And they ate grass, tearing it up by the roots, as she demonstrated. But this here was petwa grass. Kitotul's daughter Washaw got down on her hands and knees and bit grass to show how petwa ate, and everyone laughed; even Nudawah, Uduban's tall snobby wife, who usually ignored Kitotul's whole family.

Once they saw ponies around a water hole—shaggy things, with dull yellow hides and gray-striped shoulders and flanks. "Will the men hunt horse?" Esther asked.

Ahrva shook her head. "Not unless we get hungrier. They're good to eat, but mostly they're too fast to bother hunting."

"Like camels," said Washaw, proudly. "Not many men can kill a camel, like my father did."

"He couldn't have, if Esster hadn't put wazicat on it," said Tekinit, equally proudly.

"I didn't put wazicat on anything," said Esther, who hadn't decided whether this word meant "magic," or "the evil eye," or what; but was sure she didn't have any. "I screamed and ran like a rabbit. A clumsy rabbit. I didn't know about the camel."

"My father isn't oheitika like Podan and Uduban," said Washaw. "When a low man does something hard like kill a camel, there's wazicat at work. He has killed four deer and three javelinas. My brother Skedat's killed his first javelina. Wazicat is in their hands that was never there before. If it doesn't come from you, where did it come from?"

Esther didn't have the vocabulary to argue with this logic. "So does everybody think I have wazicat?"

"Yes," said Ahrva.

"No," said Otala, Mingwah's girl. "Uduban says no."

"Uduban is jealous the wazicat didn't come to him," said Emni, Kitotul's teenage daughter. She had been walking apart from the other girls for a couple of days, and veered off if anyone came toward her, but she never went far enough to not be in the conversation. "He knows she's got it, but he doesn't want to admit it. Podan tells my father, wait, sooner or later, he'll have to admit the luck has changed."

They walked along in silence for a while. Esther reviewed the conversation. She'd understood almost every word. It was time to ask the question that she'd wanted to ask for days. "So—where are we going?"

"To the next camp," said Ahrva.

"Yes, but I mean—isn't there someplace we're *going?* Where we'll stop longer than a couple of days?"

"If you stop too long, you get fleas," said Emni.

"Oh, I know!" Ahrva snapped her fingers. "She means the Valley."

"We go through lots of valleys," protested Esther.

"Not the *valley*," said Ahrva, "the Valley."

"That's clear as mud," said Esther. "Is there good food in the Valley?"

"Telapa," said Washaw. "There's grass, reeds, trees, water—everything telapa like. Everyone comes, eats, visits, and plays ball. It's wonderful."

"In a good time," added Ahrva. "Last year, there were floods, then no rain, then floods. The reeds didn't grow. The telapa didn't give themselves to us."

"Like now," said Washaw.

"We heard telabat last night," said Otala. "Where there are telabat, there are telapa."

Esther shivered. The telabat made a scream from a horror movie—a howl, a whistle, a crying baby, all at once.

"It only means there are telapa families," said Emni.

"But that's good, isn't it?" asked Esther.

"The men can't kill from the families," explained Ahrva. "Our men hunt telapa men. My father says we depend too much on finding telapa where they were before. If people don't listen, we'll live on squirrels all summer. You won't have enough wazicat to prevent it."

"If I had wazicat, I'd be with my mother now," said Esther.

"You don't have the right kind of wazicat for that," said Emni. "But there'll be dream-walkers in the Valley. They'll know what to do. They can find out what no one else can."

"Oh?" *I don't believe in wazicat.* But—if a way existed to get here, a way must exist to get back. And she had seen Tekinit first in a dream. "When do we get to the Valley?"

"When the tsik is ripe and the nights are cold."

Rats. Cold nights probably meant fall.

"Till then, tell your wazicat to find telapa," Emni went on.

"Or strawberries," suggested Otala, momentarily confusing Esther. The hardest thing about this language was that everybody was named for everyday things! Ahrva's mom was named after strawberries, and it *would* be nice to find them today, but Tekinit had another idea.

"No, sulira!" Tekinit danced, waving her stran to make the goldfinch feathers tied to it flutter. "I want sulira!"

"Weh," said Esther. "I'll work on it. If we find sulira and telapa both today, that'll prove I've got wazicat. And if we don't, you'll know I've got none."

"There won't be any sulira," said Otala. "If there were, Ehdanwah would already know where to find it."

Esther merely looked wise, wondering what sulira was. •

EIGHT

➤ SULIRA

Esther's hair was limp with sweat. The girls had lagged behind the women, who straggled along the slope of the current hill. Tall Nudawah stopped beneath a red oak at the top. Mingwah settled down to nurse her baby and Silika to rest her swollen feet. Ehdanwah stood beside Nudawah, scanning the horizon. The girls struggled to the shade and flopped down; except for Tekinit, who ran to Ehdanwah and announced: "Esster says we'll find sulira and telapa today!"

"Oh, does she?" Nudawah turned her searchlight glare to Esther. "She flew up to the stars and saw them, maybe?"

Esther shook her head, then remembered that these people only shook their heads when they were teasing children, and tried to shake her hands in the proper "no" gesture instead. She wanted to explain, but she was out of breath, and before she could start, Ahrva did. "We were talking about wazicat. Esther isn't sure she has any. So she said she would try to use it to find sulira and telapa today, and if we found both, then we'd know."

Nudawah laughed. "We know *now*. Your mouse-child maybe

60

dropped from the stars, maybe not, but my big toe has more wazicat."

"Weh, weh, I bow to the power of your big toe," said Silika, getting nervous laughs from the other women. People didn't like laughing at Nudawah. She kept track. "No one knows what a star-child can do. Tekinit wasn't born yet when we last came to this hill. There was no sulira then. Maybe there is now."

"Sulira doesn't run from place to place," said Nudawah.

"It doesn't run, but maybe it waits," said Ehdanwah, jabbing her heel into the bare dirt under the tree. "We're near the hole with the cold water. I remember a place my husband's mother liked. Some years the sulira wouldn't be ripe yet; some years the animals had eaten it all; some years, it was just right. My husband's mother died. The next senior woman didn't like sulira. Now I'm senior woman. This morning, I wondered, can I find sulira again? Who knows? How do we find out?"

Tekinit danced with excitement. "I'll help you, Ehdanwah! We'll find it!"

Ehdanwah smiled at Tekinit. "You think we should look, hey? Where should we look?"

"What was the place like?" asked Shusskt, Kitotul's wife.

"I was trying to remember," said Ehdanwah, studying the view. "We climb down. We come to the rock. To go to the hole, we turn right, but to go to the sulira, we turned left. Before the river, there were three creeks. The sulira was above the middle creek."

Nudawah looked sour, but she said: "It may be a long search for the sulira, and maybe there will be none. Ehdanwah and I will look. The rest of you will swim and catch turtles."

"If you take two girls with you," suggested Silika, "young legs can run to tell us what you've found."

So they hauled their loads and each other downhill, around a cedar brake, and down a steep slope, to a rock taller than Nudawah. Esther heard water, but the undergrowth was too thick to see any. Nudawah, Ehdanwah, and two of the girls turned left as everyone else turned right.

As they helped Silika clamber along the rocky path, Esther thought, *The trees are wrong,* and wondered why.

Then they came to the hole with cold water, and she knew.

Swallows dashed from bug to bug high above. A waterfall, bigger than she remembered, poured over the high lip of stone, feeding a green pool. Eleven thousand years had changed the land, the plants, the creek, the shape of the tiny beach; but the sloping granite would still rise from the water, the waterfall would still drag moss over the lip of the hole in the rock dome, and kids would still break into a run when they saw the waterfall pool.

Esther let the rest surge past, dropping their packs, wading into the shallow beach end. She had never been here this late in the day. Her family would come early, with a small cooler, a picnic basket, and towels. They would swim until they were hungry, then sprawl on the towels drinking soda and eating cold meat, greens, and cheese wrapped in flour tortillas. By then, people would be hauling ridiculous amounts of stuff down the nearly vertical path from the parking lot—lawn chairs, boom boxes, coolers that required two people to carry. Her own family would go back to town for an air-conditioned movie.

The last time she was here, Danny had climbed onto the slippery rocks below the waterfall, as Ahrva was doing. Dad had helped her onto the steep rocks, where a snapping turtle with a head the size of a tennis ball, like the one there now, had climbed up to see whether they were fool enough to feed it.

Tekinit slipped and fell on her behind, laughing—the floor of the pool was slippery, Esther knew, with moss and algae. The women's voices echoed off the roof. Ahrva waved from the rock. "Ess-ter! Come in!"

If there was any place where she should be able to find a gate home, it was here, where her family came three or four times every summer. Everywhere she looked, she saw the future—but only with her brain's eyes, not with the ones in her face. She took off her sneakers, bracing herself for the pain of the first step as hot feet met icy cold water, and waded in beside Tekinit, who had her arms spread wide, frowning as she balanced. Esther took her hand. "Can you swim to the waterfall?"

"Watch!" Tekinit shouted, launching herself in a series of splashes worthy of a girl three times her size. Esther followed, breast-stroking slowly, wondering whether, if she dived, she would come up in another time.

She had tried three times when the two girls, Washaw and Otala, came running, calling: "Sulira, sulira!" Tekinit cheered and swam to Esther, latching onto her back. "Ho, ho, I knew you had wazicat!"

"I don't see any telapa standing around," said Esther; not that she would have known a telapa if she'd seen one.

Silika, coming out of a back float which made her pregnant body appear like a line of islands, said: "Everyone has wazicat." She looked straight into Esther's face. "And what you have, you must use. Nudawah's jealous, because now I have three daughters and she has none. If she could leave you behind, she would. Don't help her by denying the power you have."

"Yes, ma'am," said Esther, swallowing. She wanted to ask— could Nudawah really do that? Would Ehdanwah let her? What would Silika and Podan do? But Silika turned away before she could shape the questions; and maybe she didn't want to know the answers.

Silika and Mingwah stayed to watch Mingwah's baby, but everybody else grabbed bags and headed for the sulira. Esther had hiked from the pool to the river more than once in her own time, but none of the terrain was familiar now.

Ehdanwah and Nudawah were busy in a fierce tangle of bushes, picking red berries off of thorny stems. Birds flew up, protesting, and something crashed away as the women approached. Ehdanwah grinned. "They're perfect! Tomorrow, the birds would have eaten them. Yesterday, they wouldn't have been ripe."

"Emni can have that bit over there," said Nudawah, pointing. "Watch for podans! We've seen two."

Emni retreated to the darkest, thorniest part of the patch without protest. The women wrapped their arms in animal skins and scraped berries wholesale into their bags. Thorns tore the leather, stuck their faces, snagged their blouses, and scratched their legs. As many thorns, twigs, and leaves got into the bags as berries. When all the bags they could carry were full, Ahrva and Esther hauled them back to the pool. Silika had rigged a sleeping fur into a ramp and spread another fur at the base, skin up. "Where's Mingwah?" asked Esther.

Silika pointed with her head toward the top of the sinkhole, as her hands were busy dumping sulira at the top of the ramp. "She's building a fire to bring the men." The berries tumbled down the fur ramp, leaving a trail of debris, to land on the other fur in a squishy mound, on which Tekinit pounced.

Ahrva took a handful and Esther did the same, watching in case there was a trick to the skins and seeds, like with the grapes. No, you just popped them into your mouth. Yuck! They were still dirty! Then the fruit sugar hit her system with a shock as welcome as that of the cold water. Esther tried another handful. "They'd taste better if they were clean," she said.

"Weh, weh," said Silika. "They're too small to clean."

"My mother," Esther said, slowly, trying to arrange the idea in the most accessible words, "had a . . . a gourd. With holes. She put the berries in that and poured water over them." She'd never thought of running the faucet as "pouring" before, but it basically was. "The water ran out and the berries were clean."

Silika looked interested. "Show me."

Esther picked up an empty gourd doubtfully and studied the problem. Silika passed her the piece of antler she used to punch holes in leather. All the women and children stopped to watch her picking away at the gourd as they passed from the sulira patch to the berry-cleaning ramps (one for Emni, one for everyone else) to a refreshing swim. Nudawah sniffed once and then ignored Esther. Esther worked steadily, though it made her hand and back ache, and she'd much rather have swum.

At last she was finished. As she dipped her handmade colander, full of sulira, into the pool, even Nudawah watched, sideways. Ehdanwah accepted the gourd, took a handful of berries, and ate them. "Weh," she said, her face crinkling into a smile. "Clean sulira, and cool, too! It's a good idea."

"We have one fewer water gourd than we used to," said Nudawah. "We liked sulira well enough before."

"You eat it your way and I'll eat it my way," said Esther.

"Sa, sa," said Ehdanwah, no longer smiling. "They're picky eaters in the stars. Here, we eat what the land gives us."

"Yes, ma'am," said Esther, lowering her eyes respectfully. "I won't eat it my way, if you say not."

"Esster, let me try some," Silika said.

The gourd soon emptied, amid expressions of appreciation or dislike. Emni kept to her own mound of berries, but started drilling holes in a gourd.

Howls of return echoed down from the sky. The women all looked up, as one, to see Kitotul on the sinkhole's rim, waving his stran. "Why did you stop, you lazy women? Why didn't you march bravely forward to join us? Why don't you sing the praises of Kitotul, who found telapa sign?"

The women cheered, and Kitotul dove. Esther was sure the pool wasn't deep enough for safe diving, but he came up, spouting water, and caught his daughter Washaw, twirling her around in the water. Tekinit crowed, Silika shouted, and the men above howled and shook their spears.

Nudawah scowled.

Oh, crud, Esther thought, *telapa. I guess I have wazicat.*

NINE

➤ BEFORE THE HUNT

With no lifeguards or rules against roughhousing, the grown-ups played as hard as the children, ducking each other and whooping when they got ducked themselves. Mingwah's husband, Dul, swam the baby around the shallow end, splashing and talking baby talk. Even Ehdanwah swam stealthily up to Uduban and pulled his feet out from under him. Only Emni picked her way downstream and bathed in the shallower water of the creek.

"What's up with her?" asked Esther, when certain that Emni couldn't hear her ask.

"She's yana," said Ahrva. "She's too strong."

"She looks the same to me."

"That's because life is invisible," said Ahrva, catching hold of Tekinit as her little sister barreled against her, swimming like a frog. "She's full of life-wazicat. And it's not going into a baby like my mother's is. It's dangerous for the men to get too close to her. Even if us women touch her, we might accidentally pass it to the men."

"So she's downstream so the wazicat will wash away? But life-wazicat should be good. How can it hurt anybody?"

"Fire's good," said Ahrva, "but if you touch it, it hurts. All the world's strength is in a yana woman, so she must be careful."

Since Kitotul had found the first telapa sign, he was privileged to choose their campsite. Tekinit was so tired she had to be carried to the top of the chosen ridge, from which it was easy to see both the river and, a mile or so away, a water hole in a green marsh. The air seemed to hum, as if the world was more alive than usual.

Tonight there was no fire, for fear of alerting the telapa. The women even gathered material for the shelters from the opposite side of the hill to the distant water hole. Emni set up a shelter right down behind the ridge, at the very edge of the space that could be considered safe, to guarantee that her wazicat didn't interfere with the hunting preparations.

Each man told the story of the hunt in the usual way. "This is the river where I hunted with my father," Uduban said. "I remembered the fat days when we let telapa go because they were too small." This got a polite laugh. "I went where I have been before. I found mammoth sign, but it was old. Kitotul said he would look away from the river. I thought, *That won't hurt anything.* I said: *Go, find telapa where we have not found them before, and I will find them where we have found them before, and we will all be happy.* But I had not found them yet when Dul saw the women's smoke calling us to the place with cold water."

That explained why he looked as though he was sucking a lemon. It must burn him that Kitotul did better than he; and not by luck, either.

Podan stood. "We went to the river. The grass there is too short for telapa to grip. There used to be a shallow place where we would cross to meet our cousin Fedat's people. That place is dry, now—the water has moved. Kitotul and I spoke about what telapa like. Kitotul remembered a marsh with a water hole. He thought I should mention it to Uduban. I knew that Uduban loves the river where he and our father killed ten telapa." That got a laugh; but Esther, watching Uduban, wished Podan hadn't said it.

"I knew he wouldn't go. But I also knew that Kitotul might be right. I am already oheitika. I don't need to steal his ideas. So I told him that if he would tell Uduban about the water hole, I would go with him.

"So Kitotul, Skedat, and I left the others, patiently searching. We climbed, and the grass was long. Jackrabbits ran from us at every step. They couldn't tell that we were not women." Another laugh, one that Uduban and Nudawah joined this time. "We found a tree that had been pushed over and grass that had been ripped up. At the water hole, we found telapa tracks, trampled reeds, dung. Then Skedat saw the women's smoke."

Dul spoke briefly, basically repeating what Uduban had said without the part about giving Kitotul permission to look elsewhere. Then Kitotul stood up, looking taller than usual. Everyone else had started with going to the river, so Kitotul's first words were a surprise. "I am a low man. I know this. So before I went to the river, I went to the star-child."

Esther wished the ground would suck her down.

"I took her hand and shook it. Since I have done this every

morning, my wazicat has been better. Since my son Skedat started shaking the star-child's hand, he has become as good at hunting as any boy." The way he said it, Esther was sure he meant "better than." "I followed Uduban, but we found nothing. I talked to Podan. He is a man who thinks, and he is full of wazicat from sharing a shelter with the star-child."

Esther's face burned so much, she was sure if she put water on her cheeks, it would sizzle. "Esther," she whispered. "My name is Esther, not star-child!" Ahrva squeezed her hand.

"I remembered the water hole. Once we stopped to rest near it, and a telabat came to drink. Would telabat waste his time with water telapa never drank from? But maybe it had changed, too. The only way to know was to look. I thought: *I am a low man, Podan is oheitika, he is Uduban's little brother, he should suggest this.* Podan said that it was my idea and I should speak it; but he would go with me. We told Uduban we were going. He thought we were stupid. We went anyway. The star-child's wazicat helped me find telapa sign." He grinned triumphantly at the ring of faces, apparently not noticing Uduban glaring at him.

Everyone else did, though. Dul stood up again. "Weh, weh," he said. "Maybe it is wazicat, maybe not, but telapa waits, and we must not disappoint him! We still have much to do!"

The men formed a circle and the women brought bags of rocks and gourds of water with strings of wesk soaking in them. The boys took out all the hunting equipment and examined it. The women and girls built shelters and sang about how strong the men were. Esther sang, too, watching the men. She could tell they were making Clovis points. Women often sharpened their points by taking bits off the edges with pieces of antler, but this was the first time she'd had a chance to see one made from scratch.

"Podan's points will be better than Uduban's," whispered Tekinit to Esther, as if imparting a great secret.

"Hush," said Ahrva. "It doesn't matter. It takes all the men to bring down telapa."

Esther was edgy, feeling that the ground beneath her shivered—in anticipation? In fear? "What do we do while they're hunting?"

"We wait," said Ahrva.

That sounded like great gobs of no fun. "How long?"

"Till the hunt's done," said Ahrva. "Maybe by noon tomorrow we'll feast, and maybe many days from now we'll still wait."

The sky in the east was dark blue when Uduban stood, raised his arms, and called: "Flint fathers, listen to us! Make my brother's hand sure and steady! Make his eye strong!"

At once the women and children, except for Emni, hurried to the hilltop. The men chanted: "Sure and steady, sure and steady."

Podan had several of what looked to Esther like finished points, and three pieces of antler, one with a notch cut out, about the size and shape of the point he fit into it. Holding the notched antler in place with his foot, he held a smaller piece of antler against the base of the stone point, and struck it on the end with the last, heaviest antler. *Crack!* Esther felt all the women holding their breath as Podan picked up his foot, nodded, and turned the point over. A flake of stone dropped to the ground. He repeated the process on the other side of the point. The women let go their breath when he nodded again, passing the point to Dul.

Podan put another point into the notch, and repeated the process, as Dul chanted: "Straight and sharp, straight and sharp," rubbing the edges of the new point with a squirrel skin dipped in red powder. Podan passed three points to Dul; then a groan went up, as the fourth point cracked with a different sound. Podan shook his head, discarding the broken shards.

Ahrva leaned forward. Silika chewed her lip, Tekinit clutched against her side. Esther kept her mouth shut, afraid that speaking would break whatever wazicat this was.

Podan's fifth point also broke. He passed the tools to Uduban and stood, raising his arms. Sunset changed the color of the light. "Flint father, listen to us! Make my brother's hand sure and steady! Make his eye strong!" Uduban finished five points in the same way. Only one broke.

The western sky was orange. *Oong-KA-choonk!* The nightly animal chorus had begun. The men began assembling their short strans that could function as either knives or spear fore-shafts. Uduban and Podan faced each other, eye to eye; then Podan lowered his head. Nudawah said to Silika, with a jerk of her nose: "The flint knows who's best."

Silika said nothing, but Tekinit made a face as Nudawah walked away. "He's not so much better," muttered Ahrva. "The flint favors Uduban because he's older."

"I know I ask lots of stupid questions," said Esther. "But what *was* all that?"

"Every man must have at least one new stran, for the new hunt," said Ahrva, "and the flint fathers decide who leads."

"Oh," said Esther. "So why didn't Kitotul get to try? He found the telapa sign."

"He can't," said Ahrva. "His father came to us because he killed his leader. That bad wazicat is still on Kitotul."

"But...that's not...right!" Esther didn't know the group's word for "fair," but she knew "not fair" when she heard it. "Kitotul didn't do anything wrong."

"I know," said Silika. "I'm angry at Kitotul's father every time I think of what he did. When you do evil, it casts darkness all around you. He should have thought of his childen and his grandchildren before he killed his leader."

This explained a lot about Kitotul and his family—why Uduban's son, Telabat, shoved his chores onto Skedat, why Nudawah snubbed the whole family; even why Podan and Silika were nice to them. *They're kind to us outsiders. It's a habit,* Esther thought. "You can make darkness back off with fire. Isn't there some way to make the darkness from evil go away?"

"In time," said Silika. "Kitotul's mother cut it in half for him. Shusskt cut it in half for their children. For Emni's children, it will be cut in half again, and then in their children, it will be so small, it won't matter."

Esther was still considering this bleak future, and feeling better about the idea that she had good wazicat herself, when Skedat called out, "Look! They're coming!"

Esther joined the stampede to the hilltop. Tekinit between them, she and Ahrva forced their way through the grown-ups to a good viewing position. The marsh and water hole made a dark saucer in the land, overhung with trees and shadows of the rough terrain. Esther saw movement, in rhythm with the sudden shaking of the ground.

Telapa meant "mammoth."

"Mammoth" meant "big."

One was practically a hill, its back sloping from a domed head that rose above the trees. The trunk draped casually over the tusks, which curved out and in, a circle thrusting far ahead of the face. The other mammoths—four—were smaller; which was like saying other mountains were smaller than Everest.

The mammoths splashed into the water hole in the heart of the marsh, drank, washed themselves—acting like the elephants at the zoo. Their ears were smaller than Esther would have expected, and their bodies weren't woolly at all.

"It's a family," said Skedat, disappointed.

"But the men won't be far," said Uduban.

The lead mammoth plopped down and rolled in the water hole. The earth, in a delayed reaction, trembled.

So did Esther.

The men were going to hunt *that*?

TEN

➤ STORIES IN THE MORNING

*E*sther, dreaming of mammoths, thought that a baby one had crawled in with them; but it was only Podan. He kissed Tekinit, tucking a fur round her; then Ahrva, who slid her arm around his neck and murmured, "Good hunting, Daddy. Be careful!"

"I will. Go back to sleep." He rubbed Esther's forehead. "You too, star-child."

"Good luck," whispered Esther.

He slipped out, followed by Silika. Esther wanted to cry, wondered why, and remembered how, when her father left early on a business trip, he always came in to kiss her and told her to go back to sleep. "Is hunting mammoth dangerous?" she asked.

"Once," whispered Ahrva, "Uduban and Nudawah had a grown-up son. The men wounded a mammoth. Only someone standing next to it could pierce the heart. If you don't pierce the heart, the mammoth doesn't die. Uduban's son ran forward. The mammoth grabbed him in his trunk"—she sat up, pantomiming, so that Esther understood the word for trunk though she hadn't heard it before—"and hurled him. He broke. He couldn't move his arms and legs. He couldn't even kill himself. Uduban did it for him."

"*What?*"

"A man who can't walk, starves. Ehdanwah couldn't fix him. It's better to go bravely than to drag your feet."

Esther crawled out of bed to lie on her belly in the entrance, watching the women smearing the hunters' faces with red paste. Shadows and silhouettes, the men collected equipment and hugged their wives. Kitotul and Skedat came, holding out their hands for Esther to shake. Esther did so, whispering: "Good luck." Uduban and Nudawah's surviving son, Telabat, saw them and rolled his eyes scornfully. Dul hesitated then ran up, shook her hand quickly, and ran off again. Then all the men were gone into the gray morning.

Silika waddled back to the shelter. "You go back to sleep," she whispered.

"Ahrva told me about Uduban's older son," said Esther.

"Don't think about it," said Silika.

"The sun's almost up," said Ahrva. "We can't sleep now. Tell us a story."

"It's not the season for stories."

"Esther's never seen mammoth before. Tell why she has such a big nose and little tail."

"I have to make the loud mammoth noise for that. It would wake your sister."

"Then tell how you married my father."

Silika laughed. "You don't want to hear that again!"

"Yes, I do."

"Please," said Esther. She needed a cheerful story after that one about Uduban's son!

"Nuaah," moaned Silika, which meant "Oh, all right." "When I was Emni's age, my mother said it was time to find me a husband. I cried that she wanted to get rid of me. My brother Geshwaw said that at the Valley he would find me a fine husband who would make me want to leave the group.

"We came to the Valley. My little sister Apuk and I met my friend Yahaywah, and we fished as we told each other our troubles. Yahaywah's mother, Ehdanwah, also said it was time for her to marry, and she was afraid, too. We told her what my brother, Geshwaw, had said. 'It must be a fine man to make you want to leave your family,' said Yahaywah. 'He must be as tall as mammoth.'

"I said: 'He must be able to swing a mammoth by its trunk!'

"'He must carry home two mammoths over his shoulder on every day's hunt,' said Apuk.

"'He must be so handsome, when the sleeping fur falls off his face at night, the group will rise, thinking the sun has come up,' I added. 'Grass will grow in his footprints, and he will smell so sweet, the butterflies will flutter round him.'

"'But you'd have to brush the butterflies off to kiss him,' said Apuk. 'And the other women will fight you for him.'

"'Oh, but he won't want them,' I said. 'If he doesn't think I'm as fine as he is, I want nothing to do with him, not if he were the sun come down to walk the earth!'

"Our men prepared for the big hunt. We girls were not allowed to look at the men."

"Why not?" asked Esther.

"Because if we saw one that we wanted, our desire might draw his wazicat off of him and make him weak."

"But if you couldn't look at them, how could you pick one?"

"Oh, we already knew them, and we talked to their sisters," said Silika. "All the women bragged. Nudawah bragged loudest. She had a fine son—the one who died later. She had a fine daughter then—she died the year Tekinit was born. Uduban was taking charge as Ehdanwah's husband grew feeble. Nudawah had the best children, the best husband; she had everything! And she was full of life—Telabat would be born that season. So she was loud, telling the world and sky about her wonderful family. Nudawah always knew best."

"She's still like that." Ahrva giggled.

Silika looked somber. "Knowing best is all she has left. Since then her daughter has died without children, her son has died, her son's baby has died, and her son's wife has gone to a man in another group. Remember that when she angers you."

Ahrva patted her mother's arm. "Tell about Yahaywah's favorite brother."

"You're so bossy, you had better tell the sun to get up in the morning." Silika pinched Ahrva's nose and smiled. "My friend Yahaywah's favorite brother was Podan, so as loud as Nudawah talked, she would talk louder. Apuk and I bragged on Geshwaw. We told how he outsmarted a telabat and stole its kill. But Nudawah sniffed her nose in the air"—Silika twitched her nose so exactly like Nudawah that Esther laughed, guiltily—"and said: 'I don't see anything so fine in stealing a baby mammoth. My Uduban brings home man-sized mammoths.'"

"Did you already like Podan in those days?" asked Ahrva.

"At one gathering, he had come back from the biggest hunt with his spear unbloodied. He told Yahaywah and me that he had decided to become a woman, and we must teach him to be yana. That was how I thought of him, a boy who laughed at his own failure."

Tekinit stirred, but did not wake. "Go on," said Ahrva. "Or you won't finish the story before light."

"The men hunted. We could see the mammoths. The ground shook with them! But the men lay low, in disguise, so that the mammoths would see only coyotes, bears, animals that couldn't hurt them. The wind carried the smell of the men away. Our mothers said that the mammoth herds were less than when they were girls."

"They always say that," said Ahrva.

"I thought you weren't supposed to watch," said Esther.

"We didn't, exactly," said Silika. "We looked sideways, and my little sister Apuk described what went on. Our men hunted the young and foolish bulls, driving them quietly, quietly into ambush. They were so careful that the other mammoths knew nothing of it. They took one, and another, and another.

"Then at sunset the wind shifted."

Ahrva hissed air in through her teeth.

"A mother mammoth called out. More answered. Our men scattered as the mammoths charged, but one man stumbled and fell. He was bound to be trampled! Another ran straight at the mother mammoth that was heading for his friend, holding his hands up, holding his stran up. But no one can kill a charging mammoth head on, and if he hurt a female, the bad wazicat would be on him forever. We all moaned, and we big girls closed our eyes to keep from looking. Nudawah said: 'That rock-brain is dead, but brave.'

"My heart stood still, and I thought: *The man who can run at a mammoth to help his friend is worth leaving a mother for.*

"Apuk shouted that the mammoth was rearing on her hind legs, raising her tusks and trunk against the sky. Then she trumpeted. The sound made all my hair stand up, my belly grow cold. The women jumped and screamed for joy as the man who had fallen rose. The man who had run at the mammoth veered, and they both ran."

Esther relaxed. "It was Podan who ran at the mammoth, wasn't it?"

"It was," said Silika quietly, but her smile was loud. "And the man who stumbled was my brother, Geshwaw." She looked toward the sky, green and pink in the east. "Many girls wanted the man whose courage the mammoth honored with that cry; but it was my brother he saved. And it was me, out of all the girls who wanted him, that he chose. Many men had looked at me, but no one would fight the man the mammoth honored. I wouldn't have looked at them, if they had. So Geshwaw found a fine husband for me, and though I miss my family, I've never been sorry. Now wake your sister. It's time to eat."

Ahrva woke Tekinit. Esther stretched, thinking of the waterfall, the beach, her family smelling of sunscreen on hot summer mornings. Dad would rub sunscreen into Mama's back and tell how he had proposed. "I was rubbing it into her shoulder, like this," he said. "We were all alone, and everything was perfect. So I said: 'What if we got married? Don't you think we should?' And your mama rolled over and looked me in the eye and said: 'What?' And I said: 'Don't you think we should get married?' And she said: 'Oh, all right, if you want to.'"

Mama would hit him and say: "That's not how it happened!" But she would never say how she remembered it, because Dad always kissed her then, laughing. Esther and Danny would roll their eyes and race to the water, last one in was a rotten egg.

"C'mon, God," Esther whispered to the paling sky. "C'mon. It's time to go home!"

ELEVEN

➤ WAITING AND WATCHING

*E*hdanwah and Nudawah took out foraging groups, leaving Silika and Mingwah to look after the camp. They no longer worried about alerting the mammoths, figuring that the more the animals noticed the camp, the less likely they were to notice hunters. The eskways in the marsh were no longer good, but the cattail tops—called apuk, like Silika's little sister— were ripening, and Ehdanwah found greens, mushrooms, ground squirrels, and grapes. Emni found a good trapping trail.

In the afternoon, with full stomachs and a pile of food, the girls and women ran races dribbling a ball. Esther taught them to jump rope with a grapevine. Her counting rhymes sounded funny in the group's language, but they soon invented new ones.

As dusk fell, the games stopped. No one sang, except Mingwah, when her baby cried. Deep blue clouds bunched on the horizon. Esther found herself listening for homecoming howls in the evening chorus of birds, the invisible *oong-KA-choonks*, the rumbling of the mammoth family returning to the water hole.

The mammoths used their trunks to pick grass, scratch their bellies with sticks, and touch each other. They especially liked to stroke and play with the baby, who seemed to belong to all of them. One mammoth, bigger than the baby but smaller than the others, kept wandering off, then wandering back, nudging the older mammoths' sides until they swatted him away. "What's he doing?" Tekinit asked.

"He wants milk, but all the milk is for the baby now," said Silika. "He's like you last winter!"

Tekinit made a face. "I was *glad* about the baby! But Ahrva wouldn't share her food."

"Did too," said Ahrva. "You wouldn't eat it."

"You gave me rotten fruit!"

"Did not."

"Did too."

"So why can't the men hunt these mammoths?" asked Esther. "Why do they have to go off for days instead?"

Nudawah snorted. "Star people sure are stupid!"

"Esster is like a woman newly married," said Ehdanwah. "All her old knowledge is no good. But she has come from farther away than any woman ever did, and she doesn't even have a man to make it worth her while. I think they have no mammoths in the stars."

"No, ma'am," said Esther. "I'd only heard of them."

"Then how could you know?" Ehdanwah sat cross-legged, sparks rising into the darkening air behind her. "Among mammoths, daughters stay with mothers, sisters stay together. They protect each other. But when the sons grow, the mothers drive them away. The sons wander. When they find no women, they're friends with other men. But when women are near, the men mammoths fight. When we find the women mammoths, we know there are men mammoths who won't defend each other. And the women mammoths understand that we must eat their men sometimes. But if we hunted the women, they would fight to defend each other; and then they would find the human women and trample us. In winter, you will hear the story, how our grandmothers and their grandmothers agreed, for the sake of all the babies, to keep the quarrels among the men."

Esther watched the mammoths, the biggest one wallowing, one rubbing her tusks against a half-dead tree, the baby and the weanling playing. It seemed impossible that anything so big could ever die, much less die out. "I wish I could see them close," she said. "If I ever get home, I want to be able to tell everybody about everything."

"*When* you get home, you will!" declared Ahrva.

"Maybe we'll find a tree tall enough for her to climb to the stars," said Nudawah, drily.

Darkness came. Owls and mammoths called. As Esther raked zulotuls out of the fire, Nudawah stood over her, saying softly, "Don't think I don't know what you're doing."

Esther looked down, and said, "I'm getting zulotul for Tekinit, ma'am."

"If you have any wazicat, it must be bad," said Nudawah. "Podan thinks he can use you to replace his brother. He pretends to be a good brother, and to Ehdanwah he is still her baby, but I see what he's doing. He thinks he can lead. Look out! If he can turn on his brother, he can turn on you."

Esther was so mad she almost couldn't see; but before she

could answer, Silika came up, asking, "Are the zulotuls not cooking right?"

Esther poked the cooked roots with her stran. "I'm not sure," she said. "I'm sorry to be so stupid."

"You aren't stupid," said Silika, rubbing her head.

They ate the zulotuls. Then Ahrva rubbed Silika's swollen feet and Esther combed Tekinit's hair as all the women sang to Mingwah's baby. Esther sang along. "Be sweet like strawberries, strong like mammoth, fast like pronghorn. Be tall like pine, smart like fox, beautiful like blue jay."

It was Silika's turn for first fire watch, so Esther and Ahrva put Tekinit to bed. Tekinit kept popping up to say one more thing, but the big girls took turns pushing her down and rubbing her back, until she began to breathe the breath of a sleeper. Esther closed her eyes.

"Let's go look at the mammoths in the morning," said Ahrva. "If we leave early, we can get close."

Esther's stomach fizzed. "Is it safe?"

"Sure. They'll know that you're a star-child, and that I'm the daughter of one they honor. We'll lie low and never move."

"Nuaah," said Esther. "Why not?" It must be okay, if Ahrva said it was. Besides, they'd probably both sleep too late.

To her surprise, her eyes opened while the entrance to the shelter was still black. Ahrva touched her shoulder. Without a word, they crawled into the chill, damp outdoors. Ehdanwah nodded by the fire; but as they tiptoed up to rake out some zulotuls, she said, "It's early to go anywhere, girls."

"Nudawah said someone would have to go back to the bog this morning," said Ahrva, which was true, as far as it went.

"It's a fine thing to be young and to see in the dark."

"It's a fine thing to be old," said Ahrva, "and to know what danger is. What lives in the dark that would hurt us?"

"When I was young, uduban ate a child Tekinit's age."

This statement startled Esther; until she remembered that the men were all named after predators. "Uduban likes fatter meat than us," said Ahrva.

"You could take Otala."

"She's asleep. Mingwah would be angry if we woke her."

Ehdanwah made a shooing motion. "Go. Go. When I was young, the world had more food and more danger, and I and my sister would go before dawn to see the mammoths drink. But do not push your wazicat too far!"

The girls speared a few zulotuls apiece and trotted away.

At first they ate without talking, the grass wetting their knees, the zulotuls burning their mouths. If—when—she got home, Esther wondered, would she crave zulotul as she now craved breakfast tacos? "Why was Uduban named after an animal that eats children?" she asked, to have something else to think about.

"The uduban is a great hunter, with long legs, who can bring down game that's too fast for us. His cousin the podan is smaller and clumsier, but if uduban can't find meat, he starves, and podan can live on grubs and berries." Ahrva stopped, pointing. A shadow as big as both of them was tearing up something not twenty yards away. When it grumbled, Esther recognized a bear ripping at a rotten log, licking grubs from its claws. Ahrva said into Esther's ear, "Podan. Good omen, but be careful!"

Esther nodded, numb. It looked far bigger than the black

bears at the zoo seemed behind their moat. Ahrva tugged her hand, and Esther moved with her. The bear ignored them.

The sky brightened, pink and green and yellow, above a world that still overwhelmed Esther's senses—so many birds, flowers, animals—so few traces of people. The moans and rumbles of the mammoths rolled like a bass line of music across the soprano of the morning birds.

"So what did Nudawah say to you last night?" asked Ahrva.

"She doesn't like me."

"Did she say bad things about my father?"

"Um—I didn't believe any of it," Esther said, but she wasn't sure. If Kitotul hadn't made that lucky shot at the camel when she showed up, would Podan have thought her worth adopting?

"She has bad luck because she's mean," declared Ahrva. "But she'd rather blame my father than be nice."

"I don't see what I have to do with it," said Esther. "That's all grown-up stuff."

"Grown-up stuff is our stuff," said Ahrva. "If they decide wrong, we die! Like Nudawah and Uduban's children."

"That wasn't their fault," said Esther. But wasn't it?

Like hills in motion, the mammoths milled about the water hole. The ground for yards around was churned and trampled, the hoof and paw prints of smaller animals crisscrossing broad, scalloped mammoth tracks. The weaned mammoth wandered in the grass, tearing up trunkfuls, mouthing them, spitting them out; whirling on its hind legs, trumpeting squeakily, and charging a bush, from which a bobcat darted, hissing and bounding away.

When Ahrva dropped to her belly, Esther did, too. The world quivered as they inched through trampled reeds.

Mosquitoes and gnats materialized in clouds. Ahrva coated her face with mud. Ick! But it discouraged the bugs, so Esther plastered her face, too. Red-winged blackbirds darted among nests waving in the reeds, where wide-mouthed babies peeped. Ahrva almost crawled straight into a great blue heron. At one point, the ground beneath Esther gave way to water, and she panicked; but Ahrva helped her onto semisolid ground, repressing giggles.

The biggest mammoth, a mother and grandmother, stood knee-deep in water, eating cattails. No house had ceilings tall enough to fit over her, and she was as long as she was tall. Even her skimpy tail was as long as Esther's body, and in constant motion, flicking bugs.

The baby hit the water with his trunk to splash his mother. Esther bit her lip to keep from laughing. He was so cute, with fuzz all over his head and drooping from his cheeks! Dawn light glowed on the mammoth's rough skins.

The grandmother mammoth ate her way toward Esther and Ahrva. The end of her trunk had projections, like a finger and thumb, which might be useful for picking up small things; but she yanked up cattails and shoved them into her mouth— apuks, zulotuls, and all.

The mother stroked the baby with her trunk and—incredibly—purred. Grandmother Mammoth's trunk descended between the girls, and hesitated. Esther's heart almost stopped as the trunk-fingers touched her face. *She could pull my head off like a bunch of cattails.* The fingers were warm and wet.

A scream ripped the world down the middle, and Esther thought that she had died.

TWELVE

*T*he baby mammoth plunged into the water and the mother mammoth surged to her feet, but Esther barely had a chance to see this as the grandmother whirled on her hind legs, blotting out the sky. *She can't stay up like that,* Esther thought, not realizing that she was scrambling backward until she hit her foot on a submerged rock. She yelped, but the trumpeting, the screaming, the cacophony of birds in the reeds, drowned her out.

Huge—huge—huge spotted cats, with fangs like curving butcher knives. The weanling mammoth. Blood. Lots of blood. Esther closed her eyes and put her hands over her head. The ground heaved. When she looked, she saw mammoths trampling the grass, a pool of bright red, and Ahrva. No weanling. No cats.

Esther waited to throw up, and didn't. "Wh-what was that?"

"Telabat," said Ahrva.

Esther shivered. "Will they . . . will they catch them? Can they still save it?"

"No," said Ahrva. "Look at all that blood. It's already dead.

Telabats like young mammoth better than any other meat. They aren't fast enough to catch small game. They have to surprise their prey, and if they don't get a fat animal, they break their teeth on the bones. It's not easy to be a telabat! One mistake, and they're dead. These made no mistake."

Esther closed her eyes. The picture of the telabat killing the mammoth became more vivid. It didn't look much like the picture in her book at home, but she knew what she'd just seen: a scimitar cat—like a saber-toothed tiger, but with smaller teeth. A famous cave in central Texas held the bones of one that had died of old age, along with the remains of hundreds of young mammoths. Scientists argued about how the cats used their big fangs, so unlike anything on any modern animal; and now Esther knew. She wished she didn't. "Let's go," she muttered.

Birds made a vast racket as they filled their bags with zulotuls and apuks. The dew on the grass glittered, except in the dark trail where they had passed earlier. At camp, a thread of smoke spread gray-blue against the blue-gray sky. When Esther looked back, a vulture soared above the water hole.

"What's the matter?" asked Ahrva.

"Don't you think it's awful about that mammoth?"

"It wasn't nice to see, but it's no different from us killing a squirrel." Ahrva thought. "You don't like it when we kill squirrels either, do you?"

"No," said Esther. "I wish everything lived off plants!"

"But then there'd be no plants left, and we'd all starve."

"I know," said Esther. "But the mammoths are all going to die off anyway. I don't know why telabat has to hurry it along."

Ahrva stopped. "What?"

"What what?"

"I thought you said the mammoths were all going to die."

It occurred to Esther that she probably shouldn't have said that, but it was too late now. "They will."

"How do you know?"

"Look, I'm sorry I mentioned it."

Ahrva put her hands on Esther's shoulders and her face close to Esther's face. "How. Do. You. Know?"

Esther swallowed. "I've seen it."

"Did you come here to help us prevent it?"

"I wish I could, but I don't know when it happens, or how."

Ahrva frowned silently for the rest of the walk.

Halfway up the hill, Nudawah suddenly loomed above them, huge against the sky. "So, you decided to come back. We're honored! Where did you go that was such a secret?"

"Seeing the mammoths, ma'am," answered Ahrva.

Esther held up her food bag. "We brought apuks and zulo-tuls."

"I don't care if you brought us the stars," said Nudawah. "You don't forage on your own. What if a bear had decided you looked good to eat, or a mammoth had stepped on you, or the little people stolen you? I don't expect the star-child to have any sense, but you should know better, Ahrva!"

Ahrva looked at her feet, her jaw set.

"It was my fault," said Esther. "I wanted to see them."

Silika appeared behind Nudawah. "Nudawah, my child is wise. The star-child has wazicat that ripens sulira and calls mammoth. Don't meddle where you don't understand."

"I understand all right," said Nudawah. "I understand that

you think your family is better than anyone else's and the rules are for other people. I understand—"

Someone cried out, in a voice too shrill for comprehension, and Nudawah stopped in mid-word, turning in unison with Silika and Ahrva. Esther heard Tekinit's joyful screech and saw a puff of smoke drifting in the sky to the northwest.

Nudawah charged up the hill to join Ehdanwah. Ahrva skipped toward Silika, crowing: "The men! Dad found mammoth! I know he did!"

"Maybe so," said Silika, frowning. "But why did you take Esster to see the mammoths without telling me?"

Ahrva stopped short. "Ehdanwah said—"

"Ehdanwah is wise, and loves us all. You are right to ask her permission. But I am your mother. When I wake up, I should know where you are. And we have talked about how you like to go off alone. You promised not to."

"I wasn't alone," protested Ahrva. "We were safer than Washaw and Otala were coming from the sulira patch to the hole with cold water, because we could see farther, and . . . and—"

Esther tried to think of something to say that wouldn't make things worse, and couldn't. Silika said: "And?"

"And I'm sorry," said Ahrva. "I won't do it again."

"Weh," said Silika, kissing the top of her head. "Come. There's lots to do."

Everyone bustled around talking at once. Esther couldn't make out word one, so she trailed after Ahrva, as usual, and collected a bag of rocks and a gourd of water. Emni came up, declaring that she wasn't yana anymore, and joined Esther and

Ahrva in the group that Nudawah led toward the puffs of smoke rising on the horizon.

"What's going on?" asked Esther.

"The men killed their mammoth," said Ahrva, pointing at the puff trailing bluish tendrils on the wind.

Esther had thought she was used to walking, but this wasn't the usual leisurely, child-paced stroll. Nudawah called no halts. The marsh mud plastering Esther's body and clothes dried tight, making her itch—or maybe that was mosquito bites. Though she couldn't help being last, she kept doggedly walking long after her brain had forgotten why she was doing so.

Mammoth feet had trampled the earth. Many trees were newly stripped of bark, pushed down, or both; and piles of fresh mammoth dung loomed in the ripped-up grass. Telabat and Skedat tended a fire on a limestone outcrop, holding down the smoke with a vast flap of hide, then lifting it to release a puff. When they saw the women, the boys dropped the hide, letting a half formed signal drift away. "We got him!" Telabat yelled, through cupped hands.

"A big one!" added Skedat.

"There are no small ones!" Nudawah yelled back.

Naked, bloody men poured up out of the ground, talking, waving their strans, hugging their families. Esther braced herself, hands on knees, knowing that if she sank to the earth as she wanted to she'd cramp up something awful.

The men had trapped the mammoth in a steep creek bottom. He wasn't as big as the grandmother mammoth, but he was big enough—what was left of him. The men had already skinned one whole side. That was what the boys were using to make the smoke signals—fresh mammoth hide. Another fire burned in the creek bottom, with the mammoth's tongue roasting on the spit above it.

The women and girls stripped off their clothes and went to work with strans and heavy edged rocks, like cleavers. The men told how they had worked in relays to drive the bull into the creek, which they knew got narrower and steeper, so that he gradually ran out of options. He had turned to fight, exposing his heart. Kitotul, hurling his stran with his atlatl, hit the leg, laming him. Uduban dodged a blow from the trunk when he ran in to deliver the death-thrust. All, even the boys, had touched the animal before it died, which everyone seemed to think important.

At certain points in the story, everyone would chant: "Oh, brave mammoth, mammoth who gave itself to us!" Esther did not chant along. This mammoth hadn't given itself to anybody. What was the use of pretending otherwise? She gritted her teeth, and copied Ahrva, straining to cut through muscle and fat. None of her cuts were straight, deep, or long.

"You're no good for this," sneered Nudawah. "If I tell you to collect cut meat and pile it on hide, can you do that?"

"I'll do my best, ma'am," said Esther.

"Well, since some people think you're worth the bother to feed, I guess we'll have to settle for your best."

Esther set out to be the best meat collector there'd ever been. In addition to the flesh, people lifted out internal organs in armfuls and stripped off sheets of transparent connective tissue—wesk. Men smashed the bones, taking out chunks that could be made into tools. Blood clumped nastily, every fly in

Texas descended on the site, and all Esther's muscles ached. Nudawah distributed the tongue and built more fires to cook more meat and warn scavengers away.

As Ahrva ate cooked tongue, and Esther tried to eat, Podan squatted beside them. "What's the matter with the star-child?" he asked, feeling a stran edge.

"She doesn't like for mammoths to die," said Ahrva.

"Grass dies, so mammoth can eat," said Podan. "Mammoth dies so we can eat. We die, so grass can eat. If we didn't eat mammoth, there would be no grass."

"I know," said Esther. "I don't have to like it, do I?"

"This mammoth died well. He'll be born into another mammoth next year."

"She says someday there won't be any mammoths," said Ahrva.

Podan raised his eyebrows. Esther looked away. "Maybe when there's more time, she'll explain that," he said.

One more thing to look forward to. Oh, joy.

The children twisted grass into ropes. By the time the adults had reduced half the mammoth to a skeleton, they had enough rope to tie to his trunk, tail, and feet, and haul him—with the combined efforts of all—onto his other side. He landed in the creek, damming it. Everyone was soaked with water, mud, and blood. Cleavers and strans wore out and were resharpened or thrown away, and new ones quickly made, out of carried flint or the smashed mammoth bones.

Before night fell, everyone washed in the spring, dressed in their dry clothes, and ate juicy, rare pieces of mammoth, smacking their lips and licking grease off their fingers. Esther wanted to wash again afterward. "Do you want dire wolf to catch you? How about jaguar?" Emni's mother, Shusskt, demanded. "They know we're here. They're waiting! No washing at night!" Everyone curled in one big human pile to sleep. Children with lit torches took turns staying awake to guard the carcass.

Esther's fingers were cut and bruised from inexpert handling of her tools. The smell of wood smoke, fresh meat, and unwashed bodies was solid in the air. When she closed her eyes, she saw the scimitar cats kill the baby mammoth. When she opened them, the firelight made a nightmare of dancing shadows. When Ahrva's and her turn came to guard the carcass, she was glad to get up. Chasing off scuttling creatures was better than trying to sleep.

"Do you only eat plants in the stars?" Ahrva asked.

"No. But we don't see the meat when it's alive."

"But how do you honor its spirit?"

"We don't."

"Then how does the spirit get free to become a new animal?"

Esther's head hurt. "It works all right, for the stars. What you do works for you, but I'm not used to it."

"It works now. What about when mammoth goes away?"

"They may not die off till your grandchildren are old."

"Why shouldn't I worry about my grandchildren?"

Far away, a scimitar cat screamed. "Please, God," Esther whispered at the sky. The stars glittered.

The group rose before the sun, ate meat that had cooked all night, and resumed work. Finally, in the afternoon, Uduban stood on the bloody skull, crying a long rising and falling note.

Vultures soared. "Our brother mammoth gave himself to us," said Uduban. "We give his spirit back."

Podan and Dul stroked the tusks, longer than their bodies, curving out from the mammoth's devastated face. They said together, "We thank you for your strength. Take your spirit back."

"Oh, brave mammoth, mammoth who gave himself to us!" Everyone else said—like call and response in church.

Kitotul and Skedat came next, then the women, starting with Nudawah. Esther laid her hand on the bloody ivory and said the words with Ahrva.

As they departed, laden with meat, bone, and wesk, the vultures dropped. The remains would feed many scavengers. Maybe someday, an archaeologist would find the site.

But the tusks could not tell how they had given the mammoth's spirit back. Even if Dr. Durham found the site, she would not know that Esther had been there, or that Ahrva existed.

I wish I had spray paint, Esther thought.

THIRTEEN

➤ FEAST AND FAMINE

*B*ack in camp, Esther had never seen people eat so much in her life.

Fingers were permanently greasy. Men ate, talked, and repaired strans. Women ate, talked, sewed, cut wesk into usable strips, and made needles. Ehdanwah made the mammoth's ears into bags, but the rest of the hide was too coarse to use and got piled up on the prairie, well away from camp.

By the third fly-ridden afternoon, the flavor began to change. Esther thought of her mother's freezer, but it would have been too small. "Can't you salt or dry it?" she asked Ehdanwah.

"We'd need a salt lake," answered the old woman. "What do you mean, dry it? By the time it dries out, it's spoiled."

"There's a way to do it that helps the meat last longer."

"Can you show me?"

"Um—no." Esther wished again that Dr. Durham had come with her. She might have known stuff like that. It wasn't fair!

Esther couldn't eat even as much as Tekinit. Her stomach didn't have room, and besides, the taste of meat built up on her tongue till she had to break it up with plant food. She didn't care who laughed at her. Trouble was, the plants were about used up. The mammoth family had finished the cattails at the water hole and crossed the river into "Bedabat's territory." (Esther tried to learn more, but asking who Bedabat was elicited such a cascade of names that she soon gave up.) The greens had all been eaten, and though new mushrooms sprouted, they were tiny. Esther had to eat grapes that the birds and wasps had already picked over, and it was hard to talk anybody into going with her to get them. She couldn't go alone, because of the predators.

By the fourth day, the meat definitely tasted funny, and everyone had fleas. Ehdanwah said she knew where a grove of chipays would be ripe. Podan pointed out that the grass was wrong for mammoth in that direction. "But maybe there'll be petwa."

"Petwa don't come into the hills." Uduban laughed.

"They may, if the grass is right," said Podan.

"You and your grass," said Uduban. "Our father and I killed a mammoth not half a day's walk from those chipay trees."

"I remember," said Podan. "The grass was different then."

"It doesn't matter," said Dul. "We'll hunt what we find. There are always mammoths ahead."

"Always is a long time," said Podan. "Things change, and we must change, too."

Uduban snorted. "What things change?"

"Something's bothering you," said Ehdanwah.

"Yes," said Podan. "It's too hot. This meat should have lasted longer. When I was a child, we would eat for four days and take some along when the fleas got bad. Remember?"

"Not always," said Uduban.

"I don't remember the last time a summer mammoth lasted five days," said Ehdanwah.

"And I've noticed another thing," said Podan. "In winter, it's too cold, too long."

"That's good," Dul pointed out. "The meat lasts longer."

"But the plants die sooner," said Kitotul.

"Some seasons are good, and some are bad," said Nudawah. "We can't change that."

"Bad, good," said Ehdanwah. "I know that what he says is true—the seasons are different than when I was a girl."

"Maybe it's your star-child, controlling the weather till we return her to the sky," sniffed Nudawah.

Esther, Ahrva, and Tekinit had been playing cat's cradle, only half-listening, but this exchange made them look up.

"Esster's a lost child," said Silika. "It can't be bad luck to take care of her till her people find her."

"And she's got wazicat, if we knew how to use it," said Podan. "Ehdanwah, has she told you that she sees the future?"

All eyes turned to Esther.

"Is this true?" asked Ehdanwah.

"Um . . . yes," said Esther. "But it's not useful. I only know the faraway future."

"What do you see in this faraway future?" sneered Uduban.

Esther's face burned, but if she kept quiet, Podan would look like an idiot. "Someday, there won't be any mammoths."

"Oh? Where will they go?"

"Nowhere. They'll all die."

"And why will that be?"

"I...I don't know. Maybe their grass dies out, or maybe people eat them, or maybe they get sick, or—I don't *know!*"

"The child's right," said Uduban. "Her knowledge isn't useful, even if it's true. And it *can't* be true."

"Esster," said Ehdanwah, "what happens to the people, when mammoth dies? Do they die, too?"

"No," said Esther. "They learn to eat other things. They do fine." Until the Europeans came—but she could hardly imagine that herself. "But the scimitar cats die out. And...and someday there won't be so many trees."

"What about petwa?" Podan asked.

"I don't know what petwa are," said Esther. "Lots of big animals die out. Horses. Camels. There was an animal called bison that got smaller, and shorter horns, and bunched together in herds that stretched from, from sky to sky, and people lived on those." After they got horses. She realized that she didn't know what Indians had lived on between the time the mammoths died and the time Spanish horses arrived; or why prehistoric horses had died out here and not in Spain.

"This is the stupidest stuff I've ever heard," said Uduban. "Tomorrow, we head for the chipay place—before *they* all go away!"

They burned and buried the rotting meat, but when Esther looked back from the next hill, dire wolves already pawed the remains of the fire.

They walked southeast, more or less, in rain. Esther's sneakers sank straight through the grass to sticky clay underneath, and in a few minutes she had mud shoes. Tekinit stepped on a thorn and wanted to be carried, but she was too big. Mingwah's baby cried constantly. When the rain stopped and the sun came out, they sat on wet rock outcrops, trying to dry off; but the sunny air was still full of water and the temperature soared. Esther had trouble breathing and her stomach cramped.

They reached the chipay grove in late afternoon. Chipays turned out to be mulberries, already well picked over by birds, wasps, and bears, many fuzzy with mold. "These were ripe days ago," said Ehdanwah. "I am sorry."

"It's not your fault," said Nudawah, in a tone of voice that implied that it was, really, but Ehdanwah was forgiven.

Ehdanwah snapped: "Of course it's my fault! I'm the senior woman. I'm supposed to know these things."

"Maybe the men will find mammoth," said Mingwah.

"Maybe they'll find petwa," Shusskt corrected her. Shusskt hardly ever corrected anybody. "There's no mammoth grass here."

"Ha," said Nudawah, from the bottom of her throat; a sound that meant yeah, right. "They'll find mammoth, and that'll prove that Podan doesn't know what he's talking about."

Shusskt looked as though she were about to speak, but Silika, sitting on a fallen tree trunk while Ahrva rubbed her feet, caught her eye and gestured no. "There are still chipays high in the trees," she said. "Who climbs well?"

Tekinit danced up and down and screamed: "Me, me!"

"What if you fell and broke?" Ahrva asked. "We'd have to leave you here for the bears to eat. Esther and I can climb."

Esther looked up, not at all sure that she could.

"No," said Nudawah. "Me, Otala, Emni, and Shusskt."

Ehdanwah cleared her throat.

Nudawah looked at her. "If you think that's best, ma'am."

"You bruised your foot," said Ehdanwah. "The others can climb, but you should not."

Nudawah looked as though she wanted to spit, but she said: "Yes, ma'am."

The plan was fine with Esther. She took Tekinit down to the creek to fill the water gourds, and found some relief by stretching out on a sunny rock, her aching stomach pressed against the hard surface, while Tekinit splashed, chasing fish. Her noise made Esther's head ache. "You'll never catch one like that," she said.

"I'm not supposed to catch them," Tekinit said.

"Why not? Fish are good to eat." And, with all the creeks and ponds in Ice Age Texas, an easy food source, she realized. So why had she never eaten any here?

"Nudawah says not to," said Tekinit. "Fish killed her daughter."

"Fish don't kill people."

"This one did. It choked her with its bones." She grabbed Esther's hands and tugged. "Come in the creek. You're all hot."

"I don't feel like it."

"Then the creek will come to you," said Tekinit, dumping a gourd full of water over her head and giggling.

The women made camp in an open space where bears and cats would be unlikely to sneak up on them. The men straggled in, late, to tell their stories in turn, but more briefly than usual. It boiled down to: They had seen horses, which had gotten away. People were turning glumly to the piles of mulberries that would be the only supper tonight, when Telabat stood up and said: "I am not a man, but I must speak."

"You are not a man and you may not speak," said Uduban.

Skedat looked scared and tugged at the back of the other boy's apron. "It doesn't matter," said Podan.

"It does," said Telabat. "The men were talking about how to get close to the horses. I said to Skedat, *I can get close.* Skedat said, *Your father will not allow it. Horses kick, they go fast, only men are allowed to get close.* I said to Skedat: *I will do it, and my father will be happy and forget to be angry. Make sure he doesn't know I'm gone.*" He looked at Skedat, who looked away. "I said to Skedat, *Your father is a low man: your grandfather killed his leader. I will lead and you will follow.* Now I say to Skedat, I should not have said that."

"You should not say anything," said Uduban.

"Telabat, sit down," said Nudawah. "We don't want to know."

"Would you let the boy keep poison in his stomach?" Ehdanwah put her hand on Telabat's shoulder.

"Thank you, ma'am," said Telabat. "I said to Skedat what I shouldn't say, and I crept through the grass. I picked a fat mare. I watched her. I didn't watch where I put my hands. A family of bobwhites flew up, crying, *Danger, danger, danger!* The horses ran. It's my fault we have nothing to eat tonight but mulberries."

"Horses usually get away," said Uduban. "We might be eating mulberries even if you had done as I told you."

"Would you say that if Skedat had done as I did?" Telabat looked his father straight in the eye.

"Yes," lied Uduban.

"You have spoken like a man," said Ehdanwah. "We can ask, every day, *What if this, what if that,* but it puts no food in our stomachs. We will eat what we have, and do better tomorrow."

Telabat gave his mulberries to Skedat, who split them with his sisters. "Poor Telabat," said Silika softly, so only her family could hear.

"It's about time," said Ahrva. "He picks on Skedat, and acts higher than him; and Skedat's nicer, and hunts better, too."

"Telabat knows that," said Podan. "Uduban and Nudawah are so afraid he'll die like their other children. You can't hunt without risks, so Telabat has never made a proper kill."

"I think Telabat's getting smart," said Silika. "If he killed the horse, all would be well. He didn't, but now everyone's watching. That matters to Uduban."

"But he broke the rules twice," said Tekinit.

Podan popped a mulberry into her mouth. "Rules are important, because they make things work smoothly. But if the rules aren't working, they must be broken."

"Whether Uduban admits it or not," added Silika. "Which doesn't mean you girls can go around breaking rules anytime you feel like it, by the way. Esster, you're not eating."

"I think she needs charcoal," said Ahrva.

"I'm all right," said Esther. "A bellyache won't kill me."

"Maybe it will," said Silika. "You should speak up."

The medicine she mixed in a turtle shell was disgusting—crushed charcoal, dirt, and water. "Don't be scared, Esster," piped up Tekinit. "It tastes nasty, but you'll feel better."

Esther took a deep breath. "Over the lips, through the gums, look out stomach, here it comes." She drank, thinking she was sure to throw up, but she didn't, quite.

"What was that you said?" asked Tekinit.

"My mother's wazicat. It makes things easier to swallow." Esther made herself smile at Silika. "Thank you."

"When I take medicine next, you must help me say that," said Tekinit solemnly.

FOURTEEN

*E*sther was light-headed, headachey, and cranky the next morning, but made herself forage with Ahrva and Tekinit anyway. Several ground squirrels escaped, but Tekinit spotted a black-headed snake, and Ahrva stabbed it. Esther, of course, got nothing. She was so completely useless she could scream!

The boys had dragged one of the shelters out of camp to use as a target. As the girls passed them, Tekinit held up the snake. "See? We're fine hunters, too!"

"Weh, weh." Skedat laughed. "We'll eat for days from your kill." He extended his hand to Esther.

Esther sighed and rolled her eyes, but shook it. "Good luck," she said, in English; and then, for good measure, in Spanish. "*Buena suerte.*"

"What are those sounds?" asked Telabat.

"Her people's wazicat," said Tekinit. "It's very strong."

"It didn't do anybody any good yesterday," muttered Esther.

"You were sick yesterday," said Ahrva.

"I've wasted my wazicat," said Telabat. "I should borrow yours, if you'll let me."

"Um," said Esther.

"Your father will be mad," warned Skedat.

"My father is already mad."

If anything bad happens to him today, Nudawah will blame me, Esther thought. But this luck charm business was the only thing she was good for, and it was too much work to say no. "Good luck." She sighed, shaking his hand. *"Buena suerte."*

The fire-dowsing song went up from camp with a cloud of smoke. *"Shuha!"* Tekinit exclaimed, which meant something like "Drat." "Now we can't cook my snake."

"There shouldn't have been time to get your snake," said Telabat. "It's obvious that we must follow those horses, even if we have to stay out all night to catch up. But everybody talked and talked."

Kitotul and Dul detoured to meet Esther and get their share of wazicat before following Uduban. Tekinit kept talking about the snake and how hungry she was, her voice drilling straight through Esther's ear into the headache. Ehdanwah and Mingwah had already started walking by the time the girls reached the demolished campsite. "We won't go far today," said Silika, passing out loads. "Oh, good, a snake!"

"Can't we stay long enough to cook it? Please, please, please?" Tekinit danced up and down.

"Do you think it will cook in the sun? The fire's out."

"Couldn't we relight the fire? I *want* to eat my *snake!*"

"Making fire takes forever, stupid," snapped Esther. "And it's not your snake. Ahrva only let you carry it to be nice."

Tekinit's face crumpled. Ahrva and Silika glared at Esther. "That's no way to talk to a child," said Silika.

Suddenly Esther was terrified as well as giddy, headachey, and fed up. What if these people walked off and left her? She tried to make her voice sound normal, but it came out wrong. "Kru! Kru! I didn't mean it! How should I have talked to her?"

"She's little and doesn't know better," said Ahrva. "You must make a joke. Then she'll remember."

Esther's eyes prickled. "Well, I don't know better, either. I'm sorry. Kru. Tekinit . . ." She reached out, but the little girl jerked her shoulder away.

"So, this is what star-wazicat is for," commented Nudawah, arranging her load. "Making children cry and delaying us."

"A little more delay won't make any difference," said Silika. "We're all hungry and cross. Ahrva—"

Ahrva quickly skinned the snake, split it open, peeled out the spine and ribs, and cut it into chunks. Esther held her share, trying to steel herself to eat it raw. If she refused, Nudawah would make another remark. But it was gross, and the pieces were so small Tekinit had shoved hers into her mouth whole, and what if Esther's stomach went bad again, and—

"Gckha," said Tekinit. She shook her head. "Chkachck!"

Silika slapped her on the back, but she only coughed and held her throat. Nudawah grabbed Tekinit's ankles, jerked her off her feet, and hung her upside down. "Spit it out! Spit it out!"

"Ghackhut!"

"Ehdanwah!" Ahrva screamed.

Tekinit was turning blue. Nudawah jerked her up and down, so fast she lost her grip, and Tekinit sprawled at Esther's feet. Ehdanwah started to run toward them, but Tekinit was blue now.

Esther reached down and wrapped her arms around Tekinit's middle from behind, remembering the diagram on the wall of the restaurant where they ate on paycheck nights. She made her hands into fists, placed them under the ribcage, and pulled up. The snake rib flew out, and Tekinit took a full breath.

Everyone cried and laughed and hugged. Esther sat on the ground, breathing hard and crying, letting Silika tear Tekinit out of her arms. Then Ehdanwah was there, and everyone talked at once. Tekinit's shrill voice was loudest: "I choked and Esster saved me with her wazicat!"

"Not wazicat," said Esther. "The Heimlich maneuver." But nobody heard. Nudawah looked down at her with a terrible expression. *Tekinit had said Nudawah's daughter choked on a fishbone,* Esther remembered. *They don't know the Heimlich maneuver.*

They traveled only as far as the next creek, which was deep and clear and cold—too deep and clear and cold, unfortunately, for crawdads or cattails, though fish as long and thick as Esther's arm darted away when she dipped up water. The women found plants and set snares, talking about how the men were bound to bring meat. But dusk came, and no men. "It's all right," said Silika. "They'll catch a horse in the morning and bring it in time to cook it for supper."

"I hope so," said Shusskt, feeling the stone point of her stran.

"But women must hope for the best, and plan for the worst. Esster! Do you feel better?"

"Yes, thank you," said Esther. At least she wasn't repulsed by the smell of the milkweed pods Silika was cooking.

"Could you teach me that wazicat you did for Tekinit? That is a good and useful thing."

"Sure," said Esther, suddenly feeling less wobbly. "When?"

"Now is the best time."

Tekinit leaped up. "I can help!"

So Esther demonstrated the Heimlich maneuver while supper cooked, at once embarrassed and proud to find herself the center of an interested circle of women. Soon they were practicing on each other, laughing at Esther's warnings not to squeeze each other too hard. Ehdanwah let Tekinit practice on her; but Nudawah only looked on, saying nothing.

In the morning, they fanned out in search of more food. Esther earned her keep by gathering lots of firewood, then took a break to play four-handed cat's cradle with Tekinit, Ahrva, and Otala. Most of the women were gossiping and curing hides, when Shusskt and Emni reappeared, carrying a string of fish up from the creek.

Shusskt pretended not to notice when everyone stopped talking at once. "Did anyone find any big leaves?" she asked. "I'd rather not have ashes in my fish."

"Why have you brought fish?" asked Nudawah. "The smell brings bears."

"We dumped the guts into the creek, where the otters ate them," said Shusskt. "Bear can't smell what's gone."

Nudawah looked grim. "Throw them back."

Silika said, "Nudawah, we haven't eaten fish for five summers, because it makes you sad. But we don't plan to stop eating
snake because of what almost happened yesterday. Instead, we
have learned a new thing, to make small bones less dangerous.
These fish are caught now. To waste them would be disrespectful
to their spirits. Maybe somewhere, someone is wasting mammoth, horse, and camel, and this disrespect is why they're
going away."

"Maybe, maybe, maybe," Nudawah said jeering. "Maybe your
star-child put the bone in Tekinit's throat so she could get it
out."

Ahrva drew in a sharp breath and clamped her hand over
Tekinit's mouth. Esther bit her cheek to keep from talking.

Shusskt ducked her head. "I ask the senior woman. Is it
wrong to eat fish?"

Ehdanwah sighed. "Fish makes Nudawah sad. So sad"— she
looked hard at Nudawah—"that she speaks without thinking.
To not eat fish around her is a kindness. If you do not think
that kindness to Nudawah is a good enough reason to not eat
fish, then eat it. But be careful. Because something worked
once, does not mean it will work twice."

"Ahrva, Esster, help Emni find leaves for wrapping the fish,"
said Silika. "We will eat well."

"Others will eat better," said Nudawah, as Esther and Ahrva
rose. "No one who eats fish will get meat from my man's kill."

Shusskt shrugged. "Your man may not kill anything. If my
man does, I will give you some."

Esther hurried off with Ahrva and Emni in search of the
leaves, glad to get away from the grown-ups. "Why is Shusskt

so sassy all of a sudden?" she asked. "I thought she was scared of Nudawah."

"You're stronger than Nudawah," said Emni. "You showed everyone that yesterday morning. My mother is on your side."

"That ... but ... Ooooh!" Esther moaned. "I don't have a side! Or anyway—I don't want one."

"Nudawah's afraid," said Emni. "No one wants the world to change. But on top of that, if Podan's right, Uduban's wrong. If Podan becomes leader, she won't be so important."

"If Uduban would change how he does things, nobody else would need to be leader."

Only the two families ate the fish; which was fine, because when it was gone, Esther could have kept right on eating. The women napped and foraged, occasionally scanning the horizon for the men. Nudawah spoke softly to Mingwah. At dusk, Mingwah's daughter, Otala, was the only big girl who didn't follow Shusskt into the creek bottom for a fishing lesson.

Shusskt said to pretend to be herons, stepping softly and using strans as beaks. They had to stand absolutely still, in shade so that the fish couldn't see their shadows, and watch out of the corners of their eyes for predators. Esther, Ahrva, and Washaw got wet feet, cramped toes, and sore necks. Emni got one fish, and Shusskt got seven.

"You'll all do better next time," Shusskt promised. "Here— this is how you take the insides out. Then cast the guts into the water, this way, and tell the fish spirit: *We thank you, fish who gave yourself to us. Be strong. Be swift.*"

The howls of returning hunters echoed into the creek bottom, and they hurried to finish their job and climb the bank so they could be there when the men carried in their horse. *It's no different from a cow,* Esther told herself, but she didn't join the celebration— and it ended before the meat had begun to cook.

"Fish?" Uduban's shocked voice rang out. "We don't eat fish. It's dangerous."

"All things are dangerous," said Ehdanwah. "Listen, men! Silika will tell what happened, and you will understand."

Esther hurried to join her family as Silika rose, holding the small of her back. "My children were hungry," she said. "They found a snake. The fire was out, so Ahrva cut it up to eat raw. My Ahrva has cut up few snakes. My Tekinit is small, and her good sense is small."

"Is not!" Tekinit muttered.

"Shhh!" Ahrva put her finger on Tekinit's mouth.

"She ate too fast. She swallowed a rib in the meat."

Podan gulped.

"Nudawah grabbed my Tekinit by the ankles, held her upside down, jerked her up. But the bone did not come out." Silika gazed across the fire and the creek, at the sky where the stars bloomed white on a dark blue field. "Ehdanwah ran, but she was far away. My little one would die."

A murmur went around the group.

"Esster took hold of my Tekinit and squeezed her below the chest." Silika mimed the Heimlich maneuver. "The bone came out." She looked straight at Uduban. "She has taught us this wazicat. A snake bone is like a fish bone. Does it make sense that we eat snake but not fish?" Silika sat. The fire popped.

"So, and so," said Uduban. "Ehdanwah, did you eat fish?"

"I did not. But too much sadness makes weakness. Let it be, and tell us how you came by this fine horse."

Unexpectedly, Uduban cracked a smile. "I'm not the one to speak of this hunt, Mother! I yield the fire to one who has never spoken here before, unless it was out of turn. Telabat!"

The women howled with delight. Telabat stood, and Esther saw that he had tied the horse's tail to his head, so that it bristled down his back. He bowed, trying to control his grin. "I am a boy. I could not speak when the men decided where to go. So I practiced throwing with my atlatl. I met the star-child. I said to her: *I have wasted my wazicat. Lend me some of yours.*"

"No," whispered Esther. Uduban's eyes, Nudawah's eyes, were open wide and glaring—Uduban's at Telabat, Nudawah's at her.

"I shook her hand. She said her wazicat—*Good luck*. We tracked the horses, all day and all night. We were tired. My father approached them. He was careful, and quiet, and wise. But horse is careful, and watchful, and wise. The horses ran. Our men hurled their spears, and the horses kept running. But one horse ran at me. I thought: *This horse will give itself to me, or it will trample me*. I braced my spear against the earth. The horse threw himself upon it." Telabat looked at Esther. "He said: *Good luck*."

Esther wanted to scream and run away.

*U*duban stood. "My son is young. I ask you to forgive his foolishness. His head is full of stars, but his hands were his own." He motioned for Telabat to sit down.

He didn't. "If I was strong, why did you hold me back? When you had two jobs for a boy, you gave the dangerous one to Skedat and the safe one to me. This must mean that I'm weak. I don't want to be weak. I want to be oheitika. Like my father. Like my brother. I saw that my own strength was not enough, so I went to the star-child. It isn't wrong to ask for help."

"What help can you get from that useless girl?" Uduban demanded. "If we didn't feed her, she would starve. If we didn't let her walk with us, she would have been eaten by predators long ago. And what does she give us back? Nothing!"

Podan stood. "I do not stand between my brother and his son," he said. "If they can't agree, I have nothing to say. But before the star-child could talk or cook or forage properly, my daughter Tekinit was threatened by a rattlesnake. The star-child had never used a stran, but she tried her best to kill the snake. The first time I saw her, she sent a camel to Kitotul's stran. I saw this. Yesterday she saved my daughter. She sees the future and gives us warning. I won't hear her called useless."

Nudawah leaped up. "She is a liar and a trickster! She kept mammoth away. When she couldn't hide mammoth any longer, she said: *Now I will call mammoth.* She put the bone into Tekinit's throat. Only when the star-child released it did the bone come out. Now the lowest woman defies me and my sister-in-law backs her up. My brother-in-law speaks against my husband and my son speaks against his father. She tells lies—that mammoth and horse and camel will all die. What will kill them? She doesn't know. When will they die? She doesn't know. What good is she? None! What harm does she do? Plenty!"

Esther, her arm twined with Ahrva's around Tekinit, did not know who started trembling first. She wanted to shout, *My name is Esther, not star-child! I don't have any wazicat! I didn't do anything! It's not fair!*

"Just because you and your husband don't want to know something doesn't make it untrue," said Podan. "Why should Esster try to harm us, who took her in when she was lost?"

"Because she's bad," said Uduban.

Kitotul jumped up, Dul reached out as if to drag him back down, Telabat opened his mouth, and Ehdanwah said: "Enough."

Silence fell. Nudawah turned toward the old woman standing with her palms open. "Enough," Ehdanwah said, gently. "My children, the star-child is not our problem."

Horse fat popped in the fire. Coyotes and *oong-KA-choonks* called. Esther's foster sisters gripped her tightly.

"We don't know what we would be doing tonight if she weren't with us. But Podan and Uduban have disagreed for a long time. Uduban thinks the world is the same as when he was a boy. Podan thinks it changes. Who is right? We can't tell.

"For years, I think that things are changing, and then I think that of course I think things were better when I was a girl. My grandmother always talked about how there used to be more mammoth, the grass was thicker, the trees were different, and I said *Yes, ma'am* with my mouth and laughed in my heart. But now I wonder: *What if she was right?* Fighting about the starchild, and fish, and what Telabat heard the dying horse say will not solve that problem."

Beyond the fire, the stars crowded the sky with light. Tekinit fidgeted. An owl hooted. Uduban said, humbly, "If this is our problem, how should we solve it, Mother?"

"I don't know," said Ehdanwah. "If this was about who should lead, we could put you both to the trial in any of a hundred ways. But no trial will tell us who is right."

"I don't see why not," said Nudawah.

"My mother is right," said Podan. "The flint fathers don't tell the future. They don't even promise that the best hunter will succeed. About this, no one knows anything."

"If we had a dream-walker . . ." said Dul.

"Well, we don't," Mingwah snapped at her husband.

"The star-child knows," said Kitotul. "We must ask her."

Everyone looked at Esther. Ehdanwah motioned for her to rise. She stood, hugging herself. Her bracelet made a lump against her ribs. The rattlesnake rattle in her hair buzzed.

"Tell us about the future, Esster," said Podan.

"No," said Uduban. "Tell us first why we should believe what you say about the future."

"Tell us why we should believe anything you say," said Nudawah. "This is silly. She came to harm us."

"We don't know that," said Silika. "Only you think that."

"That doesn't make me wrong!"

"Didn't I say, *enough*?" Ehdanwah sounded angry for the first time since Esther had arrived. "Sit down! Not you, star-child! I will ask, and you will answer. Then we will talk about what to believe and why to believe it."

"Yes, ma'am," said Esther. She stood in the humble kid position, hands clasped in front of her. The light of the flames caught in Ehdanwah's wrinkles, making her face ripple like a reflection, part dark, part light.

"Where do you come from, Esster?"

Esther couldn't say "From the future." Changing her story now would only prove that she was a liar. "I'm lost," she answered. "If I could point to the place I came from, believe me, I would!" She needed to talk the way they did when they stood in front of the campfire; formally, not normally. "My place is not like this place, because ... because there are so many people. Um ... in my place, some people find all of the food, and share it with the rest, who do other jobs in return."

"What other jobs?"

"Um ... like making clothes. Making sick people well. Teaching children." Lawyers, singers, accountants, computer programmers, truck drivers—

"Seeing the future?"

"Sort of." She was sure Nudawah muttered something.

"Explain what you can," said Ehdanwah.

"My people, we . . . we like to know things," said Esther. "The more we know, the better we live. We have . . . senior people . . . that spend their whole lives learning about the world. Some can say what the weather will be." No need to explain about 20 percent chances of rain. "Some can see things that are so small they're invisible. Some can see things so far they're invisible."

"Like the future," said Ehdanwah.

Esther nodded. "Yes, ma'am."

"How do they do this?"

She started to shrug, remembered that shrugging meant embarrassment here, and held up her hands in the I don't know gesture. "It's like . . . like everybody stands on a different hill and sees different things. Then we send, send signals to each other." Books were signals, right? "And I have a . . . an elder, she told me things. Mostly, what I know, I haven't seen myself. I have seen the signals or my elder has told me."

"And what have you seen in the signals?" Ehdanwah asked. "What has your elder told you?"

Frogs sang as Esther considered her answer. "The world changes. It's like, um, seasons. The world has been in winter since before people came here."

"We have had winters and summers for as long as I remember, and as long as my grandmother remembered," said Ehdanwah.

"Yes, well, but winters and summers have cold and hot days inside them, right?" Esther's head buzzed with the effort of putting these ideas into their language. "The winter season of years is ending. Anything that can't get used to the new season will die out." Esther twisted the bracelet. "My elder can't see the details. But many big animals die."

"What about people?"

"People live," Esther said firmly.

"Then why should we worry?" demanded Uduban.

"Um," said Esther. "People live, but I don't know, I can't see... *which* people. For all I know, everyone here will starve." Her throat tightened. "I don't *want* you all to starve."

It was a long evening.

Uduban listed all the reasons why nobody should believe her. Then everyone took turns asking questions. Nudawah and Uduban kept trying to catch her in contradictions, and some of the answers sounded lame even to her. "I wish I could bring my elder here to tell you all she knows," she said. "I wish I knew how to fix it. I wish I knew that it *could be* fixed."

"If it is in the future, it can be changed," said Podan.

But it isn't in the future. It all happened so long ago, it's barely real. She blinked her smoky eyes.

"My mother, my foster daughter is tired," said Silika, saying "my mother" in a way that made Esther think she was being particularly respectful. "Our heads are heavy. Let us eat and sleep. In the morning, maybe it will look easier."

"You are right, my daughter," said Ehdanwah. "We have learned enough for tonight."

"I learned enough a long time ago," said Nudawah.

Nudawah distributed the horse, as she had threatened, only to those who didn't eat fish. Esther felt it was her fault that

Silika's and Shusskt's families sat on one side of the fire eating fish while everyone else sat on the other side tearing into horse steaks. "I'm sorry," she said.

"For what—knowing more than Uduban?" Podan asked.

"That's not as hard as it sounds," said Ahrva.

"Be nice," admonished Silika. "You did fine, Esster."

"Nudawah doesn't want to be mean," said Podan, but all the women and girls interrupted him at once: "Yes she does!"

"What a hard thing it is, to have women who interrupt the men who bring them meat," said Kitotul with a grin, around his fish.

Shusskt pretended to slap him. "She's punishing us by withholding the meat, and for what? For eating fish!"

"No one else uses their sadness to control other people," said Silika. "We can't let her get away with it anymore!"

"And we girls won't either!" Ahrva declared, accidentally shifting Tekinit, who leaned against her.

Tekinit came awake. "No, we won't! You watch!"

The grown-ups smiled in the way that grown-ups smiled when they carefully weren't laughing. "Won't what?" asked Silika.

Tekinit rubbed her eyes, smearing fish grease on her face. "Hoo. We won't, we won't do that. We won't eat horse. We'll eat fish. Because fish won't die, will it, Esster?"

"No, fish won't die," said Esther, feeling herself smile the same smile.

"Whose turn is it on fire watch?" Dul asked the group in general.

"I will stay," said Telabat. "It's my horse."

"I'll stay," said Skedat; his first words all night.

Nudawah sniffed. "That won't earn you any horse, fish-eater."

"I know," Skedat said.

"We must all try to dream," said Dul. "None of us is a dream-walker, but sometimes they come even to the rest of us."

"You should try to contact your elders in a dream, Esster," said Emni. "They're bound to be looking for you. Maybe they can stay to answer questions."

"I don't care whether they answer any questions," said Nudawah, "as long as they take her away!"

SIXTEEN

➤ SPLITTING

*E*hdanwah wanted to go south, and south they went. The weather began to feel right to Esther; hot, with no weight of water in the air. When Tekinit whined, she taught the girls—except Otala who seemed to avoid her—to play Twenty Questions. Silika and Shusskt walked together and Nudawah and Mingwah walked together. Ehdanwah walked with everyone.

When Mingwah found onions, the women converged to dig. At noon they drank and rested, eating onions, seedpods, and greens. In the afternoon, they found a mound of dirt, and everybody pitched in to dig out a woodchuck the size of a spaniel. Esther enjoyed the digging and the excitement of making noise and blocking the other entrances, but not the way Nudawah beat the woodchuck over the head while it screamed and struggled to run away.

"I wonder if we'll get any," said Ahrva softly, as Nudawah hefted the enormous rodent and joked about how small it was.

"Isn't it the rule that if you help catch it, you get some?" Esther asked.

"Normally," said Ahrva.

But this wasn't normally, and everyone knew it.

When they stopped for the night, Nudawah roasted the woodchuck. The men brought two young javelinas and news of fresh mammoth sign. "We should head west," said Uduban.

"The numb-berries are south," said Podan, "and the nuga fields are south from that."

"Mammoth is better than either," said Uduban.

"Can't you have that argument in the morning?" asked Silika.

So they ate, and sang, and went to bed in shelters arranged, nearly accidentally, in two groups around Ehdanwah's shelter. Podan and Silika talked in whispers. "If we could be surer of the numb-berries, I'd feel better," said Podan.

"If you let on that you're not sure, Uduban will have it all his way," said Silika. "If the numb-berries aren't ripe, we go to the nuga fields. You'll find us."

"Nuaah," said Podan. "But you and the girls must get enough to eat. Even if you have to be nice to Nudawah to do it!"

"I'm always nice to Nudawah," said Silika. "It's not my fault she's so good at hearing what I don't say."

Esther was sure she made no noise at that, but Ahrva did.

"And our kids must sleep as much as they can," added Podan.

"Especially Esster, who must talk to her elders," said Silika.

"I don't know how to talk to people in dreams," said Esther.

"Your elders do," said Podan. "You can meet them halfway."

"You never know what you can do till you try," said Silika.

This was exactly what Mama said when her children didn't want to try something new, but Esther didn't say that her mother didn't know how to talk to people in dreams, either. Instead she said "Yes, ma'am," and closed her eyes, mentally calling her mother and father and Danny, then Dr. Durham, then God.

She dreamed she was a woodchuck, and Nudawah dug her out of her burrow above the playground. "Thank you for giving yourself to us," said Nudawah, trying to beat her on the head; but Esther rolled aside, and Dr. Durham said, "No, no, you have to mark the place where you dug her up."

In the morning, when Ahrva asked if she'd dreamed, she made the *no* gesture.

Uduban, clearly ready for a fight, proposed that they head west in search of mammoth and looked expectantly at Podan. Podan said loudly, "My brother is right. We should seek out this mammoth. But my mother is also right. We need the numb-berries and nuga. So I say, the men should go west and the women should go south. We are only men, but I think we can find the nuga fields if my mother gives us landmarks."

Nudawah stopped in the middle of sharpening her stran and glared at Silika, who smiled as she helped Tekinit pack. Ahrva nudged Esther. "She knows it was Mom's idea!"

"But why does it bother her?" asked Esther. "I bet Nudawah gives Uduban advice."

"If we follow Silika's plan, Nudawah's not the boss," said Ahrva. "You know she doesn't like that."

"So won't she take it out on us?" Esther asked.

"What can she do? We've won already."

Only if the numb-berries are ripe, thought Esther.

The men, knowing for certain that they would be separated

from their families for at least one night, probably more, took longer than usual to set out. They had to hug their kids an extra time; hang out by their wives making jokes about how they didn't think they could make their own beds; walk a few steps, then turn back with some last-minute remark. "We need extra wazicat," Kitotul said, taking Esther's hands.

"You know I don't control this, right?" said Esther.

Dul stretched out both his hands, too.

Podan hugged her. Uduban ignored her. Telabat and Skedat shook both of Esther's hands and wouldn't stop till she'd said both "Good luck" and "*Buena suerte*" twice. The women stood watching the men follow their shadows west, waiting until they vanished before setting out for the nuga fields.

Mingwah's baby cried and everyone grumbled about the heat as they walked. "It's summer, of course it's hot," said Esther.

Ahrva flipped her sweaty ponytail. "It's not supposed to get this hot till later. And it's not raining."

"It rained two days ago!"

"But look at the sky. There's no more coming."

"It's supposed to rain every three or four days in the summer, so we'll have plenty of zulotul," said Washaw.

"It was like this year before last, too," said her sister Emni. "This is what you meant about changing seasons, isn't it, Esster?"

"But you know the future," said Tekinit. "Is it going to get hotter and hotter and not rain?"

"I can only see the faraway future, remember?"

"How far?" asked Tekinit. "After the men come back?"

"Way farther than that," said Esther. "Way too far to do us any good." Time to get off this subject. "So what are these numb-berries we're looking for?"

Tekinit laughed. "You *have* to know about numb-berries!"

"Who says?"

"I say!"

"Sorry," said Esther. "Why are they called that?"

"Because if you eat them raw they make your mouth numb," said Ahrva. "There's a song about how other berries are good when you find them and go bad, but numb-berries are bad when you find them and go good."

"So does that mean we don't get to eat them today?" All these weeks without candy had made Esther appreciate the sugar content of ripe fruit.

"Some," said Emni. "As many as are good for us."

No one wanted to stop for lunch, so everyone was droopy when they heard the cacophony of bird calls that signaled nearness to a large crop of fruit. Then the women ran, with a shrill sound that caused the birds to rise in clouds. For a moment, the group was all one again.

The women shook the trees, and numb-berries, bluish-purple clusters about the size of blueberries but with a distinctive smell, rained down onto opened sleeping furs, creating new stains on impact. Ahrva passed a handful to Esther, who popped them all into her mouth at once. They didn't taste bad, exactly; but the juice seemed to wrinkle her tongue. The taste made her hungrier, though, and she reached for more.

"That's enough," said Silika. "We don't need any sick mouths. You girls get wood and forage."

Led by Emni, the girls made a trail to the inevitable creek. (Esther was certain this many creeks didn't exist in modern Texas.) More numb-berries grew there, mixed with trumpet vine and hackberry. The creek was dark and clear as sunglass lenses, with fish too small to be worth spearing. The creek bed was so steep that they had to walk in the water half the time, and Esther tied her shoes together with the laces and hung them around her neck. Tekinit wanted to use them as bags, but Esther refused, unsure which would be nastier— eating berries that had been carried in her sneakers, or putting the sneakers on afterward.

The turtles they found went, alive, into Tekinit's backpack, where they made an undulating set of lumps. The girls discussed how to go about catching ducks, and decided to come back with a net made of wesk and grass. They found a pond and dug zulotul. A brown and white wading bird, as tall as Emni, fished with its long neck bent to the waterline, watching them suspiciously from between its legs. "Why isn't that bird afraid of us?" asked Esther in a whisper, as she dug zulotul. "Couldn't we kill and eat it?"

"Probably," answered Ahrva. "But gronkha knows it doesn't taste good. It's stringy, and smells funny."

The gronkha snapped at the water and held up a struggling frog in its beak. Extending its neck to a towering height, it swallowed, and swallowed, and swallowed some more. Esther felt sorry for the frog, but also wondered: "What about frogs?"

Tekinit giggled. "Frogs aren't food!"

When they got back to the thicket, most of the women were still hard at work, pounding the numb-berries into a mush, mixing them with horse fat, making them into patties that would be easy to carry, and spreading them out to dry. As the girls trudged up the hill to Ehdanwah's fire, Nudawah picked up a pile of sticks and walked up, too.

The girls had to stand back respectfully and let her talk first. "Here's some numb-berry sticks, in case there's anything worth roasting. What have you girls brought us?"

"All we could," said Emni, as they unloaded their haul.

"Weh," said Ehdanwah, taking the turtles.

Nudawah shrugged. "It'll do for tonight, but there's not much breakfast there."

"We'll get ducks as soon as we make a net," said Tekinit.

"Emni, Esster, and I will hunt ducks," said Ahrva. "You and Washaw are so small, gronkha might mistake you for frogs and swallow you."

Washaw looked offended at being classed with Tekinit, but Tekinit got her protest out first. "If he did, I'd hold his beak open with my stran and save us. I'm big enough to hunt ducks!"

"She's not, but I am," said Washaw. "I've hunted ducks before, you know I have."

"We all have," said Emni, "in fall, when they're dropping from tiredness. It's hard to catch a duck in the summer."

"You're wise," said Nudawah, unexpectedly. "You're all too young for such a difficult hunt. I'll go."

"You've worked hard pounding numb-berries all day," said Emni. "We can do it."

"I'm not tired," said Nudawah.

"Emni's caught ducks before," said Ahrva. "We talked about it. We have a plan."

Nudawah smiled falsely. "Really? That's sweet. If there was more food to go around, it would be a good idea. But we can't take a chance, can we?" She looked hard at Emni. "Especially when the duck hunting is led by one with bad wazicat in her bones."

Emni looked at her feet.

Esther gritted her teeth. They couldn't push this without being rude to a grown-up. But winning didn't mean getting your own way, she thought. It meant not letting Nudawah walk all over everybody. "You're right," she said. Ehdanwah looked up from the turtles, and Otala from preparing zulotuls. "We don't have enough experience in getting ducks, and we need some. If you take us duck hunting, we'll do what you say, and next time we'll be better at it." She locked eyes with Nudawah. They needed the ducks. She'd been polite. Nudawah couldn't do anything but take them duck hunting.

"Nuaah," Nudawah said. "I'll take Emni and Ahrva. But you should stay with Tekinit."

Ehdanwah peeled the shell off the underside of a turtle. "Silika and I can look after Tekinit."

Nudawah turned her back on the girls. "I will not go out at dusk with the star-child. Terrible things happen at dusk."

Esther couldn't stand that. "I don't want to hurt you! I don't want to hurt anybody! I promise!"

"And if something hurts *you*? I'm not listening to Silika wonder if I let it happen on purpose."

"Esster won't get hurt." Ahrva put her arm around her.

"Because she won't go," said Nudawah.

"It's okay," Esther said. "Tekinit and Washaw and I can help Ehdanwah."

Ahrva heaved a sigh. "Nuaah."

Great, Esther thought. *We sort of got what we were after, but nobody's happy with it.*

Then Ehdanwah smiled, her face a mass of upward-curving wrinkles, and Esther felt better.

➤ SEVENTEEN

➤ FIRE WATCH

Nudawah's objections to teaching Esther duck hunting did not extend to letting her pluck them. If they wanted the ducks for breakfast, it had to be done before bed, so Esther sat up, along with Otala and Mingwah, who had first watch at the fire. Esther concentrated on pulling out the long, greasy top feathers and scraping out the small, fluffy underfeathers. Her fingers kept cramping, and every time she looked at Otala, plucking the larger duck, she had fallen further behind.

Whip-poor-wills called monotonously, mosquitoes whined, the fire popped, and coyotes yipped. The silence of people not talking to each other seemed loud to Esther. "Ducks better taste really good," she said.

"Don't you have duck in the stars?" Otala asked, glancing at her mother.

"We've got them," said Esther, remembering the ducks and geese crowding to meet them when they went to the lake with bags of stale bread. "Some people eat them. But nobody I know." She stretched her fingers. "They sure are a lot of work to fix."

"And catch. That's why we don't have them often in summer," said Otala. "But they're good. Lots of fat."

"You won't get to eat much of that fat," said Mingwah. "We'll save it to mix with the numb-berries. Too bad it's such a bad crop."

"What's wrong with the crop, ma'am? It looks like you're getting lots of numb-berries to me."

"About half of them are stunted," said Mingwah. "It takes lots and lots of numb-berries to get us through the winter."

Esther wiped sweat off her forehead with a greasy hand. "It's hard to believe it'll ever be winter."

"You'd better believe it," said Mingwah. "People die in winter. But maybe you'll be back in the stars by then, after eating up our food, and can sit up there and watch us starve."

Esther felt her face get hot, and she plucked harder. "I try not to eat much," she said.

"Mmph," said Mingwah, adding wood to the fire.

"Will we really starve this winter?" Esther asked.

"When you can't get enough numb-berries, it's a bad sign. Babies starve first." Her own baby, in the carrier on her back, whimpered in its sleep. Mingwah looked as though she were about to say something else, maybe something Esther didn't want to hear; but her expression changed and her head cocked, listening.

Whip-poor-will, whip-poor-will. From the fields.

Whiiiiiine. In Esther's ear.

Squeak, squeak. Faint and high, overhead, where dark shapes fluttered across the blaze of stars.

Rustle, rustle. From the fire.

Quak, quak, quork. From the creek.

Shuffle, snort. Soft, but close.

Mingwah turned her head, and Otala and Esther looked in the same direction. When Mingwah stood, Esther stood, setting her duck down and picking up her stran in unison with Otala. Mingwah pulled a log out of the fire, one end burning, and held it up.

Esther could see now, sort of, something big and dark and—no, two, three somethings. Near Silika's shelter. She poked in the fire until she got a log like Mingwah's, with only one end lit, and pulled it out. If Mingwah thought they needed torches—

"Yi, yi, yi, yi!" Mingwah started the cry, and Otala and Esther picked it up, moving toward the shapes as quickly as they dared. The baby wailed. The shapes loomed, not running, and Esther could smell them now, see them now, a mother bear and two cubs, but not black bears, *big* bears, with legs as long as Esther was tall, giant bears disinclined to back down until the shelters erupted with yelling women, screaming girls, waving strans. At last they wheeled, slowly, on their hind legs, and loped away faster than Esther's smoky eyes could follow. "Yi, yi, yi, yi!" she hollered, swinging her torch, running, until someone caught her and said, "It's all right, it's all right! They've gone. They won't come back."

Esther pulled up, trembling, realizing that she was halfway down the ridge. "Are you—are you sure?"

Shusskt nodded. "The uduban can get fatter meat than us. If she could have slipped in and eaten someone, she would have, but she couldn't, and now her cubs know that they should run from fire, even if they don't know why. She'll catch javelina now, or horse, or camel. Listen."

Esther caught the sound, a low retreating moan in the darkness: *Nuaah.* The bear was telling her cubs: *Oh, all right.*

"Of course, if they notice we're here by ourselves, they might decide they can have person tonight after all," said Shusskt. "You must never, never, *never* outrun the group."

Esther had seen a picture of the uduban in one of her books in the future. The caption had called it a "short-faced bear." She thought "long-legged bear" would have been a better name. "Was it really as big as it looked?" she asked, as she climbed, as fast as her suddenly shaky knees could carry her.

"Bigger," Shusskt laughed. "We don't see uduban much, but when you see one, you see a lot!"

They returned to a camp buzzing with conversation. Silika barely restrained Tekinit from running to meet them. "Esster! Did you chase them away?"

Esther's mouth felt dry. "The women chased them away," she croaked. "My feet were so scared I couldn't stop running."

Everybody hugged her and Shusskt at once, then Ehdanwah hugged her again. "Don't do that, child," she whispered.

"Weh, weh," said Nudawah. "If the star-child is done talking to her friends that came to eat us, maybe she can finish taking the feathers off this duck now."

Mingwah laughed nervously. "She's better at chasing uduban than cleaning ducks. I can finish them."

"No," said Esther, as loudly as she could without yelling. "I want to finish. I want to do my bit." She blinked through the smoke from her torch and marched back to the fire.

Otala took the torch from her. "Here. I'll help you. But first we need to singe off the pinfeathers. Like this."

Nudawah clapped her hands together. "Bed, bed! We have a lot of numb-berries to pound tomorrow."

"Not yet," said Ehdanwah. "We must move the shelters closer together. It's not good for us to be separated." She looked from Nudawah to Silika and back again.

"Let's do it fast and go back to sleep, then," said Silika. "I dreamed that the men were back. If I go to sleep again quickly, maybe the dream will wait for me."

Mingwah sent Otala to bed as soon as the shelters were moved, and then helped Esther pluck. Nudawah came out about the time they finished. "It's my turn. I'll finish."

Esther's eyes prickled with tiredness. "I need to learn to take the guts out of a duck," she said, keeping hold of the cold, slimy feet.

"You need to go to bed," said Nudawah, flopping the bigger duck over and opening its belly with a slash of her short stran.

Esther flopped her duck over, too, but before she could slash, Nudawah caught her by the wrist, so tight it hurt. "If you do it wrong, you'll ruin the meat."

"If I never do it, I'll never do it right," said Esther. She looked straight into Nudawah's eyes, trying not to blink.

"Never gut anything with a long-handled stran. You don't get enough control." Nudawah shoved Esther toward Silika's shelter, and let go. "Go to bed."

She tried to be extra quiet, but as she was settling down, Tekinit whispered: "Esster, I can't sleep."

Esther sighed. "Close your eyes. No, both of them. Now, picture a river with only one place mammoths can cross."

"And Daddy is waiting there."

"But there's lots and lots of mammoths. He has to pick the right one. How high can you count?"

"As high as my toes."

"The right one will be one more than your toes. Keep your eyes closed and watch them, and count."

"One mammoth. Two mammoths."

"Not out loud. In your head." Esther counted, too, picturing the river, and Podan lying in wait as the mammoths crossed. The shelter was muggy. A short-faced bear could kick it to pieces in a nanosecond.

Mama, Mama, Mama, Esther thought; until she fell asleep.

EIGHTEEN

➤ THE NUGA FIELD

The next morning, Ehdanwah took Nudawah to look for a nuga cache they had buried last year when they'd found more than they could carry. Esther picked numb-berries, set her first snare, learned to make patties, and played ball. Everyone looked forward to supper.

But when Ehdanwah and Nudawah returned, their bags were only half-full. "Podan dug the cache up," said Nudawah, so sourly it took Esther a second to realize she meant black bear, not Podan.

"Never mind," said Mingwah. "Look, the girls have caught squirrels, I found ground nut seeds, and Shusskt got a lot of different roots."

Nuga turned out to be some kind of bulb. They ate a few raw, roasted the rest, and pretended they couldn't have eaten as many more again. "Tomorrow, we'll go on to the nuga field," said Ehdanwah. "We'll come back when the men bring us more fat."

"*If* they bring us more fat," said Shusskt. "These berries won't get better for waiting."

"Neither will the nuga," said Ehdanwah. "If we wait too long, the stems will dry up, and then how would we find them? We'll leave as soon as we can in the morning."

So they headed out after breakfast, cleaning camp even more vigorously than usual, to eliminate all chance of the short-faced bears deciding that places that smelled like people might yield food. Esther noticed that every woman scanned the sky to the west as they walked south. The grass was drying into summery yellow-green, and the flowers had gone to seed. "What if the nuga is dried up?" asked Esther. "Could we starve this winter?"

"It's always possible," said Ahrva.

"What if I weren't here? Would the rest of you be less likely to starve?"

"Did Nudawah tell you that?"

"I have ideas of my own, you know. I eat as much as anybody, but I don't find as much. At what point does that lead to people starving?"

"A point a long, long way from here," said Ahrva.

"There's more than one way for a group to die," said Emni. "If one of us dies, we're still ourselves. If we send you out to die on your own, then we're the group that killed the star-child. No one wants us to be that. Not even Nudawah."

"Besides, you'll earn your food when we get to the nuga fields," said Ahrva. "Nuga's good, but it's hard work!"

The nuga field was a rocky meadow. They camped above the nearest spring, which wasn't that near. Silika, Mingwah, and Tekinit kept the camp. Everyone else spread out looking for short, hairy nuga stems. Ahrva showed Esther how the stems pointed at each other. The sun beat on their heads like a hammer. The ground was so hard more than one stran handle broke. The reward was a bulb about the size of an onion, which could be peeled and eaten at once, but ought to be dumped into a bag. Esther didn't complain, didn't stop for a rest or a drink unless Ahrva did, didn't eat unless Ahrva did. She was so tired that her eyes wanted to vomit. She got blisters on both hands, which she tried to ignore; but Ahrva sent her to Ehdanwah, who took her in search of a particular lavender flower and made a bandage of it, covered with squirrel hide and tied on with wesk.

Supper was subdued, everyone shoveling down nugas and berries with weary determination.

The second day was much like the first, except that they had to walk farther to find unharvested nugas; but in late afternoon they heard Silika calling. Everyone stopped and stared at the rotund figure dancing up and down, waving her arms; and Tekinit dancing and howling beside her.

"She sees them!" The joyful murmur went around the field, as women and big girls straightened their aching backs.

"We should build up the fire," said Nudawah. "We don't have anything like enough wood for roasting mammoth."

"You wives, go," said Ehdanwah. "You should be pretty when your men arrive. The girls and I can bring wood."

Suddenly everyone was in a tearing hurry; but when the nugas and all the dry wood in the vicinity were piled near the fire and new beds of the best available grass had been made—it was much too hot for shelters—the men were still only semi-visible movement flickering through brownish-green grass.

Esther stood by Ahrva, one of a line of women and children waving and disputing whether their waves had been returned. She tried counting the moving shadows, and then counted again. "Are we one short?" she asked, one eye on Tekinit, who had gotten tired of jumping and was sitting on Silika's knee, waving.

"I think so," answered Ahrva.

Esther remembered the story of Uduban's son. With the wooden end of her stran, she probed the hole forming in the toe of one sneaker, and said: "I think I'll go get more nuga."

"It's too late to dig. Didn't you hear the panther?"

She had, of course: a hideous sound, like someone being murdered with a train whistle. "Yes," said Esther, "and I've also heard everybody's stories about how easy panthers are to scare. Besides, the men have to come through the nuga field."

Ahrva brightened, and turned toward the others. "If we go get more nuga," she called, "we'll see the men sooner. We can help them carry the meat."

"We can hardly find the nuga when it's light," said Nudawah, "but you can find it as it gets dark? How clever of you."

Not even Mingwah laughed. Shusskt started downhill. Tekinit jumped up, shrieking: "Me, too! I can find nuga!"

Silika put her hands on Tekinit's shoulders. "But if Ahrva and Esster go, who will stay with me?"

"Esster can," said Tekinit. "She shouldn't dig, anyway. She has blisters."

And I don't have a daddy down there, thought Esther; but little children running around at dusk was not a good idea. "My blisters are all better since Ehdanwah put her flowers on them." Which was sort of a lie. "Besides, it was my idea."

Tekinit made a face, but didn't protest as Ahrva and Esther joined the mass exodus down the hill without her.

No one looked hard for nuga, but they got a few, looking up every few minutes. The men started to run, except for one thick figure trailing the pack. No, that was two men, one supporting the other. No one was missing! But someone was hurt.

The women ran to their hunters, hugging them, laughing, relieving them of burdens that buzzed with flies. Podan waved his stran and supported Kitotul, who flashed a fake smile as Podan relinquished him to Emni and Shusskt.

"Thanks for the double wazicat, Esster," said Telabat. The circles under his eyes made him look as if he'd been in a fight.

"What happened to Kitotul?" Esther asked.

"He went for the heart," said Skedat. "He knew better. He's never made a shot like that. But the wounded one was escaping, and he got a chance at the unwounded one, and took it, and it knocked him down. Dul's hurt, too. Not that he cares! He got the mammoth straight in the heart."

"Only because your father made it swerve," said Telabat. "And what no one will say is that my father was sneering at his double wazicat. When we found two men mammoths, that was one up for Kitotul. If they'd both escaped, my father would have never let them forget. He had to try."

"Wait a minute," said Esther. "You mean, if I hadn't given everybody double wazicat, Kitotul might not be hurt?"

"Or he might be hurt worse, or we might have no meat now," said Skedat. "Everyone took double wazicat but Uduban, and he missed his shot. Hunts get crazy. No one can blame you."

I know someone who can, Esther thought; and sure enough,

Uduban scowled as he approached. "So," he said, "we have so much daylight to spare we can stand around talking while the dire wolves watch from the hills. That's good."

The boys started walking again. Kitotul called, "Star-child! Why do you not come to greet those you helped?"

"I don't know whether I helped you or not," answered Esther.

"Sure you did," said Washaw. "You saved my father's life. The mammoth would have killed him without your wazicat."

"And it's obvious that the double wazicat brought a double mammoth," added Emni.

"But you only took one," Esther protested.

"We couldn't have carried two," said Kitotul.

Podan put his hand on her shoulder. "Anyone would think Kitotul was oheitika, to watch him on this trip."

Esther carried her share of meat and walked silently in their laughing, talking, worried bunch. At camp, Kitotul went straight to Ehdanwah and was diagnosed with broken ribs. She wrapped his torso in mammoth hide and passed burning grass over him. The group called on the flint fathers to make his bones hard. Esther held hands with Ahrva and Tekinit, blending her voice with theirs, and praying, "God, please, make him get well and stop taking stupid chances because he thinks I have magic powers!"

That night, it was Esther's bad luck that she needed to use the latrine while Uduban was on watch. She had to walk right past him twice. The first time, he merely grunted, poking the fire. The second time, he said, in a strangled voice: "Kitotul would never have tried for that mammoth, if not for you."

Esther stopped. "So what am I supposed to do?"

"I don't know," said Uduban. "Dream your way home."

"I would if I could," said Esther. She wondered how she should ask the next thing; whether it might be better to skip it. "You don't believe I'm bad?"

"I don't believe the mammoths are dying out," said Uduban. "And I don't know what that makes you, a liar or a confused child or a bad spirit. So you had better go to bed."

Esther picked her way between the beds. An owl called nearby, a whip-poor-will distantly. Kitotul's breathing was harsh, loud, and shaky. She looked down at him, with Shusskt curled beside him, not quite touching. She didn't think she made a noise, but his eyes opened. "It's all right, star-child," he said. "Every hunter gets such a wound one time or another. Do you know if your wazicat can heal?"

"No, it can't," said Esther, firmly.

"Too bad." He shifted, forcing a smile. "This thing itches. But as long as we stay here, I get to lie around and be waited on, and eat mammoth meat."

"Weh," said Esther. There didn't seem to be anything else to say.

Kitotul walked among the women for a couple of weeks. Esther's scrunch lost its elastic, so she used wesk instead. Her socks wore out, so she unraveled them for cat's cradle. They found no more mammoth. The bogs dried up. Many plants were stunted and bitter. The nuga and numb-berries would be needed in winter, so they buried most of what they harvested.

"There's no use putting it off," said Uduban, picking through another pathetic supper, of chipmunk, half-ripe berries, a nuga, and onions. "We need one group for the other numb-berry grove, one for the petwa-berries, and one to see if the late strawberries are ripe. We can meet at the plum place."

Podan frowned. "Kitotul—"

"I'm fine," growled Kitotul.

"I have no sons," said Podan. "Would you and Skedat hunt with me?"

Kitotul relaxed. "We would be pleased."

"What does this mean?" Esther asked Ahrva.

"Each family will look for food alone," said Ahrva. "We can

146

cover more ground that way." She looked at her mother. "We should be back together before the baby comes."

Tekinit's face wobbled. "Remember the baby Shusskt had in the dry time?"

"That won't happen to *our* baby," said Ahrva.

Ehdanwah went with Uduban, Nudawah, and Telabat, but she hugged everyone and whispered blessings over them before she did. The families soon vanished among the hills and trees, which seemed bigger than usual, under an unwelcoming sky. "I miss Ehdanwah," said Tekinit, as glumly as if she had disappeared five years rather than five minutes ago. "What if she dies?"

"Why should she?" asked Esther.

"Old people do," said Tekinit.

"Don't worry!" Ahrva said. "Uduban and Telabat can hunt well enough for only four people. And Ehdanwah knows where all the food is. We'll see her at the plum place."

Podan pointed toward a hump-backed hill. "We'll go up there and get a good look around," he said. "See you tonight!"

Everyone stretched their faces into smiles as the hunters left, moving at Kitotul's slow pace. "Maybe they'll find javelinas," suggested Esther, twisting her bracelet.

"Or deer," said Ahrva.

"I hope my father's pain is not too great," said Washaw.

Something thudded against Esther's shirt. Looking down, she saw a tiny, space-alien face peering up at her. "Stupid grasshopper," she muttered, brushing it off. It spread its wings, and Ahrva snatched it out of the air.

"Tilat!" she cried.

Tekinit moaned. "It takes so many to get full!"

Another grasshopper buzzed across the path, and Washaw darted forward. "But there are always so many of them!"

Grasshoppers? We're going to eat grasshoppers?

Actually, they weren't bad, with greens and salt, and nothing else to eat. Esther pretended they were peapods.

The men did not meet them that night, which the women spent hungry and worrying.

Then the next morning as they collected grasshoppers and sunflower heads, they rejoiced to see smoke rise from a hill. When they arrived, though, they found Skedat gathering wood, Kitotul roasting a squirrel, and Podan with his ankle purple and swollen.

"I'm a stone-brain," he said, with a fake grin. "We wounded a horse, but I fell into a ravine."

"Is it broken?" asked Silika, bending over the ankle.

"No, no," said Podan. "It'll be well in no time."

"Podan speaks brave words," said Shusskt, "but it'll take more than a day to walk on that foot! Emni and Tekinit must cook while the rest of us forage."

Kitotul stood. "Skedat and I'll track the horse. If you go that way"—he pointed—"there's a spring. And there are turkeys here somewhere. I heard them." He looked over at Silika, who was smearing something on Podan's ankle, and lowered his voice. "I'll tell the horse how thin she looks, so it will give itself to us."

"Good," said Shusskt. "I'll give her the liver."

"I have dibs on the tongue," said Emni; to prove that she thought the horse was a sure thing, Esther thought.

As Shusskt helped Washaw over a ledge, on the way to the

spring, Esther asked Ahrva softly, "What happened to the baby Shusskt had in the dry time?"

Ahrva whispered, "Shusskt didn't get enough to eat. It was born dead. We had told Tekinit she would have a new baby to play with, and then—I think it's the first thing she remembers."

The first thing Esther remembered was playing in a swimming pool with her father. It wasn't fair!

Skedat and Kitotul did not return that night. As they divided the two fish Shusskt had caught, Podan told how he, Uduban, and their father had once tracked a wounded mammoth for four days, and killed it.

"You have only that one story to tell," said Shusskt. "What about all the times wounded animals have vanished into the hills? We must behave as if that horse is gone forever; and then, if they find him, it will be a wonderful surprise."

"Have you no pride in our men?" demanded Emni.

"More than anyone can guess," said Shusskt, an unexpected quaver in her voice. "But Kitotul is hurt, and Skedat is only a boy, and they carry bad wazicat in their bones. Why should they do what so many have failed to do?"

They slept under the open sky. Esther took her turn watching the fire, under stars huge and bright as street lamps. She knew that they were really suns, tremendously far away; but what if they weren't? What if they were a city, with a sign on the Milky Way to tell her where she was? She would walk until she found a convenience store where the clerk would let her use the phone. While she waited for Mama to come get her, the clerk might let her have ice cream. Rocky road, or tin roof. And—

A scimitar cat screamed. People jumped in their sleep, half-woke, and settled down again. Esther poked the fire, and saw Tekinit watching her. "Esster. I can't sleep."

"Why not?"

"I'm hungry." She sat up and rested her chin on her drawn-up knees, hugging her shins. "So's that scimitar cat."

"Scimitar cats don't hunt people," said Esther.

"Not mostly," said Tekinit. "If we can't find mammoth, maybe the scimitar cat can't either."

"I don't care how hungry it is," Esther declared, "no wild animal would come close enough to the fire to hurt us."

"I would try not to mind, if one did eat me," said Tekinit. "Maybe it would feed me to its babies. It's a good thing to keep a baby alive. But I want to see *our* baby first."

"Nothing's going to eat you," said Esther.

Tekinit crawled over to her, and fingered Esther's bracelet. "What do you eat in the stars?"

Esther told her about hamburgers, ice cream, and grocery stores. Tekinit leaned against her side. Esther put her arm around her and talked about refrigerators, candy, and air conditioners; about soccer games, playgrounds, and school; but not about Danny, Mama, or Dad.

"I wish I could go there." Tekinit yawned. "Are there lots of little girls like me?"

"Not one," answered Esther. "Lots of girls your age, but not one of them brave enough to kill a rattlesnake."

"I wish we could find another rattlesnake." Tekinit's stomach growled. Esther's growled in answer. "We could eat it."

"Maybe we will tomorrow," said Esther. "But if you don't sleep, you won't be able to do anything if you do find one."

But Tekinit didn't forage the next day. She and Silika stayed with Podan and the fire. The other girls found a foamroot plant, and Shusskt showed them how to collect and use it to reduce the pain and swelling in Podan's ankle. You couldn't just yank up medicinal plants, she explained; you had to please the plant spirits so the medicine would work.

While they were trying to track down the roosting place of the turkeys Kitotul had heard, Washaw found plum trees with buggy fruit. "Hey, bugs are meat," joked Esther, but she handled them with the tips of her fingers only. Another scanty supper, another night—no hunters. Esther noticed Podan watching Silika with a worried look.

Esther dreamed of headlights moving along a highway and a haze of city light that washed out the stars. She said to Silika: "I'm going to find a grocery store and bring y'all back some food." Dr. Durham walked ahead, scanning the ground for dropped points. Esther ran after her, shouting, but Dr. Durham didn't look up. "It's later than you think," said a voice behind her, deep and slurring, like a man with his mouth full. She turned, and it was almost dawn on the hillside, almost cool.

I know that voice. From that other dream, the one about Tekinit before I knew her. She closed her eyes, reaching deep into the future, toward the night before all this began. *Who are you? What do you know about this? Are you doing this to me?*

He was gone. Or didn't exist yet. Esther realized she had

clenched her fists and teeth in her effort to sleep again. She sat up, and saw Emni drooping over the fire. "Good morning."

Emni stifled a yawn. "Morning."

"You want to go to bed? I can watch."

"It's not your turn."

"I won't get back to sleep anyway." Esther squatted beside her. "You look tired."

"My father and my brother between them only add up to about one hunter," said Emni. "What if they meet a jaguar or a bad spirit? What if the horse tramples them? I can't make it better, but I can't stop thinking. It makes me tired and keeps me awake at the same time."

"Have you tried counting mammoths?"

"Counting mammoths?"

Esther explained, rewarded by Emni's smile. "I'll try, if you're sure you won't go back to sleep."

Fire watch. As alone as you got in the Pleistocene. Esther's stomach growled. Would they find decent food today? What if Kitotul and Skedat didn't come back tonight? Or ever? Dawn crept up the sides of the sky. A turkey gobbled. She could probably catch a turkey, if she could find it. You were supposed to pull them off their roosts while they were still groggy, and wring their necks. She put more wood on the fire and checked everyone's sleep. Emni's eyes rolled under her lids as she dreamed. Esther walked in the direction of the gobbler, picking her way down unexplored hill.

Birds flew on the edge of her vision, as if teasing her, but she did not hear the turkey again. Despite the drought, everything seemed too green. There ought to be juniper scrub, and roads, and houses clustering on hilltops so rich people could enjoy the view. Two vultures soared on an updraft, wingtips spread like fingers, as they would over these same hills in eleven thousand years, scanning the highway for roadkill.

A third vulture darted sideways behind an outcrop of rock. Another rose lazily, and sank again. Esther walked past a fallen tree with green leaves, on soil that slid under her feet. Once on the secure footing of the outcrop, she heard yips like dogs laughing, and buzzing flies.

She looked down a slope. Below her a smallish mammoth lay half-buried in gravel, dead in a landslide. Coyotes wrestled over the limp trunk. Whenever the vultures got too close, a coyote rushed them, leaping and snapping at the leisurely dodging birds.

Nausea and happiness rose in Esther's throat. At home, she had never been giddy with hunger, never considered eating meat that flies and coyotes had been at.

The birdsong faded. The air shimmered, and moved, and pulsed with music.

The Beatles.

Solid coyotes darted through a blurry figure, air rippling as a woman brushed away soil from a long, curved mammoth tusk.

Dr. Durham!

*D*r. Durham! Dr. Durham! Up here!"

Dr. Durham wiped her forehead and drank from a sport bottle.

Esther slid off the outcrop. "Dr. Durham!"

The archaeologist brushed dirt away from the tusks, singing about a yellow submarine. Esther lost her footing on the landslide, and caught at the branches of the fallen tree. "Yip, yip," said a coyote from behind the solidifying archaeologist. Esther still smelled dead mammoth, dust, and smoke . . . but no food; because her friends had nothing to cook. Would they see the vultures? Would they come this way, looking for food? For her?

"Dr. Durham!" Esther screamed.

The archaeologist looked up and around, then resumed work on the tusks.

Esther saw her and the coyotes, morning sky and shimmering afternoon shade. All she had to do was climb down, dodge the coyotes, fling herself through the correct patch of air, and she'd be home. Maybe Shusskt and Emni would find the mammoth anyway. Maybe Silika wouldn't lose her baby.

Maybe. Was that good enough?

"Dr. Durham!" Esther picked up a stick and hurled it, but it didn't fly far enough. "Over here! It's me!" She picked up a handful of pebbles and pitched one down, then another, saw them bounce off the dry, old tusk.

Dr. Durham looked up. Straight at her.

"Stay there!" Esther shouted, waving her arms. "Just—just stay there! Hold the door open! I'm coming home—I want to come home—only I have to show them the mammoth first!" She raced back toward camp, crashing through brush, shouting with all the breath she could spare. "Mammoth! I found mammoth!"

She saw them before they heard her: the women and girls up and about; Podan propped on his elbow. "Mammoth!" screamed Esther, feeling the wind forcing her meaning back down her throat. "Mammoth!" She used all her voice, waving both arms. "Mammoth mammoth mammoth! *Dead* mammoth!"

Shusskt and the girls came running. Tekinit bounced to her feet, and Podan restrained her. Esther pivoted on her heel and ran back. *Please, God, please, God, please, God!* "Dr. Durham! Dr. Durham!" She skidded down the landslide into the middle of the coyotes

"Yip, yip!" The coyotes danced. The biggest one, as tall as Tekinit, moved between her and the mammoth, growling, the hair on his neck and shoulders bristling. Seizing the moment, a vulture swooped in behind him, tearing at the remains of the mammoth's face. No other sounds. No other landscape. No Dr. Durham.

Esther wanted to cry with rage and disappointment; then all

the coyotes put their heads down, bristled, and growled, and she realized that she had more immediate problems.

The biggest coyote advanced a step.

Lumps of granite and limestone rained down, bouncing off the coyotes' heads and backs like hail. Howling, Shusskt led the charge down the landslide. The coyotes retreated in a chorus of yips, and the vultures rose with a loud flapping. Ahrva ran to Esther. "Are you all right? That was brave, but stone-brained!"

"I . . . I didn't think about it," said Esther, looking at the pathetic, bloody tusks.

Dr. Durham would find them, clean and dry, in eleven thousand years.

Pebbles would bounce off them. She would look up.

What would she see?

Shusskt was talking as she examined the remains of the mammoth, something about him being dead less than a day.

Why, why, why couldn't Dr. Durham have kept the door open? Had she even tried?

That wasn't fair. Esther didn't even know how to hold the door open, and she'd seen two of them. Had Dr. Durham had any chance of understanding what was going on?

Shusskt shook her fist in Esther's face, rattling off a teasing scold about taking risks. Esther blinked and crossed her arms humbly. "I'm sorry." Maybe if she stared at the tusks and hummed "Yellow Submarine."

The girls bounced around happily, threatening the coyotes. Esther wished they'd be quiet so she could think. The coyotes had definitely not seen Dr. Durham, nor she them. That had to mean something. Esther couldn't imagine what.

"Those coyotes"—Shusskt waved at the pack pacing back and forth below—"won't leave till they're sure their chances are gone. We'll have to live here awhile."

Good. I don't want to leave till I'm sure my chances are gone, too, Esther thought.

The outcrop provided a deep shelter, where they stored their bags. Esther sang "Yellow Submarine" and imagined Dr. Durham as hard as she could, until Tekinit began singing along.

Maybe you had to be alone for time magic to work.

She wanted to scream and cry and stamp her feet. Instead she collected wood.

The group ate mammoth as fast as they could uncover the carcass, gulping small pieces of meat raw while larger ones cooked. The coyotes had scarfed up the tongue, which was universally pronounced a shame. "Usually those who bring down a mammoth eat the tongue at once," Ahrva explained. "*You* would have had it to distribute, if it had still been here." She beamed at Esther proudly. "But you can eat the best part that's left, or give it to whoever you want to."

"That's okay," said Esther. "Give it to Silika, whatever the best part is."

Under the noon sun, Ahrva and Esther dug high on the dirt-covered hump of the mammoth's side. Shusskt butchered, Silika cooked, Washaw and Emni had taken Tekinit to the creek for water, and Podan—who had almost sprained the other ankle getting here—sat on the edge of the outcrop, making new stran points. The ground around him was littered with sharp bits of rock.

"You've hardly eaten," Ahrva said.

"I'm not as hungry as you."

"What's the matter?"

Esther took a deep breath, her eyes stinging. Dust hung in the air, coated her tongue, and itched in her nose. "I don't want to talk about it."

"Have I done something wrong?"

"No!" It wasn't fair to take this out on Ahrva, or Tekinit, or anyone. But it wasn't fair for Esther to have to cope with it by herself, either. "I never told you how I got here."

"You fell from the stars."

"Not exactly. I dreamed of Tekinit, and then I saw you while I was awake. There was a . . . an entrance"—she used the Clovis word for the opening in a shelter, for lack of a better term—"and I went through, and was with you. But when I tried to find the entrance again, it was gone." She motioned at the mammoth's raw head and bloody shoulders. "Today I saw another entrance. I saw my elder, but she didn't hear me. I ran to tell you about the mammoth, I ran back, and the entrance was gone." She blinked and sniffed, wishing she had a Kleenex. "So I'm not hungry. But I'm not mad." Not exactly, not reasonably, not in a way she could express. "I g-got myself into this."

Ahrva hugged her. "We might have found the mammoth."

"And you might not," said Esther. "It's—it's okay." She swallowed. It was important to be brave. "There'll be another entrance sometime." She had to have faith in that—whether she believed it or not.

"Maybe." Ahrva's eyes were huge and troubled. "You're good luck to us, Esster. But don't let us be bad luck to you!"

Kitotul and Skedat returned empty-handed, following the

smoke. No one slept much that night, though Esther tried. This time, if she heard that mumbling voice, she wouldn't turn. She'd stare straight ahead and ask questions.

But if she slept, she didn't dream.

When not eating, they butchered; when not butchering, they dug; when not digging, they drove off scavengers. Everyone grew red-eyed and tired, their stomachs swelling in contrast to their skinny arms and legs. But Silika smiled and sang, and once put Esther's hand on her stomach, so she could feel the baby move.

"This will be a child of good luck," Silika said, "with so much wazicat around him—even that of the stars."

Esther didn't bother to argue.

TWENTY-ONE

*E*ven my eyelids ache," Esther complained, when their shift on the mammoth was over.

"But how's your belly?" Ahrva asked. "Come to the creek."

The creek was not so much a creek as a series of puddles. But the buggy plums were all eaten, and there was nothing else to drink. "In the stars," said Esther, "water's so easy to get, we're bored with it, and drink other things when we can."

"What can there be to drink besides water?" asked Ahrva.

"Kool-Aid," said Esther. "That's sweet and cold and comes in different colors, like flowers. And iced tea. That's brown and cold and tastes—oh, there isn't a word for how it tastes. And soda, which is sweet and cold . . . and . . . tickles as you drink it. And lemonade. It's cold and sour."

"Is anything you drink not cold?" asked Ahrva

"Sure," said Esther. "But when it's this hot, I want to think of the cold ones."

"The spring will be cold," said Tekinit. "Let's go there. I'm so thirsty, I could die." She staggered, crossing her eyes and hanging her tongue out. Esther made herself laugh, though she didn't feel like it. As far as she knew, Ahrva hadn't told anyone what was wrong—but Tekinit was way too sharp not to know that something was. Esther wasn't about to let her decision make Tekinit feel bad.

"All right," said Ahrva, skipping a few steps. "At the spring, we'll work star-magic, and make le-min-ade."

"Yuck!" Tekinit stopped staggering. "Not le-min-ade! Kulaid! I want to drink flowers!"

"What kind of flowers?"

"Bluebonnets!"

"Rain lilies!"

"Garlic blossoms!"

They howled with laughter, and even Esther smiled. Washaw had dared Esther to eat a flower off a garlic plant once, and she had done it. Bad idea! They climbed to the spring, and Esther, determined to show them that she was okay, struck the surface with her stran. "Abracadabra, alacazam! Turn into Kool-Aid, as fast as you can!" she chanted, in English.

"Look! Look! It's turning blue!" squealed Tekinit, falling on her stomach and sucking brown water from her grubby hands. "I'm drinking bluebonnet kulaid!"

In between drinks, they studied the paw prints left by the animals who used the spring, too. "That's a raccoon," said Ahrva, pointing to a series of skinny handlike marks. "A raccoon would be good to eat, but they're hard to kill."

Tekinit pointed to smaller, fatter prints. "Is this skunk?"

"That's right. Would you like to catch a skunk and eat it?"

Tekinit twisted her face up. "No!" she spat, giggling. "Nudawah can eat skunk!"

"Here's hoof prints," said Esther. "Is this pronghorn, or javelina?"

"Javelina," Ahrva said. "When my father is well, he will catch us a javelina."

"I bet *you* could catch one," said Esther.

Ahrva looked shocked. "I wouldn't try!"

"Why not?" asked Esther. "Why do only men get to hunt the big animals?"

"Men hunt big animals because women have more important things to do. If I killed javelina or mammoth, I'd never get yana, and never have babies. What's the good of having meat, with no babies to feed?"

"Women are good for lots of things besides having babies," said Esther. "Some star-women never have babies at all."

"Oh, the poor things!" cried Tekinit.

"They're *not* poor things," said Esther. "They *decided* not to have babies. They had better things to do."

"Like what?" asked Ahrva.

What jobs would they understand, much less be impressed by? "Making sick people well. They can be doctors."

"My mother can do that," said Tekinit.

"But a doctor might have made Uduban's son walk again," said Esther. "A doctor could have saved Shusskt's baby."

"Aiee!" Ahrva said. "That would be worth doing!"

"Not worth giving up having babies for," said Tekinit.

There was no point trying to liberate Ahrva and Tekinit. They didn't think they were oppressed. Maybe they weren't.

Maybe the men were. Maybe the whole group was. What did Esther know about anything?

Tekinit, inspired by the talk of babies, found a knobby branch and got Ahrva to scratch a face on it with her stran. She sang to it all the way back to camp.

They ate and dug and butchered in a haze of heat. The wind gave up blowing in exhaustion. Kitotul kept saying it was bound to rain, until Shusskt told him to be quiet. Even when the men went to the hilltop, to see if they could spot game, they caught no breeze. No smoke hovered on the horizon to indicate the location of other members of the group.

"The petwa are coming back from the north," said Podan, when they returned. "Petwa" must be what ate petwa-berries, Esther thought, and if they were coming back, they were probably migrating. Birds? No—she remembered that petwa ate grass, different grass from mammoths. Oh, it was too hard trying to keep track of everything.

"This is a good time for you and Kitotul to make a long hunt," agreed Silika, not looking at his ankle. "We'll have meat to live on while you're gone."

The mammoth already tasted funny to Esther. But she didn't say anything, and chanted with everybody else as Podan finished his new points. She understood this ceremony better now. Knocking out the final pieces, which made the base of the point thinner and easier to haft, was a tricky business. Most people who tried it broke their points. The fewer points a hunter broke, the better luck that meant for the hunt.

It's kind of like praying, she thought, taking her turn on watch with Emni that night. The cloud on the edge of the sky flickered like a weak flashlight. *None of the prayers I know has been invented yet. But God's here anyway.* She made up a prayer, as best she could.

A prayer for rain.

A prayer for Silika's baby to be born well.

A prayer for her family, eleven thousand years away.

TWENTY-TWO

➤ RAIN

*T*he men set off the next morning in rain so dense they were invisible before they passed the remains of the old fire. The new one under the outcrop was a smoky, miserable thing.

"Tomorrow the sun will come out, the flowers will bloom, and the animals will grow fat again," declared Emni.

"Meantime, we eat mammoth," said Shusskt. "Who'll come with me to butcher?"

Ahrva, Washaw, and Esther moaned. Tekinit, pretending to breast-feed her branch-baby, moaned in imitation. "We have enough meat," complained Washaw.

"Do you think the coyotes will be stopped by a little rain?" asked Shusskt. "If we don't want to have done all that work for the sake of our brother animals, we must keep working." She crawled out into the watery darkness.

Emni sighed and followed her.

"They'll be miserable when they come back," said Silika, lying down to rummage among the bags in the low-ceilinged rear of the shelter. She thrust a gourd at Ahrva. "Fill this, and we'll make them a hot drink."

Ahrva filled the gourd from the water streaming off the rock, while Silika built a tripod of crossed strans over the fire. As she put dried leaves called sulip into the water and hung the gourd on the tripod, Tekinit rocked her branch-baby and fidgeted. "My baby wants a story. Tell how the sky mother made the world."

That sounded interesting, but the others shushed her. "It is *not* the season for those kinds of stories," said Silika. "We'll tell our own stories, or coyote stories, or hero stories, but not making stories. Those are only for winter, when the right stars are there to hear them told right."

This made no sense to Esther. "Can you tell why mammoth has a big nose and a little tail?" she asked.

Tekinit laughed and clapped her hands. "Yes! Yes!"

So Silika told how coyote had played tricks on mammoth, so that she lost her fine fluffy tail, and got her nose stretched all out of whack. The tables were turned, though, when mammoth figured out all the things her trunk was good for—including catching sassy coyotes and tossing them into the air.

Then Ahrva told about little people who lived in tall grass, who could not be seen, but whose spears never missed, and how they would help polite girls, but harm rude ones. "I thought Esther might be one, when I first saw her; but she was too tall," she said. The sulip steamed, filling the space with a warm, minty smell but no one moved to drink it, saving it for Shusskt and Emni. Esther missed most of the next story, trying to think how to tell "Hansel and Gretel" or "The Three Little Pigs" in a way that would make sense. Washaw's story was confusing, because it was about coyote, black bear, and short-faced bear—kitotul, podan, and uduban—so it sounded as if her father were playing tricks on the other men.

"Then kitotul said: 'But wouldn't you like some tender baby mammoth?' And podan said—"

The sound that interrupted her was a vast, slow loudness, like the earth rolling over in its sleep. Esther moved before she thought, but the others were outside ahead of her. The mammoth had vanished, and Shusskt, like a woman made of mud, tore at the new landslide with her hands, crying, "Emni! Emni!"

Silika grabbed a piece of skull from the scattered bones and shoveled. Seizing whatever came to hand, everyone, even Tekinit, attacked the heap. The mud was gooey and strong, sucking Esther's shoes off her feet as she waded in to prod the mound with the blunt end of her stran. When she felt a different sort of resistance, she yelled: "Here!" Everyone attacked that spot, and Emni emerged, dripping, gasping, eyes closed under the weight of the mud stuck to her face, grabbing Esther's stran with blind, desperate hands. They pulled her out as if she were a zulotul, and Silika and Shusskt half-carried her back to the shelter, Tekinit running after. Esther, Ahrva, and Washaw remained, the mud sluicing off them, as they stared at the mound that had once been their food supply.

"We have enough meat for today," said Ahrva. "Maybe the men will return tomorrow."

"Maybe," said Washaw.

"We could dig it out again," suggested Esther.

Ahrva shook her head. "A day without meat is better than being buried alive!"

Water streamed off the rattlesnake rattle in Esther's hair. Her shoes had disappeared. *I guess this is a good site for Dr. Durham now.* Would she find fossilized sneakers?

Ahrva tugged her hand. "There's nothing we can do here."

The dry soil inside the rock shelter turned slimy. The sulip, bitter and hot, passed from hand to hand. Esther longed for hot chocolate, a bathroom, hot water, towels, soap. Emni curled inside the camel skin, shuddering, until Shusskt soothed her to sleep. "My baby doesn't like rain," announced Tekinit.

"Rain is good," said Ahrva. "You'll see how much better the world is after the sun comes out."

They huddled in the shelter all day, eating and breathing smoke. Emni woke up, drank a gourd of hot sulip, and declared that she was fine; but she kept glancing at the rock above. Silika told about the time her sister Apuk was trapped down a sinkhole, in winter, when the grass was too short to make ropes. They'd had to cut a hide into strips and tie them together to haul her out.

Emni pretended that this story made her feel better. "I'm used to this sort of thing," she said. "What else can anyone expect, with bad wazicat in her bones?"

"I don't believe there's anything wrong with your bones," Esther said. "It could have happened to anybody."

"But it didn't," said Emni. "It happened to me."

Lightning cracked so loud, so near, that the interior of the shelter lit up.

"What happens if we flood out of here?" asked Esther.

"We *won't*," snapped Silika.

Water poured off the rock, chuckling wickedly. Esther shivered. Ahrva put a cold arm around her, pressing her cold stomach to Esther's cold back. "My mother doesn't mean to be cross," she whispered.

"I know," answered Esther. She thought of the time it had rained like this every day for a month back home. Everyone had been crabby, despite hot food and dry beds. She remembered news reports about people who had gone around barricades to drive through low water crossings, and been swept away in their cars.

The hunters had no car, no policemen to erect barricades, and no emergency rescue squads. She pictured Skedat slipping and falling, Kitotul grabbing him, Podan trying to save them both, and all swirling away together.

And the others? What was happening to them?

TWENTY-THREE

By the third evening, everyone had colds. No one talked about how long the men had been gone.

Silika had been right—the shelter floor was at a good angle to the main slope, so that the water ran past instead of coming in; but every time someone entered or left, she had to wade. Esther lay in the back of the shelter, carving her name in the ceiling, wearing her stran to a nub.

"What is that?" asked Ahrva, touching a pale, staggering E with her finger. "Are you making wazicat?"

"Sort of," said Esther. "It's a message to my elder. So she'll know I was here. It's a rock signal."

"But the rock can only be seen in the cave."

"This same rock," Esther patted it, "exists here and in the stars both. Otherwise there couldn't be an entrance here. My elder won't be able to find me unless an entrance opens again while we're here, but sooner or later, she'll see this." Esther wished she had paper to write the whole story on, but paper would rot before Dr. Durham found it anyway.

"I see," said Ahrva. "What if—"

She never finished the sentence, for Tekinit burst into a fit of coughing that bent her skinny body double. Ahrva rocked her. "My throat hurts," whined Tekinit. "And I'm c-cold."

"I know," said Ahrva, taking the hot gourd Washaw, nearest the fire, passed to her. "Have some sulip."

Tekinit turned her head away. "Hurts," she croaked.

Ahrva sighed and handed the gourd back to Washaw. Silika rummaged through her medicine bag and pulled out a licorice root. "Chew that, then," she said, passing it back.

"I wish we could keep her dry," said Ahrva. "C'mon, Tekinit, you don't have to swallow, just chew."

"Here," said Esther, wedging her back against the carrying bags. "You lie by me, and we'll put her on top, and be a bed."

"Count me in," said Washaw, shivering.

So the three older girls lay down on top of a sleeping fur, with Ahrva in the middle, and covered Tekinit (clutching her branch-baby) with their arms and the woolly camel skin. Esther had trouble breathing, but it was warmer like this. Tekinit cried and coughed and could not sleep. Ahrva tried to sing to her, bringing on a coughing fit of her own. Silika sang instead, her voice a barely audible drone under the sound of the water. Esther tried to lie still. The fleas were moving in, fast; and she had scratched her head yesterday and found that her dandruff had legs. Lice. Wonderful.

It was impossible to sleep, but Esther found herself dreaming that they waited in a doctor's office. Everyone else in the waiting room was getting treated first, because Esther's group smelled so bad. She tried to explain about not being able to take baths, but the nurse, a cross between Nudawah and a vulture, only gave her paperwork to fill out with her stran.

"But they don't *have* any last names," she was explaining, when she felt the twitchy weight of Tekinit lifted from her. "No, no!" she cried, clutching for her.

Silika croaked, "It's all right. I've got her."

"We brought a raccoon and grapes," announced Emni, in a stuffed-up voice. "And I saw a break in the clouds."

Tekinit coughed, clinging to her mother awkwardly over the bulge of the baby. She got most of the grapes, squeezed out of their skins into her mouth one by one in between bouts of coughing. Emni and Shusskt, who both bore raccoon bites, cut up the skinned carcass for cooking. Silika scraped the hide.

"I wonder how the men are doing," said Ahrva.

"They're strong, clever men," said Silika. "They'll come back soon, with petwa."

"We'll have to go out in the rain, if they do," said Shusskt. "There isn't room for petwa under here."

Esther tried to put together everything they'd said about petwa and compare it to her book of Pleistocene animals, to figure out what it was, but the effort made her head ache.

They cooked and ate the raccoon in silence, except for sniffing, sneezing, and coughing. Silika brewed up leaves and a bright yellow root in a turtle shell. The result tasted filthy, but enabled them to sleep. Emni covered the fire with earth, and when Esther woke, no layer of smoke covered her eyes.

At first she didn't know what had awakened her, but then

she realized that it was quiet. Water rushed past the door, but none beat against the rock or streamed off the entrance.

Esther was suffocating in the tangled mass of bodies. Gently she extricated herself, removing Tekinit's burning-hot heel from her stomach, lifting Ahrva's head from her shoulder, sliding on her belly to the entrance.

Clouds trailed streamers across the Milky Way. Feeling giddy, Esther stood up and stretched her aching body, reaching over her head as if to grab the rain-washed stars. An owl hunted, hooting invisibly in the dark as a breeze shook wet leaves and a small animal ran away.

Esther crawled on top of the outcrop, and lay down. A cool breeze dried her skin. Her clothes were clammy and nasty. She lay her head on her arms, her view limited to the arc of her bracelet between her eye and the sky.

I know more than all the archaeologists in the world, she thought. *I know what mammoth hunters eat when they're not hunting mammoths, and what they do when they're sick, and what stories they tell when it rains.* To them, life was about finding food and having babies. Everything else—stories, singing, science, games—fit inside those two things, or didn't exist. She was beginning to see why it had to be like that; but she did not think she could settle for it.

Except that she might have to.

She breathed through her sore throat because she couldn't breathe through her nose. When the day grew gray around her, she sat up. Where had Shusskt said the grapevines were? She would fetch some so the others could eat vitamins when they woke up. They'd scold her, but it was impossible to get well without vitamins, and sleep. Whoever she woke up to come with her would get well that much less quickly. And maybe, maybe, being by herself was the key.

Both times, she had been alone near an archaeological site that Dr. Durham was working. And both times, she had dreamed of other times and the people in them. Was it important that Dr. Durham be working the site, or could it be any old archaeologist?

Maybe digging the site punched a hole through time, and the dreams held it open.

Moving softly on her bare feet, she slipped into the shelter and got an empty bag and her stran. She laid out her wet clothes to dry, turned inside out so she could pick the nits out of the seams later. One last star flamed near the rising sun. *Mama would faint if she saw me. I look like a mammoth hunter.*

But she wasn't. It would take more than a stran and a rattlesnake trophy in her hair to make her into one of the group.

Pausing often to rest and picture the effects eleven thousand years might have on her surroundings, Esther found the grapes and picked the biggest, least moldy ones, swallowing a few in spite of her sore throat.

To the west, the world extended into blue haze. She squinted, trying to picture highways and subdivisions.

And she saw the men returning.

TWENTY-FOUR

Petwa meant bison. Esther could tell by the shaggy pelt in which they had carried the meat. Now everyone rested, drying in the last rays of the sun, bellies as full of meat and grapes as sore throats could manage. Esther could even breathe through her nose, but Tekinit was still coughing.

"There are plenty more at the bison-berry place," said Podan. "If we leave today, we can have berries and bison meat to bring to the others at the plum place."

"Yes, we need to move on," said Shusskt. "This hill's full of bad wazicat."

"It could have been worse," said Ahrva. "I'm not sure Tekinit can walk far."

"Then we'll carry her," said Silika.

Washaw groaned. "She's too big to carry! Can't we drag her on the hide?"

"She's not a lump of meat!"

"We don't have to drag her," said Esther. "We can make

a . . . um, oh, I don't know the word. We could tie spear shafts
to the hide for handles, and carry her on that."

"Good idea," said Podan. "When Ehdanwah's cousin broke
his leg, he had the women carry him that way. The women
complained of how heavy he was, but his brother's leg had set
crooked from being walked on too soon, and he wouldn't take
the chance. Tekinit will be much less trouble to carry than he
was."

Skedat jumped up. "We need new shafts anyway. Who'll
come with me to find saplings?"

"I should go. She's my sister." Ahrva sat up, and stopped. "As
soon as the world comes back," she said, faintly. "I shouldn't sit
up so fast."

"We're all sisters," said Emni. "I'll go."

Esther felt vaguely that she ought to volunteer; but she had
been up a long time, and it felt good to lie here in a row with
Washaw and Ahrva, like sunbathers on a beach.

"How would a doctor make Tekinit well?" asked Ahrva.

"A what?" asked Washaw.

"A person who makes sick people well and hurt people
whole, instead of having babies," said Ahrva. "They have them
in the stars. Esther isn't one, but maybe she's seen how they
work."

"Well, I have," said Esther, "but I don't understand it. Mama
takes me to a doctor, and he—"

"You said women were doctors."

"All right, she then. She listens to my heart and lungs and
looks in my ears, and gives me . . . um . . ." No word for "pill" in
this language! "Medicine. I swallow it three times a day for a

few days, and I get a drink that stops the coughing. The doctor says, get plenty of rest, and liquids. Especially fruit juice. There's lots of good wazicat in fruit."

"We'll find plenty of fruit at the berry place," said Ahrva. "But I don't think anyone can rest much."

They couldn't; but they walked even more slowly than usual, taking turns carrying Tekinit's litter. They collected greens, mushrooms, and bark to make Esther a new pair of sandals, but were too slow and achy for anything more. Silika kept putting her hand on the baby, and she and Shusskt put their heads together and talked a lot.

In late afternoon they found a clear spring near a bog with cattails, blueberries, and grapes. It was too good a site to pass up, even if they hadn't all been bone-tired; so Silika built a fire on the nearest hill while the others gathered fruit and zulotul. When the hunters arrived, they had a deer.

"I wish we could stay here tomorrow," said Esther, as they lounged around the fire eating meat oozing grease. A few months ago she would have thought it was gross, but now she licked up the fat and wished for more.

"Tomorrow we'll be at the berry place, and that'll be even better," Kitotul assured her.

"Except that we won't be able to get there tomorrow if we detour by the medicine trees," said Shusskt. "And we should."

Tekinit stared blankly into the fire.

Podan and Kitotul looked around the circle of weary women. "We men can walk faster than you women," said Kitotul. "If you went straight to the bison-berries, and we took the detour for the medicine trees, you'd have the medicine by tomorrow night."

"Harvesting bark is women's work," said Shusskt, looking over at Silika.

"Protecting women and children is men's work," said Kitotul. "Will our hunting magic be spoiled if we pick off a little bark to help our womenfolk?"

"I don't see why," said Podan. "But what if we pick it off wrong? We don't know what part of the plant is good and what part is bad. We don't know how to ask permission."

"We could split into two groups," said Silika. "We can do that for one night."

"Are you *sure*?" Shusskt asked.

"For one night, yes," said Silika, firmly.

Emni and Esther, who had recovered best from the illness, were picked to go with Shusskt and Kitotul to get medicine, while the rest proceeded, at a leisurely pace, toward the berries. "It'll be strange to watch you leave," said Ahrva. "You're our good luck."

"Oh, I am not," said Esther. "I didn't keep that mudslide from burying Emni, did I?"

But she felt funny the next morning, knowing it would be at least a full day and a night before she met up with her foster family again. A lot could happen in a day and a night. Ahrva said, "Your stran's point is too small to sharpen. Take mine."

"Thanks," said Esther, taking it from where Ahrva had stuck it into the ground overnight.

"Maybe you'll see an entrance to the stars while you're gone," said Ahrva. "Maybe I won't see you again."

"I don't want Esther to go away," croaked Tekinit.

Esther did not want her last memory of Tekinit to be of her looking miserable. She snapped off her bracelet. "Would you keep this for me?"

Tekinit's jaw dropped. "Really?" The bracelet curled twice around her wrist, and she gazed at it in a stupor of joy.

"Come along, can't you?" called Shusskt. "We have a lot of walking to do!"

The grass was green, and plants that had stopped growing during the drought would be fit to eat soon. The four traveled fast, reaching their destination in early afternoon. The medicine trees, a kind Esther had never seen before, grew around a water hole which had probably been dry a few days before. Shusskt was picky about how much bark they took from which part of each tree, and taught Esther a super-polite chant to say as she worked: "You are beautiful and strong, Tree Mother. Your roots are deep, your branches wide. We are small and wander in your shade. Lend us your strength, please, Tree Mother. We will remember you when we are far away, and be grateful."

"If we do this wrong, the Tree Mother will be offended, the trees will die, and we won't get bark so easily again," Shusskt explained.

That night, Esther glimpsed a spark across the rolling hills, like a star settled on a ridge. She pointed. "Is that the others?"

"Yes," said Shusskt. "They're pointing at our fire, and saying: 'There're the others, eating supper.'"

"I wish we could see more campfires," said Emni. "I wonder if anyone else is sick, or hurt."

"There had better not be any more sick," said Shusskt. "I

found hardly any medicine plants. There used to be roots here that I can't find anymore." She frowned at the spark. "They didn't reach the berry place. They're not far enough away."

"Probably carrying Tekinit tired them out and they didn't make good time," said Kitotul.

In the morning, they headed toward the berry place, hoping to intersect the course of the others before too long. Pleased with themselves and the world in general, they sang: "We walk between the earth and sky; earth and sky smile on us!" But by mid-morning, thin smoke still rose from the hilltop where they had seen the spark last night. Esther nudged Emni and pointed. Emni stopped. "Mother. Father. Something's wrong."

"Wrong where?" asked Shusskt; then followed Esther's pointing finger. "Oh."

Esther hugged her arms. "You don't think—you don't think Tekinit got worse and can't be moved, do you?"

"Why aren't they signaling us?" Kitotul asked.

"Maybe they're too busy to mind the fire," said Shusskt.

They changed course, keeping their eyes on the thread of smoke. No one suggested stopping for lunch. In early after-noon, they saw figures moving among the trees, and two brush shelters as far away from each other as it was possible to get and still be on the top of the hill. They were howling to announce their arrival when a wail silenced them.

"What the—?" said Esther. "Is that Tekinit?"

"Aiee!" Emni and Shusskt broke into a run.

Esther ran, too, her heart blocking her breath. She had never heard any of the group cry, except for the baby—

Baby!

Washaw dragged her mother and Emni toward one shelter. Tekinit coughed in the other. Kitotul, Skedat, and Podan stood well away from both, slapping each other's backs happily. Esther went to Tekinit, who clutched her branch-baby and croaked: "My mother has a boy! His name is Kiraka."

They'd named the baby *Toad*? "How can he become a mighty hunter with a name like that?"

"My mother's father did," said Tekinit. "He—" Coughing interrupted her.

Ahrva crawled into the shelter, looking tired but happy. "Give me the bark, and go look at our baby."

Esther felt shy, approaching Silika's shelter, but the others made room for her. "Watch out!" cried Washaw. "If you break the barricade, *anything* can enter."

Obediently, Esther put her foot down outside the line of ash encircling the shelter, and bent over to peer inside, where Silika lay with a wiggly, tiny baby sucking at her breast. "Welcome back, star-child."

Washaw whispered in Esther's ear: "Say, 'Welcome and happiness, Mother. Welcome and happiness, new little one of the group.'"

Esther felt funny repeating the words. Who was she to welcome anybody? But Silika thanked her. "You see he was too eager to run and meet life," she said. "He didn't want to be left out." She kissed the fuzzy head.

Ahrva had lots to tell Esther as she brewed the medicine bark. Silika's water had broken yesterday afternoon, scaring Podan to death. Having a man around was dangerous to the baby and the mother both, and neither he nor Skedat could come near her. Silika had kept walking, instructing Podan and Skedat to run ahead and find a good campsite and firewood. Washaw and Ahrva made the shelters while Podan and Skedat walked the perimeter making noise so that predators would think the whole group was protecting her.

"It was awful," Ahrva whispered. "Father helpless, Mother screaming, Tekinit coughing, and Washaw and I could only give them water! But the baby came this morning, Washaw caught it, I cut the cord, and—and it was worth it!"

"He's awfully tiny."

"Yes, even for a baby," agreed Ahrva. "Mother will have all she can do to look after him. We two will take care of Tekinit."

Tekinit had no appetite. As Esther pushed grapes into her mouth, she plucked the bracelet. "I kept it safe."

"Thanks. Would you hang onto it a little longer? It . . . gets in my way."

Podan was in a good mood, although forbidden to come near the baby shelter. "In a day or two, Tekinit will be well, my son will come out where I can hold him, my wife will be strong and happy, and we'll walk to a feast of bison and berries!"

"It'll be more than a day or two before your wife and daughter can walk anywhere," said Shusskt. "Men! You lie around for three days on a sore ankle, and expect a woman to dance the morning after putting all her power into a new life!"

"My wife won't move till she knows she's strong," said Podan, grinning as if Shusskt's crossness was one more thing to be happy about. "I trust her wisdom."

"Hmph! You'd better find some fat meat, or your wise wife won't get strong," said Shusskt. "She needs bison liver."

"Yes, ma'am," said Podan. "Come, Kitotul, Skedat! We must ask bison to give us his liver."

Nursing mothers needed special foods and ceremonies to keep their milk flowing and prevent sickness, and since Kiraka had come early, Silika needed even more than she normally would. Tekinit's medicine also had to be prepared in a certain way. To make matters worse, Emni and Shusskt turned yana. This left the younger girls to do all the women's work.

Fortunately, the men got their bison, so the girls could concentrate on medicinal plants—roots for Tekinit's throat and Kiraka's gas, leaves and roots for Silika's milk production and strength, and stems to be woven into wreaths to cool the head. Esther wasn't sold on the effectiveness of this last treatment, but making the wreaths was something Tekinit could do when she felt like sitting up.

The yana women made Esther a camel-hide blouse and told her how to take the yana power out so it would be safe to wear. The men hunted nearby, letting several mammoths go for lack of enough men to hunt them safely. Silika made a baby carrier out of special wood, sang, and nursed.

Ahrva taught Esther how to make a new stran from scratch, choosing a butterscotch-colored flint. The result was sharp, but lopsided. "What about that flake out of the bottom?" Esther asked.

"Better let Podan do it," Ahrva advised.

"I don't want to wait till he gets back." She'd gotten used to carrying a stran, and felt naked sharing Ahrva's.

"We don't have to knock out that flake, then," said Ahrva. "We women don't need the flint fathers' favor so much." She passed Esther some peeled sticks and a cleaver. "Now mount it."

Esther spoiled four sticks—no big deal, since they became firewood—before she got the split right. Then she wedged in the blunt end of the blade and wrapped it tight with damp wesk, which dried even tighter. Her shoulders ached, her hands stung from tiny cuts, and one finger throbbed where she'd banged it; but she had made her own stran.

If only she could show it to Dr. Durham, and her mother!

After five days, Silika got up and Emni and Shusskt stopped being yana. They tore down the shelters with another ceremony. Tekinit drooped tiredly, until Esther thought to dress her in the T-shirt, cinched by the rattlesnake belt. Tekinit grinned proudly and paraded around camp. "I'm big enough to wear star-hills," she announced, pointing at the picture of the roller coaster under the words "Fiesta Texas."

Esther was certain both Tekinit and Silika should have had

a few more days to rest; but fleas were eating everyone alive, and they'd used up all the convenient plants. Besides, the bison-berries they'd been sent to collect in the first place would be all gone if they didn't get to them soon. They traveled in a compact version of normal progression, the men hunting but not roaming far. Silika looked funny, with her stomach flat and her back bulged out by Kiraka's baby carrier.

"I like babies," Tekinit announced. "I'll have as many as I have fingers."

"You won't live that long," said Ahrva.

"She could have a baby every year," objected Esther.

"Not and keep the ones she already had," said Washaw.

"Why not?"

"You can't feed two babies at once," explained Ahrva. "You'd kill yourself making milk. When one is old enough to walk half a day, you can feed him real food, and start a new baby. Do women have babies every year in the stars?" asked Ahrva.

"Some," answered Esther, thinking of the family at school that had a kid in every grade. "I told you we have more people."

"And more food, obviously," said Emni. "But why would anyone want to? Doesn't it wear them out?"

Esther shrugged. "Nobody makes them do it. Only women who think they can keep strong have so many."

"When I grow up, I'll marry a star-man," Tekinit announced. "I'll have a baby a year and drink kulaid. When my sister and brother are hungry, I'll throw food down."

In three days, they finally reached the bison-berries, which grew up and down a limestone cliff and on flat, sandy land where bison grazed. Esther had known bison were big, but knowing and seeing were different. Most were taller than Podan, with massive horns sticking straight out of the sides of their heads. They dotted the landscape in bunches of two or three cows with calves at heel, watched over by enormous bulls.

As the girls picked black, sweet berries, Kitotul and Podan crept out covered by the hide of the last bison they'd killed, moving at the same pace as the real bison—step, step, graze, graze. Esther had read that modern bison were too stupid to run when hunters shot at them—but was *any* animal so stupid it couldn't recognize a hide held up by two men? "Can't they smell them?" she asked.

"Look how the wind's blowing," answered Ahrva. "The scent blows away from the bison. Bison wants to eat while the grass is good. If they don't smell anything dangerous, they won't fuss about how ugly their neighbors are."

"So where's Skedat?"

Emni pointed, but Esther saw only grass, boulders, and a motte of maples. "He's working his way upwind. When the bison smell him, they'll get nervous. Then he'll stand and shout, and they'll run toward our fathers."

The campfire bragging was short that night. "Sometimes I think there must be a better way to hunt bison," said Podan, holding his side where the dying bull had kicked him. "What do you say now you've seen them, Esster? Do bison die?"

"No, but they, um, change."

"Change?" Silika repeated. "How?"

Esther had read about evolution, but hadn't understood it well. "I don't know how they do it," she said. "But they get smaller, their horns get shorter, and someday, herds of bison will cover the earth as far as the eye can see."

"Aiee," breathed Shusskt, reverently.

TWENTY-SIX

➤ REUNION

*F*ive days later they arrived, late, to meet the rest of the group at the plum grove.

They followed the smoke and howled. Answering howls went up, at first rising bodiless from the landscape; but then Esther saw Ehdanwah, a small silhouette, stand up by the fire, and Telabat drop from a tree. He and Otala ran to meet them. The grown-ups followed more sedately. Only when Kiraka woke and started crying did they also start to run.

The two groups came together with much exclaiming. Uduban slapped Podan on the back and said, "So! I'm again an uncle!"

"Yes," said Podan, trying to suppress a grin and watching Uduban's face. "I have a son. But he's only a little one."

Nudawah peered into the baby's face. "Weh, he has good lungs," she said. "But you should have waited."

"That's what I told him," said Silika, not trying to hide her proud grin. Nudawah tried to look happy, but couldn't control her eyes. *Now Silika has four children, counting me, and Nudawah only has one,* Esther thought.

They trooped up the hill, the women clustering around Silika, the men pounding Podan on the back and joking, the children forming a trailing cluster like a flock of birds.

"You've almost missed the plums," said Otala, passing out dark, blackish-purple balls frosted with the bloom of condensation that, Esther had learned, indicated plums at their peak. "But I saved some for you. And I would have saved you strawberries, but I couldn't. I ate so many, I got sick! And I helped my father butcher the horses he killed."

"Dul killed horses without other men to help? He's truly a great hunter," said Ahrva. "You must have been good luck to him. We haven't done much, ourselves. Esster brought us a mammoth, and Washaw and I delivered a baby."

Otala gaped, and Ahrva laughed. Esther's insides bubbled. *Everything'll be all right*, she thought, banishing the image of Nudawah's jealous eyes to the back of her brain.

The group welcomed Kiraka. Ehdanwah held him in her lap and asked Silika questions before pronouncing him a fine child and sending the girls to find a plant that she could mix with fat and rub on him to bring his weight up. Esther didn't see how rubbing fat on his outsides would do that, but she did as she was told. The plant in question had a sharp smell, and when Ehdanwah rubbed it on the baby, fleas jumped off of him like dirt flying off a duster when you beat it. Esther resolved to find more and mix it into her bedding.

They built up the fire till it seemed to lick the stars from the sky. Dinner was venison that had cooked since the night before, zulotuls baked in greens that imparted a salty savor, and juicy plums, one bite sour and the next bite sweet. They

sang, and ate, and sang some more. The women sang while
the men danced, leaping over each other, whirling, and
stamping; then the men sang and the women danced, circling
Silika and tossing a ball from person to person over her head.
Everyone laughed, everyone sang, everyone's mouth and
hands were covered in grease and juice; and Esther thought:
This is how it's supposed to be.

The night's campfire talk was more detailed than usual, each
man describing landmarks, animal signs, and the weather.
Tekinit fell asleep with her head in Ahrva's lap and her feet on
Esther's leg. Esther wished she could sleep, too, but she tried to
pay attention and build a map in her head of where they were in
relation to food and water and future archaeological sites. She
whispered to Ahrva: "The women should talk, so we'll know
where the plants are."

Ahrva nodded and whispered back: "They will, this time."

Silika poked them and said: "Shhh!"

Sure enough, when Kitotul finished his portion of the story
of their eventful weeks, Ehdanwah talked about nuga, numb-
berries, this plant and that plant and the other plant. Things
were blooming at the wrong time, drying up at the wrong
time. Then Nudawah said it all again, politely disagreeing with
Ehdanwah about how weird it was that the plants were blooming and bearing at the wrong times. By now Esther was having
a hard time sitting up straight. Mingwah talked about strawberries, water, medicinal plants. Esther's bottom went to sleep.

When Silika stood, she held up Kiraka. "What I have to tell,
is soon told. Others in my family did the real work. All I did
was have a son. Anyone could do it! But I am sorry I did not

wait and do it properly, with the group. I will be more careful next time!"

A laugh went round, but Ahrva puckered her eyebrows. *"Next time" was awfully close to bragging,* Esther thought. Silika sketched the outline of events, then said, "Those who did these things will tell you of them," and sat down. Nudawah looked displeased. Did she feel that Silika had shown her up, generously passing talk time to Shusskt, the least important woman in the group?

Shusskt kept it short, then called Ahrva to tell about delivering Kiraka. Esther, her arm around Tekinit, woke completely, pleased to see how Ahrva hit the right note between justifiable pride and modesty. *She's been practicing what she'd say since we sat down,* thought Esther. *It's good to go last.*

"When you have no choice, you do what you must," said Ahrva. "It isn't time for credit or for blame. But the person who makes a hard choice must tell her story. Esster, it's your turn."

Esther's brain went numb. Nudawah said, "Tonight the group shares. That star-child is not one of us. So she found a dead mammoth. So what?"

"That's not all she found," said Ahrva. "Esster, stand up."

Everyone was looking at her. Esther swallowed. "That was . . . that was . . . !" She didn't know the word for secret. "What are you doing?"

"If you know something, you must tell us," said Podan. "Esster, what happened?"

"Please. Next to helping with the baby, it's nothing. No one will eat better because I tell."

"That is for us to decide," said Ehdanwah. "Stand, Esster, and tell your story."

Esther took a deep breath. "It was morning. Everyone was asleep. I walked by myself."

"Why?" Nudawah demanded. "That is stupid and dangerous."

"Because I'm stupid!" Esther snapped. "I know I shouldn't have, but I felt... I was... In the stars, you can be alone and bears don't eat you. Do you want to hear the story or not?"

"Go on, star-child," said Ehdanwah. "We will talk about your manners later."

Esther swallowed. "Yes, ma'am. I saw vultures, and followed them. I saw the mammoth, and coyotes eating it, and... and... I saw an entrance. To the stars. And someone I knew on the other side. My elder that taught me to see the future."

Everyone drew a breath at once.

Esther kept talking, her voice gone tight and squeaky, until the story was told. The fire tossed up sparks to turn into stars above the encircling shadow of the group.

"You should have gone," Nudawah said. "They would have found the mammoth."

"You weren't there," said Shusskt. "I was up and calling for her, and I hadn't spotted those vultures."

"Oh, the star-child could kill Ehdanwah, and you'd still come to her defense," spat Nudawah. "But all the star-wazicat in the world won't make you anything but a low woman married to a low man whose children and grandchildren will still be low!"

Everyone talked at once. Tekinit was awake and trembling with the effort of not shouting at a grown-up. Ahrva looked as if a firework had gone off in her face. "Why'd you make me tell?" Esther asked her. "Everything was great, and you spoiled it!"

"I didn't ... they shouldn't ... I'm sorry."

"Enough!"

Everyone fell quiet except the babies. "There is much to think about, and it's too late to think," said Ehdanwah. "Tonight we sleep, we dream. Tomorrow, we talk."

"But—" said Nudawah.

"Tomorrow," said Ehdanwah.

TWENTY-SEVEN

*U*duban didn't want to hear how bison would cover the earth as far as the eye could see. "Isn't it handy," he said, "that the star-child sees such a bright future for the animal Podan wants to hunt!" Dul gave up talking at morning arguments, and proved to be ingenious about getting wazicat from Esther without Uduban or Nudawah seeing him. "They know you do this, you know," she said one day.

He shrugged. "Knowing is one thing, seeing is another. He's used to having me on his left hand. As long as he can pretend not to know, he will do nothing."

Whenever Ehdanwah was busy elsewhere, Nudawah talked about how evil Esther was. "Look what happens to people who trust the star-child! They sprain their ankles, break their ribs, get buried by mudslides, get sick, and have babies too soon! There was no drought before she came. Our husbands never fought."

"They don't fight now," said Silika. "No one's been hit."

"When his brother speaks against him, it wounds my husband like a stran in the heart," said Nudawah.

"Pretty lively, for a man with a stran in his heart," said Shusskt, surprising a giggle out of Mingwah; big point for Shusskt, and not one that Nudawah forgave readily. Silika and Shusskt started turning their backs on Nudawah, who made a big show of not noticing. Mingwah and Dul fought, sort of, and pretended nothing was wrong. Nudawah forbade Telabat to shake Esther's hand.

As if all this wasn't enough, the weather was muggy, with overcast skies. Some mornings, steam came off the grass as the dew dried. Tekinit could barely breathe on those days, and the babies cried incessantly.

Until, one morning, Esther woke to a change in the air. It was still hot, still humid, but—a smell? The color of the light? "We should move today," said Podan to the other men. "I have flea bites all down my back."

"Weh, weh," said Uduban. "I suppose you want to follow those bison to the west."

"I thought we could go south and east," said Podan.

"South and east." Uduban smiled. "Who says differently?"

"South and east," said Dul.

"What are they talking about?" Esther asked.

"The gathering," said Tekinit. "In the Valley."

The gathering!

Esther looked around at the people who had become her whole world, bustling about collecting their stuff. How many more groups this size? How many mammoths? And what else, all coming together in a Valley, in the junction between summer and winter? "When ... when will we get there?"

Ahrva pointed southeast. "A moon cycle or so. There'll be

feasts, and dancing, and weddings. Emni's old enough to marry."

Emni, as if she felt all their eyes turning toward her, looked up from the belt she was mending for Kitotul. "We'll run races, and play ball, and tell our news. Some will have new babies. But none will have a star-child!"

"Um," said Esther, "do we have to tell them about that?"

"But they'll wonder where you came from," said Tekinit.

Esther sighed. "Nuaah. But don't tell anybody I have wazi-cat!" She could see herself shaking hands with a line of men that stretched over the horizon.

"We won't have to," said Tekinit. "Kitotul will."

"So will Nudawah," added Ahrva. "We must tell as many people as we can before she does."

Esther wanted to say she didn't care what people thought; but she would have been lying. "Are there lots of groups?"

"Lots?" Silika repeated the word as if Esther had used it wrong and she was trying to sort out what she meant. "Enough."

"Why don't we ever see them?"

"Because they're in their own places," said Emni. "The autumn gathering is for groups from the escarpment and the low places. In the spring, we'll see the high groups." She saw her father coming, and held up the belt. "Or you all will. If I marry a low flatlander, I may never see a high group again."

"Marry on the escarpment," said Kitotul, taking the belt and her hand. "Then we'll see you in spring and fall."

"Maybe I won't marry," said Emni. "Maybe I'll do like star-women and become a doc-tor, and keep the group alive forever."

"Forever is too long," said Kitotul. "Let us die when our grandchildren have grandchildren."

If the Valley hosted the gathering every year, bones and points had to accumulate, no matter how tidy the groups were. If the cross-time warps had to do with archaeologists and the connections they made between present and past, maybe... maybe...

And maybe not. How much did she dare hope?

The nights cooled as they traveled, at the usual slow pace, southeast. Ripe fruits and seeds were easy to find, and they buried several caches of food. Birds sang louder, making restless flocks. Silika joked, when she took Kiraka out of his carrier in the evenings, that he had grown a stran's length since she'd put him in it that morning.

Emni put in extra foraging hours finding soap-root to scrub with, and mixed rosehips, fat, and roots to wash her face. "You'll wash your skin off," said Washaw, as the girls waited for their gourds to fill at a slow-dripping spring one afternoon.

"She wants to be beautiful for her husband," Ahrva teased.

"She'll be dirty again by the time we get to the Valley," said Tekinit. "She should wait till the night before."

"No, it'll take that long to work down through all the layers of dirt," said Esther.

Emni tossed her wet hair so that water spattered them all. "Maybe if you three start now, and wash every day with roses and soap-root, by the time you're old enough to be married, a man might be able to tell you from horses that have been wallowing."

"Be careful, or by the time we get there, you'll smell so sweet, the butterflies will cover you, and the men won't be able to see you," warned Ahrva.

"Good," said Washaw. "Then she won't get married, and I won't have to carry that bison hide by myself."

"Don't worry, Washaw," said Otala. "My mother says it's as likely as a bison catching a fox that Emni will get a husband."

Emni started working on her tangles, but Ahrva and Washaw stared at Otala as if she'd sprouted horns. "Sure she will," Tekinit declared. "She's pretty and tall and always finds food, and she can carry lots, and she's way way way nicer than you!"

Otala crossed her arms. "If she was Dul's daughter, or Podan's, or Uduban's, that would matter."

Washaw's face twitched.

"Your mother listens to Nudawah too much," said Ahrva. "Kitotul married a good wife. Three of her children have lived past the age of danger. Any man worth having will count that more than a shadow on her father."

"Maybe," said Otala, looking as if she would rather have stopped talking. "But my mother says it's a shame Kitotul and Shusskt didn't have only boys. Even a boy who'll never be oheitika can work hard for a wife, like Kitotul did; but a girl can't drive the shadow out."

"Otala," said Emni, in an even voice, "because something is true does not mean it must be said."

Otala looked at her feet. The water trickled, and big green parakeets chattered in the trees.

"Okay, somebody explain to me," said Esther. "How do people decide who marries who?"

She could see them remembering that she was likely not to
know the oddest things. "It depends," said Ahrva.

"On what?"

"Oh ... who your parents were. What group you're from."

"I thought people who liked each other picked each other
out. That's what Podan and Silika did—isn't it?"

"Podan saved my uncle Geshwaw. He had given our grand-
parents Geshwaw's life, and they could say: *Our daughter marries the man the mammoth honored.*"

"Silika's family can be proud of her husband," said Emni. "No
one can be proud to connect to my family."

"But Shusskt married Kitotul. He's got more bad wazicat
than you," said Esther.

"My mother is ugly—"

"No, she's not."

"Her chin is too pointy. My father knew he couldn't have a
pretty woman. He liked my mother. It took him three gather-
ings—two spring and one autumn—to make her like him. He
went to her group. They said he couldn't have her. Every morning he brought meat and asked again. They asked him to do
impossible things."

"Like?"

"Like turning blue. My mother helped him find a plant that
would do it. And he hopped on one foot all one day. My uncles
sat with their friends thinking of terrible things to make him
do, and my mother was so mad she put itching plants in their
bedding. But whatever they asked, he did. Finally my grandfather said that he might or might not find a better hunter for
his daughter, or a man who was wiser or healthier or luckier,

but he would never find a man who wanted her more. So they were married." She smiled as a cloud of parakeets rose in unison.

"But we can't do that," said Washaw. "We have to make some man want us. And they won't, because our grandfather was bad."

"But *you're* not," said Tekinit, taking her hand. "You're better than most people." She glared at Otala.

"We have to be, don't we?" said Emni.

Esther thought about Emni's problem, almost as much as she thought about her own. She was no longer a complete waste of space. She could fish and gather plants and watch for predators and carry as big a load as anyone. The knowledge that Tekinit might have died without her ached in her chest, half pride and half fear. But . . .

But she would always be an outsider, and Kitotul's family would always be low.

The group imperceptibly quickened its pace, following the escarpment above a river looping through the hills. *Dreamwalkers*, Esther encouraged herself. *Archaeological sites.* Queasy with dread and hope, she watched three or four lines of smoke rising from the horizon to join the evening clouds. Mammoths moved in slow bunches along the river valley, eating what they didn't trample, pushing down trees, not hurrying. The men did not hunt them. There would be plenty of mammoths in the Valley.

Tomorrow. They'd be in the Valley tomorrow.

The group would have walked all night if Ehdanwah hadn't called a halt. People chattered as they did their evening chores. Esther listened, silently, trying to get a head start on all the new names she'd have to learn. Silika and Mingwah's mothers, fathers, sisters, and brothers would see their babies for the first time. Silika especially looked forward to seeing her sister Apuk, who had been pregnant with her first baby at the spring gathering. The children bragged about how they would win the games and contests. Tekinit pretended to be a mammoth, making the babies laugh till they hiccuped, and Mingwah's baby crawled after her making trumpeting noises.

The married couples paired off, and the girls and boys slept on opposite ends of the camp in open-sided arbors. The girls kept giggling and thinking of new things to say about people Esther didn't know and games she had never played.

"Look," said Otala. "A star's falling. Maybe it's Esster's home."

Esther wanted to say: *It's a rock burning in the upper atmosphere,* but she would have had to say "top part of the sky" instead of "upper atmosphere," and what was the point, anyway?

"Esster's home is fine," said Ahrva. "Don't be mean. We'll find a dream-walker to find Esster's elders, and when she goes home, we'll all miss her."

"You *really* think a dream-walker could get me home?" Esther asked.

"If they can't, nobody can," said Ahrva.

Not a comforting thought. "But how?"

"Well—you know how when you dream, you're lost, because you don't know you're dreaming?" Emni said. "Dream-walkers know exactly where they are and can go everywhere in dream space. Visit the dead, those not yet born, everywhere! They must be able to find the stars, too."

Esther was afraid to believe it. "What happens if I can't ever go home?"

"You'll stay with us," said Ahrva. "You're our sister now."

"So's Emni," said Esther. "She's not staying. I don't see why girls have to leave the group and men get to stay."

"It's easier to learn where plants are than to hunt with men you haven't known your whole life," said Emni.

"Men make the groups, but women make the families," said Ahrva. "When Emni leaves, her new family and her old family will be connected."

"So—if I grow up here, who do I marry?"

"Telabat likes you, I happen to know," said Emni.

Esther pretended to throw up. "And have Nudawah for my mother-in-law? Don't even joke about that!"

"Nudawah picked out Telabat's wife a long time ago, don't worry," said Otala.

"Marry Skedat," said Washaw. "I bet star-wazicat would burn our badness out of your children."

"You think my wazicat's powerful enough for that?"

"Sure," said Emni.

"Probably," said Ahrva.

"No," said Otala. "You could make it worse. And even if you burned all the bad out, how would you prove it? If everyone thinks they're shadowed, it doesn't matter if they are or not."

Which was the whole point.

Esther propped herself up on her elbows, choosing her words carefully. "I've been wondering how it works here. Because where I come from, nobody has to live with a shadow.

We have a wazicat that takes it out. And I think I could work it. But it takes—it takes a lot of people, and I don't know—maybe I'd do it wrong." Her stomach hurt with the hugeness of the lie.

"But maybe you wouldn't," Emni said. "Tell me about it."

TWENTY-EIGHT

They followed the escarpment toward the rising smoke. Quail flushed, unpursued, under their feet. Two boggy places fringed with cattails went unharvested. The girls sang all of the Clovis songs Esther knew, and a few that she didn't. She sang them anyway, and in turn taught them to sing "Ta-ra-ra-boom-de-ay." Nudawah wanted to know what it meant, and Esther, who had no idea, said: "It means 'we're strong and happy,' more or less."

She did not teach them the version about eating beans today. It didn't seem fair to trick them into singing about farting.

The trumpeting of mammoths and the smell of roasting meat kept them walking with stomachs that growled and calves that ached. The Valley was full of mammoths. They milled about, talking in low rumbles and shrill trumpets, hugging with their trunks, drinking, wallowing, running, clashing tusks, butting heads. They were so huge and moved so lightly, though they shook the ground; and each one was different from the others in size or shape or coloring, in the ways they moved or sounded. *They can't die out. It isn't real,* Esther thought.

She wasn't sure where she was, but she remembered that on the map, Interstate 35 followed the curve of the escarpment through central Texas. Six lanes of traffic, gas stations, outlet stores, fast food, billboards. *They would have found the archaeological site when they built the highway. Wouldn't they?*

If they had, Dr. Durham couldn't dig here, because the site would already have been dug, or destroyed by construction crews that didn't care and wouldn't know a Clovis point if it leaped out of the ground and whacked them on the noses.

Dream-walkers. Maybe the dream-walkers will know what to do.

At last Esther heard a low, continuous roar. "The falls!" Uduban cried; and they broke into a tired run, howling: "We are Uduban's group! We are all well!"

The falls spurted from the escarpment in a dozen places, tumbling down steep, thickly wooded hills. The group shed their burdens and clothes and ran into falling water that couldn't have been any colder if the limestone had concealed a refrigerator. "We have to wash the year off," Ahrva shouted in Esther's ear. "I'll scrub your back and you scrub mine."

When they couldn't stand any more they bounced out, shivering and blinking. Esther threw herself onto the grass and rolled to dry off. "This one's new," said a strange voice. "Who had the fast-growing baby?" Strange hands helped her roll.

Esther squealed and sat up. A woman laughed at her. "Yahaywah!" Ahrva shouted, throwing her arms around the stranger.

The space around the falls was full of people—strange people—and Esther was stark naked, dripping wet, and freezing cold. *I don't want to be here, I don't want to be here, I don't want to be here!* Dry strangers helped wet familiars roll themselves dry, bundle the babies and young children back into their clothes, and comb out their wet hair. Nudawah hugged an old man; children jumped and shrieked; babies were passed around and admired. *I used to see more people every day in school,* Esther told herself, but that had been different.

She'd belonged at school.

Podan's sister Yahaywah and her husband, Silika's brother, Geshwaw, had brought their children—Kordak, a boy about Ahrva's age, and Wahay, a little girl to whom Tekinit at once showed off her bracelet, T-shirt, and rattlesnake belt, directing attention to Esther—not that everyone wasn't looking at her anyway. Podan put his hands on her shoulders. "This is Esster," he said. "She fell from the stars. We're taking care of her, and she shares her wazicat with us."

"Did it hurt, falling from the stars?" the little girl Wahay asked.

Esther shook her head. "I didn't fall, exactly."

"Who is here that can dream-walk?" asked Silika.

"Well, there's Jul," said Yahaywah. Podan and Silika shook their heads. "Bedabat's group isn't here yet. Are you sure Jul won't do? He's behind you."

With a sinking heart, Esther saw Nudawah and the old man coming toward them, trailed by an embarrassed-looking Uduban. The old man limped, his shoulders hunched, and his mouth collapsed in upon itself. Wrinkles dragged his face down; he would have had to fight gravity to smile.

"We are happy to see that you still live, Jul," said Podan.

Jul sniffed skeptically, and Esther thought: *So Nudawah got that from her dad. Or was this her granddad?*

"I am happy to see that the group my daughter married into has done so well this year," said Jul, in a deep, slurring voice. He had so few teeth, it took several seconds for Esther's understanding to catch up to his meaning. "But some of her news troubles my old heart. Let me see this star-child who makes the future sound so dark."

Podan stepped aside. Ahrva took Esther's hand on one side, and Tekinit on the other, but they both kept their heads down respectfully, so Esther did, too. When Jul put his hand under her chin, though, she looked him in the eyes, which were bloodshot, with one cloudy pupil. His breath was warm and smelled faintly rotten. "So, you are from the stars."

"Yes, sir." Why did he sound familiar?

"And you see the future."

"Yes, sir." Who did he sound like? Not Nudawah.

"And the mammoths will all die."

"Yes, sir, someday." Maybe she was imagining it.

"And what about people? Will we all die, too?"

"Everybody dies, sir, but in the far distant future I see, there are plenty of people."

"And when will I die?"

"When you're ready, sir."

It would have been the right answer for Ehdanwah, who was

pretending not to listen in. Jul made a wheezy attempt at a laugh, and looked sour. Podan and Silika were silent. So was Kitotul, though he looked as though he wanted to speak.

To Esther's surprise, Uduban rescued her. "My father," he said, "it is late. We have walked far. I have not yet embraced my sister. And the star-child isn't important enough to keep us from the meat I smell."

"I gave my daughter to a wise man," said Jul. "This child will not destroy the mammoths overnight! Tonight my daughter eats at my fire. All is well."

He moved away, and the group, with bits of other groups attached, straggled toward the campfires, grown-ups leading, kids falling behind.

"Aiee!" said Kordak. "Are you really going to kill the mammoths? Or did you just make Nudawah mad?"

"Nudawah was mad before I came along," grumbled Esther, "and it's not my fault the mammoths are going to die!"

"It'll be all right when Bedabat's group gets here," said Ahrva. "His mother, Pezha, is the best dream-walker in the hills."

Kordak had a crooked nose and a nice smile. "She probably already knows you're here. And she'll be on our side, because her grandson married our aunt."

Our side. It should have made Esther feel good that Kordak counted himself as her ally; but she didn't want to need allies. The group should be the group, not opposing factions—especially not opposing factions defined by how they felt about *her*!

TWENTY-NINE

➤ THE GATHERING

*T*hey ate roast mammoth with Geshwaw and Yahaywah, were fussed over by Silika's mother, Wasitay, told stories and were told stories. People came by to hug and laugh and greet; and also, it seemed to Esther, to goggle at her. When everyone was full, Silika put Tekinit and Wahay—who seemed to be glued together—to bed and took Ahrva and Esther around the camps.

Friends mixed with strangers: Kitotul and Shusskt with the brothers who had made him hop on one foot through the campgrounds; Ehdanwah with another old woman; Otala with cousins. Over and over Esther made polite greeting gestures and said: "I am Esther. I came from the stars. Podan and Silika are looking after me."

"It will be easier tomorrow," Ahrva said when they went to bed at last.

"Nudawah's dad—how important is he?" Esther asked.

"He's the oldest man in the world," said Ahrva.

Old equaled important. Nudawah's father was the most important person in the world. Oh, joy.

"Nudawah's his youngest child, by his second wife, and the only one still alive," Ahrva went on. "He stays with his oldest grandson's group. His grandson's the leader, but we call it Jul's group. And he's a dream-walker."

"So," said Esther, "if he decides my wazicat's bad, people will believe him."

"You can't live that long without strong wazicat," said Ahrva apologetically. "But here's what I think. If he decides you're good, then good—it will shut Nudawah up. But if he decides you're bad, he'll want to get rid of you, and the best way to do that is to send you home. So don't be afraid of him."

Esther tried hard to dream that night, and failed. When she heard men's voices outside, she gave up and crawled out. In the chill morning, Silika's mother, Wasitay, stirred the fire and men checked strans and cut strips off last night's mammoth. "Good morning, Esster," said Podan. "Have you come to give us wazicat?"

"If you want it," said Esther. "Um—you never asked the flint fathers who would lead. Is this hunt different?"

"Everything is different," said Podan. "When we are all here, we'll let the flint fathers choose leaders for the Big Hunt. Until then, we choose who we will hunt with, and who will lead." He slapped Geshwaw on the back. "I haven't hunted with my brother-in-law in a long time."

"I never heard of a girl with hunting wazicat before," said Geshwaw. "Is hers really any good?"

"It's the best," said Kitotul, jogging up with Skedat in tow.

"Don't be fooled by the wide eyes and the questions. She's made of wazicat like a strawberry's made of juice."

It scared Esther when Kitotul talked like that. "Wazicat's no substitute for common sense," she said.

"If you give us wazicat today, then we'll have both," said Kitotul. "Podan, is there room in the hunt beside you?"

"There's always room for you beside me," said Podan.

"And me," piped up Geshwaw's son Kordak, crawling out of his shelter. "I'm old enough."

"No, you're not," said Geshwaw.

"Old enough for what?" asked Podan. "To hunt mammoth? No. To carry spare shafts and do as he's told? Maybe."

"He carries shafts well, but he hasn't got much practice at doing as he's told," said Geshwaw, grinning proudly.

Kordak argued; other men turned up; the men painted themselves with red powder and gossiped. When Esther shook Kitotul's hand and said, "Good luck. *Buena suerte*," the strangers watched curiously.

"I spoke to Telabat," Skedat said, extending his hand. "He told me to tell you, he and Dul would have liked to get your wazicat, but Uduban said no one who did would hunt with him."

"That's okay," said Esther. "My feelings aren't hurt."

The younger men made one band, around Geshwaw and Podan; the older men made another, around Geshwaw's uncle; and the hunters headed out, Kordak proudly carrying the spare shafts and water gourds in the rear. Esther sat next to Wasitay, and looked out over the Valley. The black bulks of sleeping mammoths loomed out of mist as if they slept in cotton batting.

A few got to their feet, stretching, scratching their backs with sticks. "Usually the men are quiet before a mammoth hunt," said Esther.

"And they will be, when they get down there," said Wasitay. "Most won't kill today. They'll stalk, and judge, and study. Someone will kill, and feed all of us. But the real hunt won't happen till everyone gets here." She rubbed her sticklike hands over the fire. "Is it not so when the star-people gather?"

"We don't have any mammoths in the stars," said Esther, already tired of explaining.

When the others emerged from the shelters, not long after, Esther started right in combing Tekinit's hair. "So what do we do today?"

"We need to make our camp," said Silika.

"Nuts," said Wasitay. "We need all available hands to keep our share away from the squirrels."

Tekinit bounced, clapping her hands. "Nuts! I can climb!"

"I know you can climb, it's sitting still you have trouble with," said Esther. "Let me braid your hair, so the nut trees don't grab onto you and keep you."

"Braid mine, too," commanded Wahay. "I bet I can climb higher than Tekinit."

"I'll need you and Tekinit here, to help me crack the walnuts we picked yesterday," said Wasitay. "That's hard work. I can't do it all myself."

"We'll take you all over the grove and introduce you to everybody, Esster," said Ahrva.

"This is such a strange thing," said Wasitay. "No one has ever come from the stars before. And she brings with her hunting wazicat and bad news. I don't know what to think."

Silika hugged her. "Neither does anyone else, Mother. But she's a good child. Nudawah is the problem, not Esster."

"I believe that," said Podan's sister Yahaywah. "What does Ehdanwah say?"

"Not much," said Silika. "You know her. She wants to be sure everyone talks to her, however mad we are at each other."

"She shouldn't have let Uduban choose Nudawah," said Wasitay.

"That's not how it was," said Ehdanwah, coming into camp.

Yahaywah leaped up. "Mother!"

They hugged as long and hard as if they hadn't seen each other yesterday. "So. I see most of my grandchildren survived the night. Where's Kordak?"

"The men let him carry their shafts," said Wasitay, passing her some mammoth. "Did you sleep well in your sister's camp?"

"Well enough," said Ehdanwah. "But I will be glad to sleep in our own camp tonight. And it's not my fault Uduban married Nudawah! She'd made up his mind, and my husband liked her."

"Why?" Tekinit twitched as Esther pulled her hair tight.

"She was beautiful, and knew how to talk nice to an old man," said Ehdanwah. "She still knows! Jul thinks the sun rises in her hair and sets in her feet. And no one argues with Jul."

Esther had been thinking hard. "I have to meet all the oldest ones, don't I? To convince them that I'm honest." Which she wasn't, exactly, but she couldn't let that stop her.

"Tonight, I will bring you to the elders' campfire, and you will tell your story," said Ehdanwah. "Only you, and only us."

"That's a lot of old people for a girl to stand before," said Silika. "Shouldn't Podan or I come with her?"

"I should go," said Ahrva. "I found her."

Ehdanwah gestured *no*. "The star-child has good manners now. When she answers our questions well, all alone, no one will say: *Podan is signaling to her. Silika has told her what to say.* They'll know that her words are her own."

"You're right," said Wasitay, "but shouldn't we wait until everyone gets here?"

"No," said Ehdanwah. "She must tell her story before everyone gets used to believing the one Nudawah will spread. I'll have to visit each old one. It makes my bones and ears ache to think of it! I'll have to admire ugly babies and eat mammoth that's cooked wrong."

"Yes, no one but us knows how to cook mammoth right," said Wasitay, and they laughed, in the way that people laugh over punch lines so old no one bothers to tell the joke anymore.

THIRTY

➤ TSIK

When Ahrva said she would take Esther around the grove, using the word "tsik," Esther had pictured a clump of trees or bushes. Not for the first time, she found that she didn't quite have the language down. Everything from the rim to the Valley floor was the tsik. Shrubby bushes with filbert-type nuts, towering pecans, trees that would either go extinct or move elsewhere in Esther's time, black walnuts, white walnuts—each in its own environment, clinging to rocky slopes or shading rapid waters or leaning at angles all over the floodplain.

Sky-scraping sycamores dotted the campgrounds, the survivors of yearly harvests of saplings for shelters. The Valley was full of trees worn smooth from scratching mammoth shoulders or ragged from assaults of mammoth tusks; of reedy cavities left when a mammoth uprooted a tree, using her tusks as levers.

Esther learned the names of a dozen new plants, how to make a new type of bag, and a separate name for every level of the Valley. Women were everywhere, picking nuts and throwing rocks at black squirrels as big as cats, spreading walnuts to dry in the sun, watching mammoths, minding children, gossiping. Sisters who hadn't seen each other for six months worked the slopes together, catching up on each other's lives. Cousins roamed, eating as many nuts as they stored. Old men and women supervised little children and talked about the good old days.

All the while the mammoths went about their business, trampling and eating, crowding the water to pull up reeds. Mammoth reed, Emni explained, as they ate a nut lunch with girls from different groups. "Mammoth reed doesn't grow everywhere," she said. "And they need it. It makes them strong for winter."

"My grandmother says when she was a girl in the high flatland, mammoth reed grew from one side of the sky to another," said Helad, a big girl whose sleek braids fluttered with cardinal, parakeet, blue jay, and egret feathers. "She wants me to marry a high flatland man in the spring."

"And you are obedient, and do nothing to attract the notice of these men here," said Emni, flipping the other girl's braid and making the feathers flicker brightly. "How long did it take you to collect those?"

"Two days," said Helad's little sister. "We all helped."

Helad tossed her braids, so it looked as though her head was about to take flight. "I *won't* marry a high flatlander!"

"I hear they're tall and handsome," said a low flatlander.

"And they think the sun rises in their hair," said Helad. "My grandmother says they take women mammoths. She says once I taste unborn mammoth, I'll understand what good eating is."

All the girls recoiled. "They kill pregnant mammoths in the high flatlands?" Ahrva demanded, shocked. "I never heard that!"

"They don't like to tell us, because they know it makes us sick," said Helad. "But my grandmother is so old, she doesn't care anymore. And her teeth are all gone, so she likes to think about the soft meat she ate when she was a girl. She also likes to brag. They hardly ever stayed in the same place for more than a day and the women were strong and carried more than us and blah blah blah."

Esther wondered if this grandmother was one of the elders she had to impress tonight. She didn't sound very impressible.

"If we see an entrance to Esster's star, maybe we can call some star-men through," suggested another big girl. "What are the men like where you come from, Esster?"

"She's too young to think about men," said Emni. "She's never told us anything useful."

This was true, because what could she say? The only hunters she knew sat in deer blinds with rifles. Her father worked for the phone company and Danny wanted to be a lawyer or maybe a Tejano star. She couldn't explain any of that! "Please, if you see an entrance, leave it alone," she said. "For all I know it closes as soon as someone goes through."

"It's not so bad here, is it, Esster?" Washaw expertly smashed a fistful of nuts with a rock. The shells cracked but didn't fly in all directions or get buried in the nut meats.

"No." Esther forced the word out. "If I live here the rest of my life, I'll be fine." *But it isn't home,* she thought. There was no word for "home" in this language.

"Don't worry, star-child," said Helad. "We'll spread the word.
If an entrance opens, even people who didn't know you existed
last night will know that it's for you."

As the girls resumed working, mammoths trumpeted. Two
bulls charged each other, heads down; but at the last moment,
the smaller one whirled aside. Some mammoths watched, their
trunks curling around their tusks, while others went on wallowing, eating, and playing with babies. "All dead someday, and
no new ones," said Helad. "Are you *sure*?"

Esther made the *yes* gesture. It was getting harder to talk as
the day went on. She let the other girls deal with the reactions
to her story—friendly, incredulous, suspicious. She made eye
contact in the right way for each age group, was polite, stood as
tall as she could, picked as many nuts as she could, tried to
remember everyone, and tried not to think about telling this
story yet again tonight to a bunch of strange old people who
could decree that she be abandoned.

Ehdanwah wouldn't let them do that.

Compared to Jul, Ehdanwah was hardly old at all.

All these people were what Dr. Durham would call Clovis,
but low flatlanders talked more in their noses, used a different
kind of wood in their strans, and decorated their clothes with
porcupine quills. Some groups wore moccasins instead of bark
sandals or cut their hair short on the sides. Some had special
knives, curving blades without points, and laughed at people
who made strans do all the work. It was a lot for Esther to keep
track of, without worrying about what she couldn't help.

In late afternoon, Esther and her friends were in a thick
stand of chestnuts, where they rooted among fallen leaves in

company with other women and girls. "The stars, huh," said a wall-eyed flatlander woman. "You expect us to believe that?"

"You must believe what you think deserves to be believed, ma'am," said Esther, splitting open a prickly chestnut burr to get at the ripe nut inside. "I can only tell you the truth the way I understand it."

"Do juripa die out, too?" another woman asked.

"I don't know that word, ma'am."

"Like mammoths, but they're smaller, have low foreheads, and live in the thick woods," said Ahrva.

Mastodons, thought Esther. "They'll die, too," she said.

"Maybe they only hide," suggested the wall-eyed woman. "You'd be amazed how well something so big can hide in woods."

"No, ma'am, I'm sorry. They all die."

"When?"

"I don't know, ma'am."

"And who kills them?"

"I don't know, ma'am."

The wall-eyed woman snorted. "So what good are you?"

"I don't know that either, ma'am," said Esther, winning a laugh.

"I think people are coming to the falls," Washaw called from the top of the tallest tree.

"I thought you were supposed to be watching so mammoth didn't step on us," Emni called up.

"I am, but listen."

Geese honked across the sky. Mammoth voices rumbled. Javelinas rustled round the edges of the tsik. Howling drifted from the top of the valley, distorted with distance.

"Bedabat's group?" The wall-eyed woman took a stab at interpreting the sound.

"My aunt is in Bedabat's group," said Ahrva, "and Pezha, who we want to dream-walk to Esster's parents."

"Go," said the wall-eyed woman. "Your nut carriers are so heavy, it will be hard to climb. By the time you reach the top, your aunt will have eaten and gone to bed."

The best paths were the ones used by the mammoths to get from the high country to the Valley, but these went the long way around. The alternative was to cut across the tsik or along the creeks, a chancy proposition because of loose rocks, bears, and big cats. They started by following the shortcuts, but Esther slipped and nearly dropped all her nuts. Emni declared: "I'm too tired to come this way, and she's not my aunt, anyway. I'm taking the mammoth path."

"Shusskt will be angry if we let you walk the mammoth path alone," declared Ahrva. "We'll go, too."

"You don't have to cover up for me," said Esther. "I don't mind that you're taking the easy way so I can keep up."

"Hey, now we're offended," said Emni. "It's our job to make you tough and strong. Are you saying we're shirking our job?"

"We'll have to be mean to her, and show her." Ahrva giggled, breaking off a filbert wand and swishing it through the air. "Here, you must run ahead, or we'll beat you!"

With much giggling and helping each other along, they found a mammoth path, and Esther ran while the others chased her noisily. The nut bag bounced against her behind, making a comfortable chunky sound; the camel shirt flapped, briefly cooling her with every step; and her body vibrated with the pumping of her blood. *Four months ago I couldn't have done this,* Esther thought, skidding around a pile of mammoth dung and startling a cloud of small birds. *I'd be out of breath and my legs would ache. I'm getting stronger. If only—*

That vibration wasn't her blood pumping!

She looked up in time to see the mammoth's domed head swaying above the treetops as it rounded the bend. "Mammoth!" she shouted, swerving. Scattering like startled birds, the girls hurled themselves into the pecan trees on either side of the path as a bull picked his way down the slope past them. Esther hugged a tree, shaking with the force of her heartbeat.

If the mammoth had stepped on her, she would have been nothing but a smear of blood and bone on the path right now.

It wasn't even that big a mammoth.

Ahrva dashed over and hugged her. "You're all right?"

"Oh, yes," Esther gasped. "Wasn't he wonderful?"

All the girls looked after the retreating wall of animal. "Oh, yes," said Emni.

They proceeded in a tighter bunch, and met Yahaywah and Shusskt with Shusskt's sister-in-law. "Where's Mom?" Ahrva asked.

"She's gone to meet Bedabat's group," said Shusskt. "It should be a happy meeting."

"Speaking of happy meetings," said her sister-in-law, "Emni, I think I have a marriage for you."

Emni's smile flickered. "That's good. Who is it?"

"He's oheitika." Her aunt didn't quite meet her eyes. "His wife and baby died, and he's sad. But he has three children who won't raise themselves. The little one pines and won't eat. You're so good with the little ones."

"Oh," said Emni.

Three children plus a dead baby, and you had to wait four or five years between babies. This guy must be older than Kitotul.

"It would be like Emni, to take an old man for the sake of his children," said Yahaywah, unenthusiastically.

"But she wouldn't have to do it, if she didn't have the bad wazicat from her grandfather," said Esther.

"She doesn't *have* to do it," said Shusskt. "It's a possibility she should consider."

Emni made eye contact with Esther and made the *yes* gesture. "What if she didn't have that bad wazicat?" Esther asked. "What if I knew a way to burn it out of her?"

"No one can do that," said Emni's aunt.

"I asked her not to mention it till I'd had time to think," said Emni. "But if marrying an old man is a good prospect for me, I should try."

"How will you know if it works?" her aunt asked.

Screams ripped through the sky.

"Mother," said Ahrva, and began to run.

"Wasitay," said Yahaywah, and ran after her.

THIRTY-ONE

➤ MOURNING

*E*hdanwah let Yahaywah and Ahrva run past, but stopped the rest. "Silika's sister, Wasitay's daughter, is dead," she said.

Tekinit and Wahay clung together, their hands black from husking walnuts. "She tried to have a baby," Tekinit informed them. "But she couldn't." Wahay cried too hard to talk, great hiccupping sobs that turned into coughing.

Esther felt relief that nothing had happened to anyone she knew, then shame. "What do we do to help?"

"That's the spirit," said Ehdanwah. "Ahrva will get Kiraka for Mingwah to nurse tonight, and we'll have the mourners in our camp."

Wails rose from the falls, making the hair stand up on Esther's arms. In the Valley, a mammoth screamed.

Esther followed Ehdanwah and Emni to find the nearest suitable bedding. Most of the grass nearby had already been cut, so it was quite a hike. "No one I know ever died," said Esther.

"No one? You're lucky!" said Ehdanwah. "It is hard for a woman who dies in childbirth to leave the world. Don't say her name. If she hears her name, it will confuse her, and she will come. This would be bad for everyone."

"So—where is she? What happens when you die?"

Ehdanwah gripped a bunch of grass and cut it near the roots. "Your body's no good anymore. You rise out of it to the dream place. That's where we came from, when the world began. Those who dream-walk can go there while living and control where they go, but the rest of us can't. The dead talk in dreams sometimes, but their wazicat doesn't mix with the wazicat of the living. Yana women and babies must stay far, far away from death."

"There's always mourning in the Valley," said Emni. "When we look forward, we think of new babies and games and marriages. But we know, in the backs of our hearts, that some will be dead. We would be made weak, if we thought about that. The mourners will be well tomorrow. Don't be frightened tonight."

Frightened? Was this another word she wasn't translating quite right?

Uduban's camp was cluttered with relatives. Nudawah turned chunks of mammoth hindquarter on a spit. Mingwah nursed her baby with Silika's baby, Kiraka, also in her lap.

Ehdanwah spread the grass. Nudawah took a deep breath. "Mother, I don't think we should have mourners here."

Emni and Esther stole sideways glances at each other and continued to spread bedding.

"My heart is sore for them," said Nudawah. "But we already have the star-child, and Kitotul's family, and now mourners? It's too much. We will be the unluckiest camp here."

"Silika, Wasitay, and Geshwaw must mourn together," said Ehdanwah. "Our camp is where they should be."

"We could make a special mourners' camp," suggested Nudawah.

"Such a thing has never been done."

Another woman spoke up. "Such a thing has never been done in the hills. But I married a flatlander, and his brother married a saltlander, and they make mourning camps."

"Have they no big cats, to smell the weak blood that the mourners spill?" Ehdanwah asked. "No bears? No wolves?"

"You would have to ask him."

"I think I won't," said Ehdanwah, while Esther was still repeating to herself: *the weak blood that the mourners spill?* "I think I'll do right by my daughter-in-law's family. When Nudawah is senior woman, she may treat my mourners anyway she sees fit."

Nudawah became busy with the spit. "Yes, ma'am."

They were still erecting a shelter when Silika, Wasitay, and Geshwaw staggered into camp. Esther thought that they had smeared themselves with red powder, until she saw flies rise from Silika's cheeks, and smelled blood.

Their faces, their chests, their arms, their legs were crisscrossed with bloody lines. They had cut up the soft, strong leather of their clothes and the tender parts of their skin and hacked out random chunks of their hair. Tears and blood and snot clumped on their faces as they cried, shaking all over. Tekinit and Wahay stepped toward their parents, their eyes wide. Ahrva spread her arms to hold them back. Tekinit dodged her. Esther caught hold of her, putting her mouth close to the little girl's ear. "No," she said. "Not yet."

"Geshwaw will want to see you later," said Ahrva to Wahay.

"You'll fill your father with gladness, later. But now, all he feels is pain and all he sees is tears and all he knows is he'll never see her again and he'll never see the baby at all. We must keep them safe while they mourn. You understand?"

Wahay nodded, blinking. Esther wanted to scream, *Of course she doesn't understand! I'm twice as old as she is, and I don't understand!* But she hugged Tekinit as the mourners collapsed on the grass beds. She didn't know what else to do; but fortunately Ahrva did. "Mingwah needs help with Kiraka," she said, and the little girls went with her.

Esther sidled up to Emni. "What did they . . . Why did they . . . How could they *do* that?"

"Do what?" asked Emni, piling up more branches between the world and the human heaps of misery on the beds.

"Cut themselves up!" Esther whispered. She wanted to run screaming home, where if you did things like this you were given tranquilizers and put into therapy.

"They have to let the pain out," said Emni. "It takes too long to let it all out through your mouth and eyes. The pain would stay and make them weak and then they'd die, too."

"And cutting themselves to bits doesn't make them weak?"

"Not for as long." Emni piled up the last branches. "What do they do in the stars?"

Esther made a helpless gesture. She had no idea how people coped with death. "What about Tekinit and Wahay?" And Ahrva, having to be calm for the little ones while her mother fell apart? *And me, what about me? I can't stand this!* "Won't it make them weak, to see the grown-ups like that?"

"They'll learn that when some must be weak, the others will be strong for them. You'll see."

No I won't, thought Esther.

The rest of the group came in, laughing and talking in low voices, around and under the terrible sounds from the mourners' shelter. The big boys had been on the team that won the relay race, and it was visibly hard for them not to strut around crowing. Tekinit sat with her arms around Podan's neck and ate meat that he fed her, though since Kiraka's birth she had been eating like a grown-up, holding the meat in her mouth and cutting it off at the lips. The meat tasted like ashes and rubber to Esther, but she ate anyway. It was almost a relief when Ehdanwah said, "Now Esster must come with me to speak to the elders."

Nudawah sniffed.

"You should feel honored, Esster," said Uduban. "It's not every child who calls all the elders together to listen to her. You must explain well to them how to make the world better."

Esther swallowed, though her mouth was dry. "This world is fine," she said, "but if the elders can make it better by sending me out of it, that would be good enough for me." She could tell this wasn't quite the right thing to say; but could anything be the right thing to say with Silika bleeding?

She walked to the elders' bonfire a respectful two paces behind Ehdanwah, her head down, rehearsing her speech.

THIRTY-TWO

Each group's eldest will be here," said Ehdanwah, as they picked their way between the camps. "Pretend they're all me."

Esther swallowed. "Even Jul?"

Ehdanwah hugged her and kissed the top of her head. "You'll do fine, my star-granddaughter."

Esther stood up straighter as she entered the bonfire's light. The elders sat on skins—eleven old men and women, plus a boy at the knee of an old man with one eye squinted shut and a puckered scar where the other should be. Jul leaned on a spear with a huge point that seemed to be dark red with white stripes, like mammoth meat. Eagle feathers fluttered from a stran of bone so pale it seemed to glow. "Hello, Ehdanwah," said Jul.

"Hello, elders," said Ehdanwah. "Let us be wise together."

"Yes," said the elders. "Let us sit and be wise."

Ehdanwah sat on a bison skin, and Esther sat looking at the ground, in imitation of the boy with the blind man. A woman shook two red-painted gourds with the seeds still inside.

"We are old, rain mothers," chanted the women.

"We are old, flint fathers," chanted the men.

"We have lived, rain mothers."

"We have lived, flint fathers."

"We will die, rain mothers."

"We will die, flint fathers."

"Let us give wisdom to our daughters."

"Let us give wisdom to our sons."

And all together: "Then we will rest."

"I am the oldest man," said Jul. "Maybe this is my last year. The rains were scarce and the mammoths shy." His voice was slow and formal. Esther's nose itched, but she didn't scratch.

One by one, in age order, the elders talked about drought, mammoths, who died and how, babies, berry harvests. The low flatlanders passed on news from the saltlanders, and the hill people passed on news from the high groups. When a woman with ragged hair and cut marks on her face told how a man had been swept away by a flash flood, everyone wailed. The reaction to the news of Silika's sister's death, delivered by Bedabat's mother, Pezha, was more subdued. Esther paid particular attention to Pezha, wanting some sign that this dream-walker knew enough magic to get her home; but she was just an old woman whose nose wasn't quite centered in her face.

When Ehdanwah, sixth oldest, gave her report, Esther braced to tell her story, but Ehdanwah never paused. Esther kept her mouth closed on a yawn, tired and tense and sick of waiting all at once.

When the youngest elder finished, Jul said: "It has been a strange year. Floods and droughts, mammoths avoiding the rivers, bison where bison did not used to go, children delivering babies. Who knows what the other elders will tell us, when they come?"

"Ask the star-child," said the oldest woman. "I hear she can tell the future."

"I hear she has hunting wazicat," said the blind man.

"I hear she has bad wazicat and holds the rain back," said Pezha, "and I hear she has good wazicat and gives power to those who have none. Let us hear what she has to say for herself."

"Yes, let us hear," said someone else, slapping his hands on his knees, and the others started slapping their knees and chanting: "Let us hear! Let us hear!"

"Now, Esster," whispered Ehdanwah. "Don't be afraid."

Ehdanwah might as well have instructed her not to sweat. Esster stood with her hands clasped, until the knee slapping stopped and Jul said, in an almost-sneer like Nudawah's, "Nuaah, star-child, if that's what you are. Speak now."

"My name is Esther," she started; and the rest was easy. She'd already said it all, so many times!

The elders didn't take long to pry out of her the little she knew about megafaunal extinction and global warming. For the most part they were patient when she groped for concepts, or described something that she had never heard the word for. She learned the word for ice, and described how, far to the north, the world was covered with ice that was melting. No, she didn't know how long it would take, and no, not all the ice would melt; and no, she couldn't describe how far away it all was.

The megafaunal extinction upset them. "There must be something we can do about this," said Pezha. "It shouldn't happen if we treat the animals right."

"Not everyone does," said another woman. "I hear they kill pregnant mammoths and eat the babies in the high flatlands."

"Nothing tastes better than tender unborn mammoth!" That would be Helad's grandmother. "You hill people are weak."

"Naa," Ehdanwah said, "you've been hill people for most of your life now. Our ways have kept you alive."

"Not for much longer, by the sound of it," said Helad's grandmother. "Why do you believe this child? People don't drop from the stars."

"If not from the stars, where?" asked the blind man.

"Ehdanwah said she had strange clothes, but I don't see any," said Pezha. "What happened to your clothes, child?"

"My foster-sister Tekinit is wearing my shirt and bracelet," said Esther. "I lost my shoes and my, um, hair holder wore out. But I still have my, um, the word in my language is *shorts*."

"Well, let us see, then."

Esther pulled up her blouse and walked around the ring. Jul snapped her waistband. "Heh. Say she is from the stars." He sounded familiar again now that he wasn't making speeches. "Ehdanwah's quick to think she brings good wazicat. But my daughter has watched her, and she says, *This girl is tricky and sneaky, sets brother against brother and sons against fathers, creates trouble among the women.*"

"There is always trouble among the women when your daughter is around," said Ehdanwah. "She is too beautiful and wise for anyone's peace of mind. Fortunately she is a faithful wife."

Esther could tell by the reaction among the other elders that most of them knew Nudawah better than that; but Jul smiled. "It is not always a person's flaws that cause trouble," said Ehdanwah. "Flies follow good meat. Troubles follow good people. Esster's knowledge is different. Even her words are different. It's not her fault she sees the future. She has warned us that the mammoths will die. She has tried to find out how, but she doesn't know. Well! She's not a dream-walker! She's not an elder! She's the child who wakes the camp when a bear comes. Do you expect her to drive off the bear? It's for us to do something about the mammoths, not for her to instruct us."

"I suppose we could stop killing them," said the youngest woman.

"That won't work," said someone else. "Not when the high flatlanders are killing pregnant ones. They're the ones breaking the bargain our grandmothers made with the grandmothers of the mammoths."

"My grandmothers made no bargains," retorted Helad's grandmother. "My relatives kill maybe one, two pregnant mammoths a year, and you act like that makes us bad. But we're not bad when you want to trade for red flint—oh, no, we're all friendly then! High flatlanders are few and far-walking, and don't kill anything like as many mammoths as hill people do. If the mammoths die, it won't be our fault."

"We can kill more bison and fewer mammoths. I don't have a problem with that," said another man. "But I for one am not going to tell my sons not to pursue a mammoth when we've been hunting for days and not seen anything bigger than a rabbit."

"This girl can only tell us what she knows. If you stand on a hill and see that the next hill is burning, then the hill is burning," said the blind man. "But does she know which hill it is? She does not. She cannot. Our dream-walkers must walk, our hunters must study. We must know more. This is not one night's problem."

"True," said Jul. "Our problem tonight is not the mammoths. Our problem tonight is the star-child." He swung forward expertly on the spear, looking down his long nose. "Ehdanwah says, *This is a good child.* My daughter says, *This is a tricky, evil child.* You will say, *Of course Jul believes his daughter.* But when I look at Ehdanwah, I remember how she gave a woman to the murderer. This is a soft-hearted woman. It would not be the first time evil fooled her."

A murmur went round, and a man stood up. "Jul is right," he said. "The killer of my cousin went to this woman and her husband and said: *I killed my leader and I am sorry now. My kin have turned me out, but my sister married into your group; let me in.* He should have wandered until something ate him, but they gave him a wife and let him hunt with their sons. And what came of that? His wife died young! All but one of her children died, and that one is a worthless half-man."

Esther ground her teeth so she wouldn't shout: *Kitotul isn't worthless!* Ehdanwah said: "Hunumand, you honor the memory of your cousin, and that is good. But you did not know my husband's sister well. She was born weak. I'm surprised any of her children lived. It was a rest to our hearts to keep her by us, among those who knew that it made her sick to eat strawberries, that liver was too strong for her stomach. The man worked hard for a year. His sister pleaded for him, and she was kin to the dead man, too. He did wrong to kill his leader, but his leader also did wrong in his life, and they are all dead now. His son Kitotul is a faithful friend to my son Podan."

"You mean he knows if Podan didn't look after him his life would be harder," sneered Jul. "What does it say about the star-child that the users of her wazicat are those with bad wazicat in their bones?"

"That those who need most, get most," said Ehdanwah.

"It's bad wazicat calling to bad wazicat!"

"It's good wazicat acting against bad wazicat."

"Is it? Show me. You can't!"

"No, sir," said Esther. "She can't. It's my wazicat, and I have to prove whether it's good or bad. So I will." She looked all the way up Jul's nose to his eye. "I will teach the elders to clear the bad wazicat out of Kitotul's family."

"That's not possible," said Helad's grandmother. "You might as well claim you have a way to cook without making ashes."

"We do," said Esther, glad to tell a full truth for once. "But I can't teach you that."

"Why haven't you mentioned this clearing of the bad wazicat before?" Ehdanwah asked.

"Because it takes lots of people we didn't have. You need elders, and someone that Kitotul's father wronged. And a . . . a woman who's done having babies but isn't senior woman yet. And a dream-walker to check that it was done right." And time alone to work out the details.

"Ha," said Jul. "I will dream-walk. It's too late in my life to fool me!"

It's too late—oh. Oh, *that* was how she knew his voice! She'd heard it in her dreams!

"I don't know," said Hunumand, the man who thought Kitotul was worthless. "Is it good to learn this? Men will do wrong, thinking: *My family is safe.*"

Esther fought to focus on the matter at hand. Maybe Jul had dragged her here; maybe he could get her home; but as long as she was stuck here, she must improvise the right answers, for her friends' sakes. "No. The family can only use this ceremony after the wrongdoer is dead."

Jul waved his spear, fluttering the eagle feathers. "We must discuss this."

"The star-child is tired," said Ehdanwah. "Finish asking her questions, and let her go."

"We will never be done asking her questions," said the blind man. He patted the boy. "Walk her to Uduban's camp, so she doesn't get lost again. She's obviously good at getting lost."

Esther, long beyond feeling offended at such remarks, followed the boy past firelight, laughter, and singing, under an autumn gold moon.

It's too late, star-child, Jul's voice had said, the night before she walked backward in time. And, as she'd chased after Dr. Durham through another dream, the night before she'd had her one chance to go home: *It's later than you think.*

She couldn't think about this now. She'd think about Kitotul's family. Whatever else happened, they needed her help. "Do you think they'll let me try?" Esther asked the boy.

"How would I know?" the boy grumbled. "Maybe. My grandfather likes you, in case you couldn't tell. He's grouchy sometimes, but underneath he's nice. Not like Jul. Jul's grouchy all through. I don't think you should let him be your dream-walker. He *doesn't* like you."

"That's all right," said Esther. "If a dream-walker who liked me said the ceremony had worked, some people wouldn't believe him. But if Jul says so, everyone will know it's true." So she had to make 100 percent sure he believed it!

Too late for what?

THIRTY-THREE

*I*n Uduban's camp, people talked in low voices. Tekinit lay half-asleep in Podan's lap. "Hello, Neerup," said Podan to the boy. "How did our girl do?"

"Well," said the boy. "Except when she spoke out of turn."

"You know better than that, Esster," said Podan.

"I expect she had a good reason," said Shusskt.

"Yes, ma'am," said Esther. "I asked permission to teach them how to clear the bad wazicat out of your children."

"Can you *do* that?" Kitotul demanded.

"No one can do that," said Uduban.

"There's no reason not to let her try," said Shusskt.

"What happens if she tries and it doesn't work?" Nudawah asked. "Kitotul's father's bad wazicat is packed away in their bones. We can handle that. What if you let it loose on us all?"

"I won't," said Esther, wishing she had a wazicat rule book so she wouldn't have to keep inventing things on the fly. "The worst thing that can happen is . . . is that the bad wazicat goes

into the person using the star-wazicat. Which will be me."
There! They couldn't say fairer than that.

"You never mentioned that," said Emni, horrified. "We can't
let you take in three persons' worth of this!"

"If we all do it right, it won't happen."

"How will we know if it hasn't been done right?" Skedat
asked. "Will you burst into flames? Wither and die? What?"

"It won't look like anything happened, either way," said
Esther. "You need a dream-walker to tell if it worked or not."

"Jul volunteered," said Neerup.

Kitotul's family groaned as one. Podan said, "There are other
dream-walkers."

"But Jul is the best," said Uduban.

"Don't worry. Esster will do it right," said Ahrva.

"She'd better," said Uduban. "Or we might have to leave her
behind."

"That's not funny," said Podan.

"No, it's not," said Uduban. "I've been patient, my brother.
But she has disturbed our family, and now she's handling
power that no child should have. If she can't control it, if her
ceremony hurts anyone—"

"It won't!" She was too tired to care that everyone looked
at her disapprovingly. All the same, she lowered her voice. "I
wouldn't have brought it up if it could hurt anyone but me."

"So you say."

"Don't call my girl a liar, Uduban," said Podan.

The fire crackled. Tekinit coughed; a harsh, rattling sound
that called a sudden echo from Geshwaw's camp. In the camp
on the other side, a burst of laughter shot into the sky like

sparks. "Whatever the elders decide is good enough for me," said Kitotul. "Bedtime, children. Don't you think so, Shusskt?"

"For the children, yes, but none of us will sleep if Tekinit doesn't get her throat clear," said Shusskt. "Ahrva, did you see where Ehdanwah put her stickyflower?"

"I want licorice," said Tekinit.

"That's not working," said Ahrva. "But you can have some if you drink all the stickyflower."

"When did she start coughing again?" Esther asked.

"This afternoon," said Tekinit. "Wahay's is worse."

"Some sickness always goes around the Valley," said Ahrva. "It's so warm this year, it shouldn't get too bad."

I guess we're swapping germs as well as salt and flint, Esther thought, paying attention as Shusskt demonstrated how to prepare the stickyflower.

Lying awake that night, Esther's brain tiredly chewed over ideas that led her nowhere. Would it do any good to ask Jul about her dream? The thought of approaching him directly made her queasy. She couldn't expect kindness from Nudawah's father. But he was part of this. If he couldn't, wouldn't, didn't help her, who could?

If she knew his voice from her dreams, why didn't he seem to know her from his?

The only way she could stop thinking about Jul was to review everything she had told people about this ritual, wishing she had a notepad and pencil. She'd told the elders she needed certain specific people. She'd told the girls that they could make flower wreaths. And that there had to be lots of people, and chanting. The safest thing would be to chant hymns, but that seemed disrespectful. After all, this ritual was a big lie. Just because the commandments hadn't been written yet didn't mean she could go around breaking them.

Her head ached. Far away, a scimitar cat screamed. Esther slept, straining her ears for Jul's voice; woke; slept; and woke with a picture in her head of her and Emni holding hands and Nudawah dancing the schottische around them.

The gym teacher had gotten sick last winter, and the substitute was a little old lady who taught line dancing. Schottische was the hardest. Esther needed to be sure her feet remembered how to do it before she showed anybody.

She crawled outside. The color of the sky and height of the moon told her that dawn would come soon. No one watched the burned-down fire, since no predator would come into so big a camp. The wind buzzed in her snake rattle, flapped her shirt, and raised goose bumps along her ribs. Geese honked overhead. A baby wailed. On her way to the latrine they shared with two other groups, she kept her eyes open for a suitable dance floor, and on her way back, she stopped there.

"Vine left, hitch right," Esther muttered, shivering in the breeze that kicked up the trampled grass. Step left, rock back on your right foot. "Vine right, hitch left." The tricky bit was to change from hitching right to vining right. "Buffalo gals, won't you come out tonight, come out—Whoops!"

Vine left, hitch right. Vine right, hitch left. What if she used her stran as a balance pole? "Buffalo gals, won't you come out tonight, come out tonight, come out tonight?" What if she kept going right every time she sang "come out tonight?" Then forward instead of sideways for "and dance by the light of the moon." That mostly worked. "Buffalo gals, won't you come out tonight, come out tonight—"

"What are you doing?"

Esther jumped, though she knew the voice. Before her stood Telabat, Skedat, Kordak, Neerup from last night, and several boys she didn't know—what was this, a boy convention? "It's been a while since I've done this," she said.

"How do you even know to do it?" a strange boy asked. "Neerup said you said old women danced this ceremony."

"Everybody in the stars learns it," Esther said, wondering if everybody in the Valley knew about her ceremony already. "Boys, too."

"Boys and girls don't dance the same steps."

"Yeah, you know how things are done in the stars," said Telabat sarcastically. "You'd better get back, Esster. You know you're not supposed to wander around alone."

"What, is a bear supposed to come out of the ground and grab me?" But Ahrva would need help with Wahay and Tekinit.

At camp, men checked their strans, women and girls milled about working, and a stranger hunched by the fire. When the stranger turned her head, Esther's heart felt wobbly. "Silika!"

Silika's eyes looked raw, her ragged hair stuck out around her blood-striped face, and her blouse hung in tatters, all the squirrel tails pulled off; but she nursed Kiraka and smiled wanly. Esther hugged her. "I'm so sorry!"

"I'm all right now," said Silika. "I hear you're no longer shy about your wazicat."

"It's not mine, exactly," said Esther. "Are you *sure* you're all right?"

"We have to be," said Silika. "Our mother will take longer, but Geshwaw and I are ready to live now. Can you really help Kitotul's family?"

"If Jul lets me," said Esther.

"Esster," said Nudawah, "Ehdanwah was looking for you."

Esther clasped her hands and ducked her head. "Sorry. I didn't mean to worry you."

Nudawah snorted. "I was hoping you'd found an entrance to the stars, so we wouldn't have to deal with your tricks!"

"That's enough," said Ehdanwah, striding into camp from the one next door. "Your father is seriously considering her ceremony. A little girl isn't likely to trick him."

"When do I find out?" Esther asked. "I need to teach people the song, and the dance, and we'll need the right kind of wood, and flowers, and—"

Ehdanwah patted her shoulder. "Tonight. Relax."

"What kind of wood do we need?" Ahrva asked.

Soon girls swarmed over the tsik, breaking branches and dragging deadfalls, looking for "sweet wood." Girls from the different groups flocked to help, even girls like Helad, who said, "Kitotul's kin remember the killing. They won't allow it."

"Yeah, somebody like that Hunumand guy would ruin it," said Esther. "But usually what happens is, the relatives say they're going to stay mad, but when the time comes, somebody does the right thing."

"If it is the right thing," said Otala. "Nudawah says it's no good trying to change the way things are."

"Nudawah can kiss my big toe," said Esther, intending to make a joke, but losing control of her voice halfway through.

"Of course *she* doesn't want to help. She's scared that Skedat would outshine her precious Telabat if he ever got a chance."

"What if I tell her you said that?" Otala asked.

"You do what you want," said Esther. "I can't stop you."

"This is stupid," said Otala. "I'm going to play fox and quail with my cousins."

Washaw and Ahrva looked grim. The gathering was supposed to be a big holiday, and Esther was ruining it. "I'm sorry," she said. "I don't know what's the matter with me."

"I do," said Emni. "You want to go home, and you want to help us, and what do you do if you see an entrance before you can do this ritual? Well, I'll tell you. You go through, and don't worry about my family."

Esther wished this were the problem. "Nuaah," she said. "This is all the wood I can carry."

They piled wood in the field where people had been cutting extra bedding and playing ball. "That's enough work," said Esther. "If we're allowed to do it, everybody can bring wood. And stones, to mark out a circle around the bonfire."

"Does it matter what kind of rock?" Ahrva asked.

"Not particularly," said Esther, "as long as it's bigger than a fist."

"Pretty rock is probably best," said Helad. "Do we have to leave it here afterward?"

"No," said Esther, though a part of her mind whispered that a circle like that, made permanent, had potential as an archaeological site. But it wouldn't work. "Animals and people playing ball would kick them out of order, and then somebody's wazicat might get trapped inside. Everyone should take their rocks away again. Meantime, can you teach me that game with the double ball?"

As they were using branches and rocks to mark goals, though, two boys from Bedabat's group ran up. "Our dream-walker is ready to talk to you," they said to Esther.

"Nuaah," said Esther, around the heart suddenly beating in her throat.

Pezha, the dream-walker, and Ehdanwah waited together. Esther clasped her hands and bowed her head. "You sent for me, ma'am?"

"You have a problem, star-child," said Pezha. "Ehdanwah thinks if we can contact your people, they will fetch you. I think she is right. But I wonder—why have they sent no dream-walkers after you?"

"We don't have dream-walkers," said Esther. "And everyone thought it was impossible to get here. So they're looking for me in the stars."

"I see," said Pezha. "Have you dreamed about your people?"

"Nothing useful," said Esther. Should she tell about Jul's voice in her dreams? Or wait till she'd had a chance to ask him about it? Would he be angry if she told someone else first? Probably. "Usually I think I've gone to my . . . my camp. I try to talk to my people, and can't; or I know something's wrong and can't remember what; or people from here are mixed up with people from there. You know. Normal stuff."

"You couldn't dream about them at all if we didn't share the same dream place," said Pezha. "It sounds as though your parents have tried to find you, and you've tried to tell them where you are, but neither of you can make yourselves clear. I should be able to reach them."

"Um. They don't use your words."

"Sa, sa. You let me worry about that." Pezha patted the ground. "You must tell me everything!"

*P*ezha had a day's worth of questions. What was similar on either side of the entrance, and what was different? Who was Dr. Durham? How close had she been to the entrances? Was Esther sure Dr. Durham hadn't seen her the second time? What did the dreams she'd had the nights before she saw the entrances have in common? How were they different? She decided to tell Pezha about the voice, but not about her identification of it with Jul. Ehdanwah sewed and listened. It was mid-afternoon before Pezha said: "I will try to reach your people, if you will help me build a dream-shelter."

So Esther learned yet another new skill. Dream-shelters had to be lined up with moonrise, made of a particular wood, and erected while singing a song appealing to the dead for help. They worked quickly, hearing the laughter and cheering from the ball field, and echoes of their own song as other shelters went up around camp. They had barely finished when Jul's granddaughter found them. She bobbed her head at the senior women, but looked down her nose at Esther. "Come, my grandfather wishes to talk to you about this ceremony of yours."

Esther sighed. "Okay."

Jul grilled Esther about the ritual, apparently hoping to catch her in a contradiction. Esther's head hurt, and she wanted desperately to be rude; but she kept her eyes down and her hands clasped and her voice low. He never paused for her to ask any questions of her own, and interrupting him would be fatal.

At last he stood up and said: "So! I am done with you! Run along and play."

"Um," said Esther, not moving. "If I could ask you something first, sir?"

He snorted. "Nuaah. What do you want?"

"Before I came, before I knew anyone could get here, I had a dream," she said. "I saw Tekinit, before I knew her, and some others. I heard a voice behind me. Your voice, sir." She swallowed, pausing long enough for him to say something if he wanted to. "You said: *It's too late.*" As she spoke, she remembered the rest. "You said: *You can't save her.* And later, the night before I saw the entrance I didn't go through—I was running after my elder, and you said: *It's later than you think.* Do you . . . do you remember these dreams?"

He was quiet so long she couldn't take it, and looked up. "I have never had such dreams," he said, but slowly. "You must not lie to me."

Crud, crud, crud. "Maybe you haven't had these dreams yet," said Esther. "My elder says time is different between here and the stars. That's why we can see your future."

"You must be careful, star-child," said Jul, "and we must be careful around you. Even if you aren't as bad as Nudawah thinks, you are dangerous. No one who knows as little as you should carry power." He frowned at her until she dropped her eyes again, then shook his hands in a releasing gesture. "Go, go. You're too big a problem to solve all at once."

So. At least he hadn't flatly denied her any help. Maybe he'd talk to Pezha. Maybe he wouldn't. The deserted camps were filling up again; the ball field had fallen quiet. Esther went back to Uduban's camp and chewed bark for her aching head, greeting the others as cheerfully as she could as they came in.

In the evening, Silika's mother, Wasitay, came out of the mourning shelter. The mourners broke it up for firewood, washed in the falls, and put on new clothes, burying the old ones. Then they returned to their own fires, talking, smiling, acting normally—except for the cuts and the ragged hair.

Esther was showing the girls how to French-braid, using Tekinit as a guinea pig, when Jul and Hunumand, the man who remembered Kitotul's father, came. "We have an errand with your people, Uduban," said Jul. "May we enter your camp?"

No one had ever asked permission before. Esther looked sideways at Ahrva, who motioned her to keep demonstrating the braid.

"You may enter, elders," said Uduban, clasping his hands.

Nudawah hurried to offer them the best meat, hot chestnuts, and the water gourd. They talked, a stiff, unnatural conversation, like a set of passwords and countersigns that everybody had to exchange before getting down to business. At last Jul cleared his throat and said: "Uduban, a matter has been brought before the elders, which concerns your group."

"I listen well, sir," said Uduban.

"In your group, you have a child who fell from the stars. You also have a family tainted with a wrong done to the family of this man with me, Hunumand. Your star-child says she can teach us to remove the bad wazicat from the family. Hunumand has talked to the spirits. I have walked with his murdered cousin in a dream and talked to the star-child. If an evil can be healed, let it be healed. If an evil can be revealed, let it be revealed. Is it true, that divisions began in your group when the star-child came?"

Nudawah glared at Podan, who watched his brother. Dul, cutting wesk into usable strips, looked from one face to the other. Everyone else kept their heads down. At last Uduban said, "My brother and I do not agree on how best to hunt the territory we hunted with our father. Our wives do not agree on anything. The star-child brought bad tidings, which may or may not be true. Divisions that were weak before are stronger now."

"I have heard it said that some of us prefer our own strength to the strength of all," said Hunumand. "I have heard it said that if the taint were removed from this family, it would be good for everyone. That if I cannot let go of my anger, I weaken everyone. And I think—this may be true. If an evil can be healed, let it be healed."

"A strong man forgives," said Ehdanwah.

Jul looked at Nudawah. "I have heard it said that one of my blood prefers division to harmony, her own will to the good of all. I know that this is not true."

"It was an ill mouth that spoke such lies," said Uduban.

"It would have been, if it were a lie, and not a mistake," said

Ehdanwah, raking chestnuts out of the fire. "A chestnut is all prickles on the outside, but the heart is soft and good. One who doesn't know chestnuts may be forgiven for mistaking them for bad plants, but show them the soft heart, and they will know better."

The chestnuts passed from hand to hand. Nudawah ate hers with an expression that seemed to be trying not to be sour. Jul said, "The star-child is strange and she knows little; but for good or ill, she has wazicat, and I think she does not lie on purpose. We are many, and we are wise. We can control her ignorance. We can use her knowledge. She says that many people are needed to work this purifying wazicat and drive the shadow from the killer's grandchildren. A dream-walker. I will do this. A male elder. I will do this. A female elder."

"I will do this," said Ehdanwah.

"The kin of the murdered man."

"I will do this," said Hunumand.

"A man who will stand with the grandson."

"I will do this," said Podan, smiling broadly.

"A woman who will stand with the granddaughters."

"I will do this," said Silika, taking Shusskt's hand.

"A girl to stand with the granddaughters."

"I will do this," said Ahrva and Tekinit, at the same time.

"One is enough," said Jul, looking to Esther.

"You have to put wreaths on their heads," said Esther. "Let Ahrva do it. She's taller."

"You mean older," grumbled Tekinit. "Can I make wreaths?"

"Absolutely," said Esther.

"A boy to stand with the grandson," Jul went on.

Telabat said, loudly and proudly: "I will do this."

"A woman, not an elder, but one past the age of bearing children." Jul looked straight at Nudawah.

Nudawah breathed a sigh. "I will do this, though I do not know if it is wise."

"Someone who carries the wazicat of the stars, who will take all the bad wazicat if it cannot be destroyed," said Jul.

"I will do this," said Esther, light-headed.

"And kin and friends of the wronged and the tainted, to witness and chant."

"We will do this," said everyone.

"All the groups are here," said Jul. "Tomorrow, we must prepare the big hunt, which will last until the female mammoths end it. Star-child, can you teach this ceremony in that time?"

How long was that? "I can do anything I must," said Esther, hoping this wasn't another lie, "and I must do this."

"If the ceremony fails," said Nudawah, "you must admit that your wazicat is not good for us, and find another way to live."

"My daughter, reflect on what you say," said Ehdanwah.

Esther swallowed, her eyes on Nudawah's face. "If the ceremony fails, I fail," she said. "It is in the power of anyone who takes part to spoil the ceremony. I am not afraid to help my friends. If an evil can be healed, let it be healed. If an evil can be revealed, let it be revealed."

Shusskt flicked her eyes at Esther, and Esther knew that if Jul dreamed that the ceremony had failed, the theory that Nudawah had spoiled it on purpose would spread like wildfire.

There, she thought. *That's all I can do!*

THIRTY-FIVE

*U*sually, if the men couldn't find a lone bull, they would spend hours tracking a male herd, patiently maneuvering one member away from the others. The targeted bull would scream as soon as he got hurt, but if the men did it right, the other bulls would arrive too late and would disperse again, knowing that if they tried to avenge their friend, the men would kill more.

At the Valley, the plan was for everyone to get as fat as possible before the uncertainties of winter. The fat they wouldn't eat on the spot would be mixed with nuts and berries, meat would be salted to carry along, and—if the weather turned properly cold—the cooked meat should last awhile.

The mammoths understood the hunt as well as anybody, and they outnumbered the humans. Any number of mammoths might come to the assistance of a victim, including females, who must not be killed. The trick was to pick the most defensible places to kill bulls and hide from cows. Fortunately, the mammoths couldn't resist coming to the danger zones to stroke the bones of old kills (obviously, visibly, mourning their dead);

but they came in pairs and were wary.

Podan declared that killing the maximum number of mammoths was no longer a good idea. He thought the important thing was to kill the mammoths that would do the most good for the people, and the least harm to the herd, without killing so many at once that half the meat spoiled. Not everyone thought this was even possible. He started a lot of arguments. "If you hadn't said the mammoths would die, the men would have started the big hunt by now," said Nudawah.

"Yes, ma'am. Shall we try the step again?" Esther asked. "Or do you need to rest some more?"

"I was never tired," said Nudawah. "I stopped because you were obviously worn out and too stubborn to stop before I did."

"Yes, ma'am," said Esther. "Thank you. Now, on three. One, two, 'Buffalo gals, won't you come out tonight?'"

Nudawah was a good dancer. They spent most of one afternoon coordinating the steps with the music; then taught Uduban's and Jul's groups to sing the song at the right tempo. People taught their friends, until by the second day of the Big Hunt the cliffs resounded with clapping hands and voices fitting themselves around unaccustomed sounds: *Buf-ala-gahls wuncha koma tahniit, koma tahniit, koma tahniit! Buf-ala-gahls wuncha koma tahniit andanss bithu liitah thamun!*

"What does it mean?" Tekinit asked. Tekinit and Wahay were running mild temperatures, and Tekinit had given Wahay her Fiesta Texas T-shirt, because she thought Wahay was sicker than her. The act made Esther so proud, she ached. "Buf-ala-gahls is what we call the spirits of the female star-bison," she said. "They're big enough to carry the bad wazicat away."

Tekinit bounced. "So andanss bithu liitah thamun must mean 'take away our bad wazicat!'"

"More or less," said Esther, smiling.

"But what do the buf-ala-gahls get out of it?" Wahay asked, worriedly. "Doesn't the bad wazicat make them sick?"

"They're too strong to get sick," Esther assured her.

"But it must be lots of work to come from the stars," said Tekinit. "Why would they want to, even if it doesn't hurt them?"

"Well," said Esther, speaking slowly and thinking fast, "why did Shusskt and Emni and I go all the way to the bog to get medicine for you?"

"Because..." Tekinit's forehead wrinkled. "I'm part of the group. You have to take care of the people in your group!"

"Okay, then, why did the group take care of me?" Esther asked. "I'm nobody's relative. I was useless and ate food you all could have eaten, and I could have disappeared before I got a chance to be useful, for all anybody knew."

Tekinit and Wahay puzzled over this. Ahrva—sewing together otter skins that she'd traded raccoon skins for—asked: "Why does mammoth give himself to us? Why did you give Wahay your shirt? If everybody gives, the world works. If everybody takes, it doesn't work."

"Exactly," said Esther, as the sound of a mammoth dying in the Valley shattered the air. She smiled at Tekinit, but inside she was cold. The groups could no more repay the mammoths than Esther could repay the group. *All I can do is the best I can do,* she reminded herself, shivering.

"Are you cold?" asked Ahrva.

"I'm fine," said Esther. "A goose walked across the ground I'll be buried in."

The little girls giggled. "Shush, she didn't mean that," said Ahrva. "It's a long time since you got a word wrong, Esther. Buried means put under the ground."

"I know," said Esther. "When my people die, we put our bodies under the ground."

"Eeuw," said Tekinit. "Then you *must* be going home. Nobody here would bury you. It'd be too much work."

"Hey, hey, hey," said Wahay. "Maybe the buf-ala-gahls will take you away when they take away the bad wazicat!"

Tekinit hugged Esther tight. "I don't want you to go away!"

"I don't want to go away from you," said Esther, ignoring the snot Tekinit was getting on her shirt, "but I want to go toward my own group. It's not up to me, anyway. Here, let's clean your face out. If you can't breathe, you can't sing."

Pezha came out of the dream-shelter and straight to Esther every morning. Esther tried not to hope. Dreams were always bizarre. When Pezha saw a woman whose face "echoed" Esther's, that was only because she knew Pezha was looking for her mother. Her descriptions of strange, regular cave systems full of bizarre objects only sounded familiar because Esther wanted them to. And the fact that she described an elder with her hair covered with a multicolored skin didn't mean she'd seen Dr. Durham and the gimme cap that Esther *hadn't* described to her.

"Your mother only cries," said Pezha. "Your elder, this Doctor-Durm, is strong and strange. Her mind is full of stone and her heart is troubled. I say that I come from you, and she says:

Take better care of her than I did. I tell her you are not in the stars anymore, and she says she can't go that fast."

You have to go faster than light to reach the stars, thought Esther. "Don't tell her where I'm not. Tell her where I am. Her word for this place is Pleistocene," she told Pezha. "Her word for the groups is Clovis. Tell her the Pleistocene and the . . . the Holocene touch sometimes." Holocene was the word for the present—the future. Dr. Durham might understand it. But would she, could she believe it, or do anything about it? "Ask her for ideas on what I can do to get home," Esther said.

In addition to Pezha dream-walking to find Esther's family, other people were dream-walking to learn about the megafaunal extinction. So far, this had only caused more arguments, as one dream-walker got one bit of information from the spirit of mammoth and another dream-walker got another bit of information from the spirit of scimitar cat. These arguments always ended with someone asking Esther for clarification. Maybe a team of ecologists, paleontologists, meteorologists, doctors, and hunters could have helped them, but Esther, alone, was woefully inadequate. She wanted to cry with frustration, but she was never alone enough, so she practiced the dance instead.

The ceremony also gave her an excuse not to watch the progress of the Big Hunt much. The married women and little girls would cluster at good vantage points and watch the Valley all day as they sewed winter clothing. Most of the time the men weren't visible, but experienced watchers could judge what was happening based on the behavior of the mammoths.

The silent thunder changed its tone, buzzing in Esther's bones like flies. Some of the females actively protected certain bulls, presumably their sons, or herded their families out of the Valley, abandoning the mammoth reed. A ring of hunters formed around every downed mammoth, and the men inside would butcher frantically, convoying the meat away, smashing the bones while the women on the cliff honored the dead. The air reeked of roasting meat and blood. Scavengers were everywhere.

It was the worst thing Esther had ever seen, heard, and smelled; but she ate mammoth meat till her stomach swelled, for four days.

She was walking Silika, Emni, and Washaw through their roles, when a warning ran through the camp from the watchers on the cliff, "Here they come! Hunt's over."

The women scattered, scooping up whatever child came to hand as they dashed for the nearest tree. Esther ran with them before she felt, heard, saw the mammoth burst out of the Valley into camp.

She had a torn ear and a broken tusk longer than a person, and as she charged she trumpeted, answered by more shrill trumpets behind her. Esther climbed, pushing Tekinit ahead and keeping an eye on Silika, top-heavy with the burden of Kiraka. Another mammoth, and another, and another, and the sycamores were too smooth, too slender, too *short* to protect anyone!

Grown and juvenile, red and black and brown, the female mammoths crashed through the camps, stamping out fires with their huge round feet, sending shelters and woodpiles flying through the air. The main support branch holding up Pezha's dream-shelter shot up to strike Pezha on the leg as she clung halfway up a tree. Babies bawled in maddening counterpoint to the trumpetings. Only the yana women and the blind elder stood stock still while the mammoths tore the camp to shreds around them. Esther wanted to shout: *Over here, over here! You'll get trampled!* But her muscles were locked around the lowest branch of the tree, and her jaw was locked shut around screams, and any minute now a mammoth would realize how easy she was to kill.

The tree trembled, out of synch with the pounding of Esther's heart, as a young mammoth walked up. Its tusks might not be big enough to uproot the tree without help; but its trunk was plenty long enough to pluck Esther like a ripe plum. Dozens of possible, horrible fates went through Esther's head as the mammoth halted in front of her; but all she could see was an eye, as blue as Dr. Durham's, in a vast expanse of wrinkled, reddish skin. Esther heard herself whimper, and wondered if her breath smelled like mammoth meat. "Please," she said. "I'm sorry. I don't know what to do."

The blue-eyed mammoth shook Esther's branch with her trunk, snorted, and ran straight over the family shelter.

The mammoth with the broken tusk trumpeted again, and the blue-eyed mammoth pivoted to follow her westward, faster than anything so big should be able to run, until they vanished among bleached grass and wooded hills.

The elders climbed down and walked among the ruined camps, kicking aside lumps of mammoth dung and poking the fires in search of live coals. Esther shook too hard to move. "What did you tell her?" Tekinit asked.

She must have spoken English or Spanish to the mammoth. "I asked her to forgive me for eating her relatives."

"I guess she did," said Ahrva. "I thought for a minute she was going to pick you up and break you. They do, some years."

"Does—does this happen a lot?"

"Every year, the mammoth mothers decide when it is time for their sons to stop dying, and tell us to go, yes."

Every year? And people kept coming back?

A woman left the yana area, walked to the falls, and let loose a long, piercing whistle that rose into the air and fell into the Valley like a shrill, invisible firework.

"So—the Big Hunt's over?" Esther asked.

"That's right," said Silika. "Tonight, we will hold your ceremony. Climb down. There's a lot to do."

THIRTY-SIX

➤ CEREMONY OF THE STAR-CHILD

*E*sther was still shaky at sunset. The moon was not yet risen and the evening was chilly, though everyone had been saying for days that it was too warm for the time of year. Every member of every group had added a rock to the circle. Esther walked the circumference, poking a few stones into alignment, getting some other kids to help her fix one place where the arc was flat. Then she was out of excuses. "We can start anytime," she said.

"Usually, when a large ceremony is performed, the stars must be in certain places," said Nudawah.

Nice of you to mention this before, thought Esther, but she said: "Since this ceremony was designed in the stars, that wasn't practical, ma'am. I stand in for the stars this time."

Ehdanwah made fire, the crowd singing the fire song with her. Telabat and Ahrva held garlands of autumn flowers—goldenrod, aster, vervain, paintbrush. Emni, Skedat, and Washaw—the focus of the ceremony—made one tight clump; Nudawah, Jul, and Hunumand made another. Despite what he'd said,

Hunumand had been expressing doubts about forgiving his relative's murder that afternoon; Esther had been relieved when he'd shown up. Silika, looking odd without Kiraka on her back, leaned against Podan, who wrapped his arms around her so that they were both enclosed in the bison hide he wore around his shoulders. People coughed in the audience.

The fire caught. A thin wind blew smoke into Esther's eyes and buzzed the rattle by her ear. *I can do this, I can do this, I can do this,* she told herself, and held up both her hands.

Kitotul's children and Nudawah backed up to the rim of the circle, to the big rock that marked where the sun had risen that morning. Podan and Silika, holding strans, and Hunumand, holding bunches of juniper, took up their positions by the bonfire. Jul and Ehdanwah stood by the stone that marked where the sun had set that night. Esther made eye contact with Jul, and nodded. He raised his fine spear and howled.

The murmurs of the spectators stopped. Crickets chirped, like a quick, steady drip from a thousand synchronized bad faucets. Jul brought his spear down. Esther started clapping and singing: "Buffalo gals won't you come out tonight?" She sounded lone, small, and pitiful; but then the spectators joined in; a dozen or so groups, all keeping time: "Koma tahniit, koma tahniit! Buf-ala-gahls wuncha koma tahniit andanss bithu liitah thamun!" Nudawah vined right and hitched left. Ahrva put a garland on Emni's head, and kissed her. Esther danced to her, clapping. "Will you come with me, and lay your burden down?"

"I will," said Emni.

Vine right, hitch left, they danced, holding hands, to the

middle of the circle, to Hunumand. "This child has done you no wrong," she said to Hunumand. "She comes to you to humbly ask that you will forgive the wrong her grandfather did to you."

They knelt, Esther holding Emni's hands and reciting the Lord's Prayer in Spanish. Esther felt better for saying the words, holding Emni's eyes with hers, as Hunumand lit his first juniper branch in the bonfire and walked around them, chanting: "May the fires of my anger blow away like smoke!" His chant, and Esther's prayer, and the slow singing blended in a way that Esther hadn't been prepared for; not exactly like church music, but not so different either.

When he had smoked them four times, Hunumand threw the branch into the fire. "Will someone stand for this child?"

"I will." Silika raised Emni to her feet. "Emni, I am the friend of your mother. You are as a beloved daughter to me. Will you renounce all evil and swear to be as good as your grandfather was bad? Will you walk with my children in peace all the days of your life?"

"I will," said Emni, in a fine loud voice.

Silika held out the stran. Emni gripped the blade and drew her hand back. She didn't flinch as the flint ripped through skin and blood scattered; but Esther did. She had thought long and hard about this part; but no one would believe in the ceremony if it was too easy. With the bleeding hand, Emni took off her wreath and gave it to Esther. "Take my badness from me," she said, "let it blow away in smoke."

Esther walked as close to the fire as she could, chanting the Twenty-third Psalm, and hurled the wreath into the bonfire.

Silika took Emni's hands, and they danced toward Ehdanwah and Jul. Esther danced, vine left, hitch right, vine left, hitch right, vine right, hitch left, vine right, hitch left, to fetch Skedat.

He danced as if he expected the ground to bite him. Esther kept her eyes on his as she prayed and Hunumand smoked him with the second juniper branch. Emni hadn't been afraid, but Skedat was. Of what? Podan said: "Skedat, I am the friend of your father. You are as a beloved son to me. Will you renounce all evil and swear to be as good as your grandfather was bad? Will you walk with my children in peace all the days of your life?"

"I will, sir," Skedat said, in a hoarse whisper, and grasped Podan's stran.

Esther, tiring, danced back for Washaw. Nudawah seemed to be still going strong, thank goodness! Washaw danced with as much spring as a pronghorn and gave her responses without hesitation. She looked into Silika's face and grasped the stran with only a small whimper. Esther chanted the Twenty-third Psalm as loudly as she could, watching the bloody flowers shrivel in the bonfire like bad dreams in daylight.

Hunumand raised his arms and cried: "I am satisfied! I am satisfied! I am satisfied!"

He timed it perfectly, the last syllable of "satisfied" matching with "moon" in the song and the moment Silika handed Washaw off to Ehdanwah. Nudawah stopped. Silence fell over the audience; until someone, in the back, cried out: "We are satisfied! We are satisfied! We are satisfied!"

Esther felt something in her let go.

Podan hugged her. "You have done well, star-child."

"So far, so good," said Esther. "Jul still has to dream-walk and say if it worked."

"He will," said Podan. "Come, we must build his shelter."

➤ THIRTY-SEVEN

➤ THE SCATTERING

Esther half-expected, in her half-sleep, to be woken by a foot the size of a truck tire coming through the roof of their rebuilt shelter. Tekinit snored, her nose too clogged to breathe properly. Esther and Ahrva woke her up periodically to make her blow her nose into a fistful of grass, which Esther would then burn. In between, Esther drowsed, trying to invent a vaporizer out of the materials at hand, and wondering what Jul was dreaming. What if, despite the damage it would do to Nudawah's reputation, Jul dreamed of failure?

What if he dreamed the truth, that the ceremony was a lie?

She must have slept eventually, because she and Ahrva were hiding mammoths in gourds when a woman's scream woke her. Kiraka started screaming in sympathy, causing Silika to scoop him up and make soothing noises without even opening her eyes. Podan picked up his strans and dashed out.

It was Nudawah, screaming Jul's name and cursing Esther. Skedat came. "Nudawah had a bad dream," he said. "About Jul.

She's going to the dream-shelter. It may be nothing. We're following her and—Esster—we think you'd better come."

"We'll all come," said Ahrva.

Esther swallowed. "No," she said. "If there's a bad thing, it's my bad thing. I don't want it getting on anybody else." She crawled out, and said to Skedat: "Stay here. I mean it."

"You're very bossy for a little girl," said Skedat. "Go, then. Podan didn't wait."

It was the dark, cold hour before dawn, and she could barely see Podan and Kitotul, picking their way between ragged-looking camps. She ran to catch up. "Did she say what she dreamed?"

Podan gestured *no*. "It can't be good."

The hunters in Jul's group had camped in the field, guarding the dream-shelter by the burned-down bonfire. Uduban stood back as Nudawah argued with her nephew Chul, who was older than she was. "I don't care what you say," he said. "It's dangerous to disturb a dream-walker before dawn."

"He's not alive to be disturbed!"

"You're not a dream-walker. Your dream means nothing."

"I *wasn't* a dream-walker. He came to me, your grandfather, my father. He said: *My daughter, the ceremony has succeeded beyond all hope. Those children are clean and their paths are straight, but I see the way to the stars. I will seek out the star-child's people so they will send for her. But I am old. I will not come back. You must walk in dreams, and in dreams you will see me again. I will learn the truth about the mammoths, the horses and camels, and I will tell you what I learn.*" Nudawah was crying so hard Esther could barely understand her; and when she did understand the words, she still didn't understand.

If Jul was dead, he couldn't help Esther anymore. Could he?

He had been eleven thousand years dead the first time Esther had heard his voice.

"If what you say is true, dawn is time enough to know," said Chul. "Come, sit. I have a soft bison hide. We have hot meat."

"I don't want hot meat! I want my father!"

But she waited, and they all waited, until the deep grayness in the air turned pale and a star hung low and hot amid the pink and blue clouds on the cold horizon. Esther hugged her knees and rocked back and forth, hoping Nudawah wouldn't notice her. The megafaunal extinction was what interested Jul, not her. Maybe that was what he meant by "too late." Maybe the "her" Esther couldn't save was mammoth.

Too many maybes. Not enough facts.

I need to learn to dream-walk for myself.

At last Chul took Nudawah's arm, and they went to the entrance of the shelter, chanting: "The dawn is come, dream-walker! Return to us, dream-walker! The sun is come, dream-walker! With him you come, dream-walker!"

But he didn't come.

Podan said, "If she says truth, Chul will not be pleased. Everyone thought his mother would get the dream-walking."

"If Nudawah is a dream-walker, she is one to be reckoned with," said Kitotul. "The first thing she learns as a dream-walker is that a ceremony she didn't want to do worked for people she doesn't like, and the second thing is that her father is dead. Nuaah! We must be kind to her, no matter how unkind she is to us."

Chul and Nudawah went into the shelter. After another long moment the wails began.

Podan went to Uduban. "What do you want us to do?"

Uduban sighed. "Tell the others. I will look after her."

"She is our sister," said Podan. "We will look after her."

"I know you would, my brother," said Uduban, "but—honestly—I don't think she would like that."

It was a long, strange, hot day.

Jul's group—Chul's group, now—mourned loud and hard. The last mammoths ripped up the last of the mammoth reeds and fondled the bloody bones of their dead in peace. Two couples stood up to say that they were not married anymore, and the elders divided their children among them. The oldest woman and the new oldest man presided over a great wedding of two dozen couples, including Helad and a low flatlander.

And all the time, Nudawah and her kin were in their shelter, slashing themselves and wailing to let the pain out; and the mammoths in the valley mourned.

Next morning, some of the groups began to pack. "Too many fleas." They laughed. "If it was colder, we would stay longer."

Nudawah and the other mourners carried Jul down to the falls and washed him, wailing and singing. "Our father has run ahead of us. Our father is dancing up in the sky. Don't look back, Father. Run ahead, Father. Your father, he waits for you. Your brother, he waits for you. Your wife, she waits for you . . ."

Esther did not attend the funeral. She started to, walking up to the falls with Podan and Silika, Ahrva, and Ehdanwah; but Nudawah came to meet them. "I do not say there is bad wazicat on her," she said. "My father was old, and he did not blame anyone. But my father is dead, and I don't want her here."

"It shall be as you wish," said Podan.

"And when I leave here, no star-child will be in my group," she said. "I don't care where she goes, or with who, or who goes with her. But my husband, my son, and I, we are done with her. Is that clear?"

No, thought Esther, in a panic.

"Yes," said Ehdanwah. "But I am *not* done with her. When I leave, the star-child will be in my group. Is *that* clear?"

Uduban made a small sound, a strange sound to come from a grown man. But Nudawah didn't flinch. "Yes, ma'am," she said.

Esther practically ran back to camp. Shusskt said, "It's not your fault, Esster."

"But—what happens now?" Esther hugged her knees. All her work to belong and now—what was left to belong to?

"Now you make a new group," said Silika's mother, Wasitay. "Podan's group. I am sure my Geshwaw will want to go with you." She looked at Yahaywah, who nodded.

"Kitotul will go where Podan goes," said Shusskt. "But what about Dul? He likes Podan better, but Mingwah's spent a lot of time keeping in good with Nudawah, against the day she'll be senior woman, and now—here the day is!"

"But—where do we go?"

"We'll work that out with the elders," Wasitay assured her. "Once we know for sure which men each group has, we'll have a good idea of what space will be best for them to hunt in."

Tekinit hugged Esther. "Don't worry, Esster! You can always stay with us, forever, and we keep Ehdanwah!"

Yahaywah looked at her mother-in-law, Wasitay. "What about you?"

"I have three living children, and two of them will be in this group. What mother could resist that?" Wasitay smiled. "Ehdanwah will be senior woman. She was born on the first day of the spring gathering, long ago, and I was born on the last."

"But you will know best sometimes," said Ehdanwah.

"When Ehdanwah says I do!"

➤ THIRTY-EIGHT

➤ THE FIRST NORTHER

The morning that they left the Valley, Esther was woken by the departure of the mammoths—not by the noise, but by the stillness. The sparkling, invisible, humming quality of air—as if the whole world were more alive than usual—that was the presence of mammoths, vanished. She woke, sweating. *Today's the last chance for Pezha to come through with a useful dream.*

Dul didn't believe Esther was bad, and told Podan he thought his ideas were right. But he and Uduban had hunted well all their lives, and (Esther knew) Mingwah had cried all night. Otala drifted by before they left with Uduban. "I'm sorry, Esster," she said.

"I'm sorry, too," said Esther.

Telabat forgot one of his bags on purpose, so he could come running back for it. He pounded Skedat on the back, and then held out both hands to Esther. "This is the last time I can get star-wazicat until spring. I will understand if you refuse."

"I don't mind giving it to you," said Esther, "but if you know your folks won't like it, are you sure you should do it?"

"Star-wazicat is good. My mother and father can't see that, but I can't *not* see it. What you give to me, I will take."

Esther shook both of his hands, wondering if Emni was right about him liking her. If so—gross. Of course, if she stayed, she'd have to marry somebody. *Still gross.* "Good luck," she said. "*Buena suerte.*" *Pezha, where are you?*

The old woman showed up in late morning, discouraged. "I told Doc-tor-Durm about the Pleistoseen and the Holoseen touching, and she said: *They are the same.* We never seemed to me to be talking about the same thing."

Esther swallowed, keeping her face carefully still and polite. "Thank you for trying."

Pezha patted her shoulder. "In the spring, we will all meet again. Maybe we will know what to do by then."

You knew it wouldn't work, Esther told herself; but a part of her hadn't known at all, and that part ached.

The weight of guilt for dividing the group remained on Esther's mind; but the fact was that without Uduban and Nudawah, the morning arguments were short. Ehdanwah didn't mind taking Wasitay's advice, and Wasitay joked that she would live to be the oldest non-senior woman in the world. The women walked in harmony all day. Esther gave star-wazicat to the men openly. The new hunters—Geshwaw and his cousin Bzzna—were shy, but their wives, Yahaywah and Shimatash, treated Esther as a little sister. Shusskt added fringe to her daughters' clothes. Emni, Washaw, and Skedat all walked tall and smiled more. *I may not be good for much, but I did that,* Esther thought, when she felt low, which was at night when she lay down and at dawn before she got up. The rest of the time she was too busy to think about it.

Despite a final, thorough wash in the falls, it took a couple of days to leave the fleas behind. Also, though Wahay's congestion soon cleared up, Tekinit still snored, woke daily with a sore throat, and tired easily. The air was so still, so warm, and so full of unreleased rain that everyone had some trouble breathing. The mammoth meat lasted a few days, not as long as hoped. Deer, camels, and horses were audible all day long, calling to each other—"Fighting over women," said the men. "It makes them dangerous. We'll get them when we need them."

Meantime, ducks and geese filled the sky, and the women made nets with which to tangle them when they came wearily to the water holes in the evening. They dug roots from a field Wasitay knew, many of which were too small; on the other hand, plants bloomed and bore fruit that shouldn't have. "I don't mind if the world stays warm," said Tekinit, eating grapes one evening. "But I'm tired of carrying all these hot clothes!" Tekinit's load consisted of two rabbit-skin caps, an otter-skin shift, a water gourd, her branch-baby, and a garlic root around her neck, intended to keep her nose clear.

"It won't stay warm forever," Esther warned. "One day old north wind will make you glad you carried those clothes."

"Nuaah," Tekinit said, and started coughing, bringing up phlegm along with her grape skins and seeds. Esther's chest ached in sympathy.

That night, Tekinit didn't sleep. In the morning, she didn't wake. She coughed, eyes shut, and whined for Silika, who didn't come near, for fear of getting the sickness on Kiraka. Ehdanwah fed Tekinit, and the girls made a litter. "You men, find us strong liver," Wasitay instructed. "A big plant-eater."

"You can't stay here," Podan pointed out, obediently collecting his strans. "There isn't enough food."

"We'll meet you at the bitter spring," said Ehdanwah. "There should be late grapes there, and the water is medicine."

We can't live on grapes, thought Esther. *We'll get the runs.* She transferred Tekinit's load to her own back and said nothing. The morning weighed her down, but this much hot stillness, this late in the year, could only mean one thing. She made sure Tekinit's fur clothes were on the top of her bundle.

"What a strange look the sky has," said Shusskt. "What does it mean?"

Wasitay said, "I don't know."

Esther studied the sky. It looked plain enough to her—an old-fashioned Texas blue norther. She would have expected northers to happen all the time, with Ice Age glaciers sprawling across Canada, but what did she know? "I've seen this before," she said. "That's the cold wind coming from the . . . the place where it's always winter."

"So the weather's finally going to turn normal?" asked Shusskt. "That will be good!"

"Well—except that it hits all at once," said Esther. One morning it had been eighty-five degrees when she left the house, and forty degrees when she got to school, and her with no sweater.

"As long as it waits till we get to the bitter spring!"

But it didn't.

They topped a hill a little before noon. Ehdanwah called a rest stop, wiping her sweaty face. "The spring is there," she said, "that white scar, you see? Near the pines."

As she pointed, the air stirred, suddenly cool. A sigh of welcome went around the group, but Esther threw open her pack and grabbed Tekinit's otter shift as the world rustled.

The sky blinked. Esther grabbed Tekinit and pulled her arms up to slide the shift on.

The sun went out. Tekinit whimpered and resisted.

Icy wind slammed into Washaw and Wahay first, pulling their hair straight into the air. The girls cried out; then it hit all of them, hard and fast and mean.

Kiraka wailed.

The norther wailed louder.

The world smelled like rain. As they hurried to wrap themselves in the warm skins they'd carried so long, the black sky rumbled, and the wind pushed at the tops of the pines, sycamores, and oaks that loomed, suddenly dangerous, over their heads. Dust, pollen, and plant fragments battered their faces, and they walked with their eyes half-shut. Esther and Ahrva carried Tekinit's litter until their arms and shoulders ached, and then kept walking. Under a mound of furs, Tekinit breathed in short gasps, through her mouth. Silika carried Kiraka across her chest inside a bison-hide poncho, like a walking tent. Esther's ears and toes and fingers and the inside of her nose hurt with cold. She wished that her socks hadn't worn out.

At last they set the litter down by the bitter spring, which stank and bubbled and steamed. Unlike other water holes, this one had no fringe of trees and cattails, only some discouraged-looking grass. Esther drank eagerly. It tasted like liquid rust, but was warm.

"Nothing ever happens when it would be best," grumbled Shusskt. "If we'd been here this morning, we could have bathed Tekinit. If we put her in now, we won't be able to take her out till the wind stops blowing."

"At least there's shelter," said Silika, pointing to an outcrop of limestone some yards away.

"That isn't a shelter," said Shusskt, looking at the pines all around. The wind had already blown some dead branches down; big ones—not that little ones would be any fun to be hit on the head by either.

"It'll block the wind," said Ehdanwah.

So they built three shelters in the outcrop's lee. Ehdanwah held Tekinit in her lap, making her drink the mineral water, while Wasitay built the fire. Ahrva, Washaw, and Esther decided they'd better fish, which meant standing naked in water so cold they quickly ceased to feel it. They sang about the Valley, but the wind scattered their voices so they could barely hear themselves. Washaw's teeth began to chatter, so they gave up. While they dressed, an opossum crept out for a drink. Esther, closest, threw her stran, and hit it in the side. It squealed and ran, but Ahrva stabbed it, snatched it up, and wrung its neck. "Thank you, Brother Possum, for giving yourself to us," she said. She grinned at Esther over the body.

Esther grinned back, though a part of her brain protested: *It looks like a rat! It's bleeding!*

Why did she still *have* this squeamish part of her brain?

The men did not come that night. "It means they're on the track of something big," said Silika, and no one argued.

Esther, Ahrva, Tekinit, and Ehdanwah crowded into one shelter. The thunder rumbled, and animals cried differently, so Esther could not tell wolf from coyote from owl. Only the scream of a scimitar cat ripped through the darkness with its accustomed sound, to make her spine shrivel and her hair stand up as usual.

Esther dreamed of popcorn bouncing in a popper while she waited in an icy theater, impatient because she was going to miss the movie, but when she woke, the sound continued—pea-sized chunks of ice bouncing off the stony ground, burying the fire in a slippery white layer. "That's big raak-han," said Ahrva. "It covers the ground so, at first I thought it was oosha."

Raak-han—"ice rocks." Esther decided not to tell her about golfball- and baseball-sized hail. "What's oosha?"

"Softer, white, falls in big piles."

Snow. "Will there be much this winter?"

"Probably," said Ahrva. "Usually it falls and takes four or five days to melt and then falls again, but sometimes there isn't time to melt. Those are bad winters."

Then the sky cracked open and let water down, as if through a gash in the bottom of a heavenly lake. They all curled up together, with Tekinit in the middle. "The men must be freezing," said Ehdanwah. As soon as the rain stopped, she organized a search for dry wood.

Ahrva went for medicine water, and Esther made Tekinit eat cold cooked milkweed root. Tekinit was hoarse, headachy, and tired, with dry, hot skin. In between bites, she plucked at the bracelet, watching the stars floating inside the dirt-dimmed plastic. "When will you want this back?" she asked.

"Keep it," said Esther. "You gave me your rattlesnake rattle, didn't you?"

Tekinit smiled, though it didn't look right with her eyes almost gummed shut. "Did you ever know a girl as small as me who killed a rattlesnake before?"

"You know I didn't," said Esther. "All the little girls I knew in the stars would have run away, screaming." She waved her arms, softly imitating a scream: "Aaargh! Snaaake! Save me!"

Tekinit giggled, but the giggle turned into a cough that shook her until she started to cry. When it subsided, she curled against Esther and said: "I wish I'd get better."

"I wish so, too," said Esther, stroking her dirty hair.

Kiraka wailed. The wind howled, as if frustrated that it couldn't quite get to them.

"Maybe the wind will carry my cough away," croaked Tekinit.

Esther thought of all the things Mama would do, if she could take Tekinit home. She'd be tucked under an electric blanket, with a vaporizer steaming the air, in a room that didn't let in sifting sand and minuscule drops of wet. She'd have Vicks VapoRub on her chest, and take antibiotics and decongestants and cough medicine. She'd spend most of her time sleeping or watching cartoons.

Would Tekinit like cartoons?

Silika sat outside, stroking Kiraka's fuzzy head as she sang. "Little one, sleep. Don't be afraid. Your father will bring you a star from the sky, only sleep. Your mother will bring you the sun for a ball, only sleep." Esther rocked in rhythm, and sang along. Tekinit leaned against her, her mouth leaking onto Esther's blouse, the harshness of her breath mingling with the harshness of the wind. Esther's legs fell asleep. She tried to shift her muscles without moving her body.

"Here." Ahrva passed in two gourds of nasty-smelling water, then crawled in, slid an arm under Tekinit, and moved her.

"Thanks," whispered Esther, stretching her legs.

Ehdanwah built a shelter over the fire, and smoke gathered underneath, jerked back and forth by the wind. Ehdanwah and Wasitay talked in low voices and drew maps in the dirt with their strans. Thunder rumbled, and lightning flickered around the edges of the sky. "A different kind of milkweed grows on the other side of the hill," said Ehdanwah. "Who comes with me?"

In moments, Wasitay, Ehdanwah, and Silika's cousin Shimatash had gathered their things and set out, looking cold and small. "They and the men will have a miserable time, walking into this," Silika said.

Wind, and spitting rain, and coughing; food that at best was barely warm. Darkness came, and neither the men nor the milkweed gatherers returned. Emni crawled into their shelter. "Your mother says we must each think of three good things about our situation. I'll start. It's good that Nudawah isn't with us. Esster?"

"You took mine. Um—It's good that the bears and jaguars and dire wolves don't know how bad things are for us."

"Those are things that aren't bad," said Ahrva. "We need

All the little ones woke up bawling. Esther and Ahrva bent over Tekinit, trying to shield her from the rain. Silika, her hands full with Kiraka, shouted: "Get her into the lee!"

Esther and Ahrva picked Tekinit up and pressed against the wet outcrop, following it until they rounded the corner. The relief from the wind made an illusion of warmth, but the water poured down, splashed back from the rock, and oozed up from the ground. Tucking Tekinit into the most protected portion, Esther and Ahrva made themselves into her wall and ceiling.

This is still no good, thought Esther, as water dripped from their clothes and hair onto the little girl. Tekinit curled up tight against the rock, breathing in short gasps, shivering violently inside her otter skins. Telling herself she couldn't possibly get any wetter, Esther pulled off her camel blouse and draped it over Tekinit's head. Rain pelted her skin like chips of ice. Ahrva pulled off her own dress and wrapped Tekinit in it. Tekinit looked like a mound of wet skins now.

Esther, shivering all over, felt Ahrva shivering, too. A dreadful clacking noise—their teeth, banging together in their uncontrollably shaking jaws—competed with the thud of rain.

Something bulked behind them. The rain lessened. Esther turned her head. The women held up bison hide. Carrying the baby beneath her, still wailing, Emni crept in underneath, followed by the other girls. The women made a tent with all the children inside, not dry or warm, exactly, but not getting much wetter or losing much heat. Tekinit coughed violently.

"It can't last long!" shouted Silika. "Not with this wind!"

But how long is long? Esther wondered. She hugged herself, listened to teeth chatter, wind howl, thunder crash, rain drum upon the hide and beat against the rock.

At last the noises began to die out, one by one, all except the chattering of teeth and the hollow sound of Tekinit's coughing. Shusskt slipped away, draping her hide over the shoulders of the other women and cutting the size of the tent. Esther was too miserable to wonder what she was doing. When the rain slowed to a pattering, Emni gave Kiraka to Ahrva, and took Silika's place while Silika slipped away.

"It-t's g-g-good that we're near pines," stuttered Ahrva through her unruly teeth. "P-pine burns well."

"W-wet p-p-pine is still w-w-wet w-w-wood," griped Washaw.

Wahay, the Fiesta Texas T-shirt plastered to her body, lifted a corner of otter skin and peered in. The sound of harsh breathing emerged. "T-t-tekinit?"

Tekinit made a noise that might have been "Weh."

The rain stopped. A blackbird called, experimentally. A mockingbird answered. The wind tugged the edges of the hide.

Yahaywah sank to her knees, trembling, and reached for Kiraka. Washaw changed her position, eased her head out. "The sun!" she said. "Aiee!"

Esther's nose ran and her head ached, but she barely noticed in the frantic, hopeless effort to get Tekinit warm and dry. Everything in the world was soaked—all the wood that should have made a fire, all the skins that should have wrapped Tekinit. Even the waterproof otter and beaver hides had gotten splashed on the insides. They stripped Tekinit's clothes off and marched her up and down, trying to walk her dry. Tekinit's legs and arms shook so she could not hold herself up. Her body was rough with goose pimples. Ahrva took her in her lap and rubbed her.

Esther rubbed, too, till her arms ached. Tekinit's skin felt hot, and her eyes looked wide and blank. She talked when she wasn't coughing, but her voice was too hoarse and fast for Esther to understand. Far away, Esther heard Kiraka crying, and wished the baby had never been born, so Silika wouldn't have to take care of him. He must be as frozen as Tekinit, as all the rest of them; but Esther didn't care. Kiraka had never killed a rattlesnake or begged for a story. She didn't care how Kiraka felt, not when Tekinit was suffering like this!

Wahay came over, carrying the T-shirt. "This is mostly dry," she said. "Star-hide dries fast."

It was also thin after months of constant wear, but Esther pulled it over Tekinit's head gratefully. If only it covered more! Shusskt brought raw bark and other plants. "We can't light a fire to make a brew," she said, kneeling down. "Even the pine's too wet. Tekinit. Tekinit. I want you to chew this."

Tekinit gabbled something Esther didn't catch.

"The baby's fine," said Shusskt. "You must get well so you can help take care of him. Now chew. Come on. Good girl."

Tekinit took the bark, chewed once, and made a face.

"Go on," urged Ahrva. "You can do it. You're brave."

Tekinit chewed, her face screwed up. A new fit of coughing overtook her, and the bark flew out, along with a clump of snot.

I can't take this, thought Esther; but she retrieved the nasty mess, wiped off the mud and phlegm on her shorts, and coaxed Tekinit to take it back into her mouth. "Over the lips and through the gums," she said.

"Luukhat stomaach herit kahms," croaked Tekinit.

Esther had no idea what anyone else was doing, as she and Ahrva hovered over Tekinit, tried to force her to be warm, to eat, to drink mineral water that, refreshed by rain, was less nasty now, once the leaves and twigs had been strained out. She ate a little herself, when Silika prompted her to. She was vaguely aware of the attempts to start a fire, but paid them no mind till Washaw cried in triumph, "Bring her here!"

It was a small fire, and the smoke gathered beneath the hide propped up on strans to keep the wind off. The warmth was so small it would not have been warm at all, except in contrast to the icy air three feet away.

Emni and Washaw dragged Tekinit out of Esther and Ahrva's arms. "Eat!" they commanded the two girls. "You'll be warmer. You won't do her any good, wearing yourselves out."

So Esther and Ahrva walked up and down, eating cold nuts. Silika brought them their clothes, which had been in the wind all day and were nearly dry. They probably would have stunk, if Esther had had a sense of smell. "How's Kiraka?" asked Ahrva.

"I think he will do well," said Silika. "Thank you for taking care of your sister."

"But we're not taking care of her!" cried Esther, on the verge of tears. "Nothing we do helps!"

"We must keep trying," said Silika. "Ehdanwah will be back soon."

So they kept trying.

The wind died at dusk. Tekinit coughed and babbled. It took two people to force her to drink medicine when it finally brewed up, and she spilled half the contents of the shell. Silika chanted to Grandmother Turtle, to the rain mothers, to the flint fathers, to everyone she could think of. Esther, certain chanting couldn't help, chanted, too. Deep in her head she prayed, but she wasn't sure that would help either.

By now, Tekinit was too weak to either fight or swallow the medicine. Esther nearly choked her before she got the hang of pouring the stuff in. They slept and worked in relays through the night, chanting over Tekinit, willing her to be better.

The first that Esther knew of morning was the sound of howling, from the west and from the south. The women did not look up from Tekinit. Esther climbed the outcrop. From the south came the men, intact, striding through grass white with frost and carrying spears bent with the weight of meat. To the west, the missing women made one hobbling figure. In the half light Esther couldn't tell who was hurt.

The chanting straggled to a halt. Esther saw the men see her, saw Skedat wave. She did not wave back, too tired to lift her arms.

Below, Silika let out a wail like the call of a scimitar cat.

Podan dropped his end of the spear and began to run.

The returning women stopped; and then one broke from the others—Ehdanwah, running on a lame foot until she fell, screaming.

FORTY

Silika's scream stretched from one side of the sky to the other. Ahrva howled like a hurt wolf. Kiraka and Wahay wailed. Podan swooped down on Tekinit, threw back his head, and let loose a scream that silenced the birds.

No, no, no, no, no, thought Esther.

Ehdanwah was half-carried toward them, her good foot encountering the ground only to repel it with a thrust that sent her soaring ahead of her helpers. She landed on all fours by the tiny figure that hadn't coughed now in ages. She snatched up her granddaughter, bent her head to her chest, pried open her mouth. Yes! Esther thought. *Ehdanwah can fix it!*

Ehdanwah held Tekinit to her chest, rocking, as a strange, long, wheezing sound rose from the older woman; the sound of pure pain forcing itself out through the mouth and nose.

Silika snatched up her stran and slashed her arms, her face, her legs. Bright red lines tore the brown of her skin. Esther leaped up. "No! Stop her!"

Ahrva grabbed her stran and slashed her own cheeks.

Podan drew a stran across his chest.

Shusskt, Emni, and Washaw stood back, moaning like wind among rocks. The other women carried Wahay and Kiraka, screaming in rhythm with Esther's pulse, to the other end of camp. The men and boys stood with their heads bowed, the meat forgotten on the ground. Ehdanwah laid Tekinit in her lap and took up her stran.

Esther jumped off the outcrop. "Are you crazy?" she yelled, not caring if she spoke English or Spanish or what. "Stop them!" She ran toward Ahrva; but Shusskt caught her by the blouse and pulled her back. "Let me go!" Esther bellowed.

"Leave them be," snapped Shusskt.

"But—" Esther saw Shusskt's tear-wet face. "But—" Pain welled in her like water in a spring, clogging her throat, spurting through her eyes. "But Tekinit's *dead*!"

Someone thrust her stran into her hand. She smashed it against the outcrop and collapsed, wrapping herself in her own arms, rocking. Someone—probably Shusskt—closed her in another layer of arms. "Sh, sh, sh. Let the pain out. You'll feel better."

"I don't *want* to feel better!"

It was true, but it wasn't. She was sure of only two things: that Tekinit was dead, and that she wasn't going to cut herself. She could eat grasshoppers, she could butcher animals, she could blow her nose with handfuls of grass; but she *could not* cut herself and let the pain out. Not and still be Esther.

Somebody cooked the bison. Maybe somebody even ate some, Esther wasn't sure. A mourning shelter went up around the family. The others sang as they worked. "Our little sister has run ahead of us. Our little sister is dancing up in the sky. Don't look back, little sister. Run ahead, little sister. Your grandfather, he waits for you. Your cousin, he waits for you. Your grandmother's mother, she waits for you . . ."

They could have waited eighty years longer, thought Esther bitterly.

Cool, still afternoon passed into cold, still evening. Esther wanted a Kleenex.

She wanted a hospital.

She wanted her mother.

The sun went down.

Esther got up out of her body and tried to lift Tekinit, to carry her toward the pickup parked in the lee of the outcrop, but she couldn't get a grip. "Oh, no," said Dr. Durham. "I wish I'd got here sooner."

"It's too late," said Jul. "You can't save her."

"Shut up, you nasty old man!" Esther shouted; and woke.

It was not quite dawn. The mourners crouched around Tekinit's body, as quiet and still as she was. Esther crawled into the shelter, and hugged Ahrva. Tekinit looked like a wadded-up rag doll. "I'm so sorry," whispered Esther. "Te—"

"Shhh!" Ahrva clapped a hand over Esther's mouth.

The lines of dry blood where Ahrva had slashed her cheeks were dark, but her face was calm. No one made a sound as the moon sank, the sun rose, color returned to the world. Birds sang. Kitotul came to the entrance. "It's time," he said.

Podan grunted, putting his hand on Silika's shoulder.

"There's a hollow tree in the pine grove," said Emni.

"That's good," said Podan hoarsely.

Podan mixed red powder into paste, as if to paint a hunting party. Ahrva and Silika, wordless, picked up Tekinit's body and carried her to the bitter spring and washed her, singing. Esther knew she should help. Instead she cried. Emni sat by her.

"You should have cut yourself," she said. "Now the pain will make you weak. You might die."

Esther choked on a sob. "What happens now?"

"First she must be clean. Then they'll tie her arms and legs with wesk, so she'll stay curled up even when the stiffness goes. Then we'll take her to the pine grove."

"Why?"

"Because there's a hollow tree where she will fit nicely."

"So you'll leave her there? Inside the tree?"

Washaw crept up on her other side. "In the tree, the birds and bugs will take her body slowly. The coyotes won't scatter her bones. If her bones get scattered, she'll be lame in the dead place, and she'd hate that." Washaw rubbed her nose and looked at the ground. "She'll teach my brother to run. He was too little, when he died, but he'll be bigger now."

That sounded all right, not too different from burying her. But—"They didn't do that with Jul, did they? Where would they get a hollow tree big enough for him?"

"They tied him up tight and put him in the top of a tree," said Emni. "Where the branches are too weak for the bears and big cats. Next season they'll gather his bones and put them in a hollow tree, with the others that have died at the Valley, and in a few seasons, they'll all be dirt together."

Esther imagined Nudawah and Chul hoisting Jul into a tree like a bundle of meat, and wished she hadn't. Silika and Podan tied Tekinit's arms and legs in place, smoothing the T-shirt to cover her. Podan, chanting a chant that was half a moan, painted her face and hands red. He picked Tekinit up, as if afraid to wake her, and walked toward the pine grove. Silika walked behind him, Kiraka bobbing on her back, then Ahrva, then Ehdanwah, leaning on a spear shaft, her swollen ankle wrapped in strips of hide. Esther made herself follow. The rest came in no particular order, quiet, only Wahay sniffling as she carried Tekinit's branch-baby alongside her own.

Rain lilies had popped up in the sparse grass between the spring and the pines. Ahrva picked a few. Esther did the same. In wavering voices, they sang: "Run ahead, little sister. Your grandfather, he waits for you. Your cousin, he waits for you. Your grandmother's mother, she waits for you . . ."

It was dark, cold, and damp among the pines. A woodpecker rapped. The hollow tree gaped like a mouth. Podan inserted his burden, carefully smoothing the T-shirt. Silika broke Tekinit's stran in half and laid the pieces beside her. Ahrva and Esther dropped in their flowers. Wahay tucked the branch-baby into the crook of Tekinit's elbow. The plastic bracelet pressed against her cheek. Silently, they walked away, except for Ahrva and Esther. Esther leaned her forehead against the tree.

"Nobody coughs in the dead place," Ahrva said.

"I guess not," said Esther. Tears prickled behind her eyes again. "How can you cut yourself up? How can you not cry at your own sister's—" She didn't know the word for "funeral."

"It's done, now," said Ahrva. "It would be a shame to run ahead, as—as my sister has—if I could prevent it."

Esther's knees buckled. "My mother must think that I'm

dead." And she *was* dead, in her mother's time. How would she die here—illness? Eaten by a bear? Killed by her friends after a mammoth broke her back at the end of next year's Big Hunt? Or in old age, leaving behind grandchildren who would be dead centuries before her mother was born?

Raprapraprapraprap! The woodpecker worked at the pine tree, digging out bugs. Eleven thousand years from now, there would be no pines, only hills of live oak and juniper. Maybe she was in the middle of a highway, heat mirages shimmering off of the asphalt. Maybe this was one of those fancy subdivisions, perched high to gaze over "Hill Country" views. She saw the area in her head, ranches and twisting roads and little towns full of antique stores and fast-food restaurants, all traces of Tekinit and her family gone, except for the outcrop, and maybe a few scraps of stone buried beneath eleven millennia of dirt . . .

She blinked, but the air still blurred and shimmered.

Ahrva's hand tightened on her arm. Esther saw through the trees, heard drums through the rapping of the woodpecker, as the sight of her mind and the sight of her eyes came together.

The grass was yellow and singed-looking, the trench extending almost to the outcrop, which was too small. Dr. Durham rested on a pickax and talked to Mike, while Delia worked at the sifting frames, running water through a hose from the container in the back of the pickup. Drums pounded in the portable stereo.

"Is that—is that the stars?" whispered Ahrva.

"Yes," said Esther. "And that's my elder." She looked into Ahrva's face, blinking rapidly. "And I—I—"

Ahrva's face twisted. "Go! Go!" Her voice sounded shrill and wobbly, as she shoved Esther toward the trench. "You belong to the stars. Find your mother, be a doctor, but don't—"

"I think this is about as far as we can afford to run this trench," said Dr. Durham, a yard away.

"But don't forget us!"

"Never," said Esther, and ran, feeling branches slap her face, seeing heat shimmer off the bare ground. "Dr. Durham!"

The archaeologist turned, but Mike did not look up. "What the—?"

"It's me, Dr. Durham! It's Esther!"

The sun and heat struck her so hard, it was like walking through a wall. Esther looked back, and saw Ahrva, lifting a hand, face dirty with tears and blood. "Good-bye, Ahrva! Say good-bye for me!"

Then there were no pines; only a bare dirt hillside, widely spaced power lines, and a distant straggle of mobile homes.

FORTY-ONE

*D*r. Durham and Mike stared.

"Boy, am I glad to see you!" Esther stopped at the trench, scared by their expressions. If Dr. Durham didn't know her—!

"Esther Aragones?" said Dr. Durham. She still wore a globe map gimme cap, and a vest full of pockets; but she didn't look scrawny. Esther knew by now what scrawny looked like!

"Yes! Yes!" Esther realized what was wrong, and switched to English. "I'm sorry! I didn't pay attention to what language I was using."

"Where have you been?" Dr. Durham seized her by the shoulders. "What's happened to you? Where did you come from?"

Esther looked at herself. Her rattle buzzed. "Oh," she said. "I forgot how funky I look. I bet I stink, too."

"Are you okay?" demanded Dr. Durham. "You've been crying."

Esther scrubbed her cheeks. "Yeah, but—but it's all right." Tekinit was dead—and so was Ahrva—and Emni; the group, and every mammoth, scimitar cat, and short-faced bear on the planet, gone and forgotten. Her brain felt numb.

"We need to call your parents," said Dr. Durham.

Esther seized on this. "Yes! I want to talk to Mama!"

"You keep digging," Dr. Durham said to Mike. "Five more feet." She led Esther along the trench. The ground was sandier than it should be, the grass sparser. No mineral spring bubbled out of the ground. The creek was a mere ditch where juniper grew. The main excavation was neatly laid out in squares in front of the diminished outcrop. Delia watched them. Dr. Durham waved at her to go back to work.

"Have . . . have you found much?" asked Esther.

"Some Clovis and Plainview points," said Dr. Durham. "I'll show them to you, later. But first we call your parents."

Esther pointed. "You might be able to find a hearth about here; or another one on the other side there. That's what you like to find, right? A hearth with charcoal that you can send to the lab for carbon dating."

"That's right," said Dr. Durham. "I guess whatever's happened to you, you haven't suffered that much, or you wouldn't be asking questions."

Esther swallowed the pain in her chest. "I don't—I don't think I have suffered," she said, following her to the pickup. "Not compared to the others."

"What others?" Dr. Durham turned off the boom box and got a mobile phone out of a pack on the front seat.

"The people I was with," said Esther, taking the phone.

Dr. Durham looked at her oddly. "Would you like a soda?"

"Yes, please." Esther dialed her home number, not forgetting the area code, and sat on the hot pickup seat. The sun was too high; the dusty wind too hot; the steep rocky land too empty of birds and bugs. A billboard near the entrance to the site advertised homes between $80,000 and $100,000. Miles away, a phone rang, once, twice, three times. "What day is it?" she asked Dr. Durham, accepting a can of Dr Pepper that dripped melted ice onto her lap. "Mama may be at work. I'm not supposed to call her there unless it's an emergency."

"This *is* an emergency," said Dr. Durham. "Maybe—"

"Hello?" said Mama.

Her heart leaped so high in her throat she had to clear it out of the way before she could answer. "Hi, Mama!"

"Esther!" Her mother's voice went shrill and loud and joyous like a grackle in spring. "Where are you? How are you? Where have you been?"

"Um—I'm fine, but I want to come home."

"Tell me where you are. I'll get you right now!"

"I—Dr. Durham's here. She'll know."

"Dr. Durham?"

"You know, the archaeologist? She's right here."

"But what happened? Were you kidnapped? Are you hurt?"

"No, I'm *fine*," repeated Esther. "I went back in time and I kind of, got stuck, till—"

"Esther, honey, I can't hear you right. Back in *what*?"

"I was really, really lost, but I'll tell you about it when I get home." Her voice wavered. "I want to go home!"

"Of course, honey! Let me talk to Dr. Durham a minute."

Esther passed the phone and popped open the soda. The can had already numbed her hand; and the soda tasted strange, too sweet. The carbonation reached inside her nose and started it running again. She wondered if she was going to cry some more. "Ms. Aragones?" said Dr. Durham. "Sorry to spring that on you, but all I could think was that you needed to hear her voice . . . Yes, she looks"—her eyes flicked Esther up and down—"uninjured. We're outside this podunk town . . ."

Esther grabbed a tissue from the box on the dashboard and let her eyes wander as Dr. Durham gave directions. She couldn't tell if the outcrop looked too small because the wind had worn it away, or because dirt had piled up around it. The mobile homes on the horizon seemed to be part of a quarry that had sliced away big chunks of hill. The grad students did their jobs, but kept looking toward her. Esther's stomach growled. Locusts buzzed. A grasshopper whirred from the ground to her knee. She pinched its head. Only when Dr. Durham's eyes widened did she realize how peculiar this was. She folded her hands around the soda can.

Dr. Durham handed the phone back to Esther. "Listen, we've got it worked out," Mama said. "We'll be there in a couple of hours. You do whatever Dr. Durham says, okay?"

"Sure," said Esther.

"Sit tight." Mama's voice went funny again. "I love you."

"I love you, too," said Esther, as the line cut off.

Dr. Durham looked toward the trench, where Mike was a blur of blue shirt. "I don't want to make you talk about anything you're not ready to talk about," she said. "You'll have to explain things over and over for your folks and the police. But I would like to know—where did you come from? The bulldozers had squashed everything flat before we got here. There's nowhere to hide. But you surprised us."

"That's because I wasn't coming from a where," said Esther, getting a fresh tissue. "I was coming from a when."

"Which means what?"

Esther took a deep breath. "I went to Clovis time. And we camped there." She pointed, and swallowed. "A little girl, named Tekinit, she, she coughed herself to death before her grandmother could get back with medicine. So we put her in a hollow pine. Over there by the trench. I'd let her wear my bracelet. She let me wear her rattle." Esther choked.

"Why didn't you come home sooner?" asked Dr. Durham. "Two and a half months is a lot of worry to put your folks through."

"It's been more than that," said Esther, when she could. "I wanted to come home the first day, but there's this . . . shimmery area, where I could see both times; and it went away. Well, I had one chance, but I blew it. When I found the mammoth and saw you digging up the bones. But I had to tell them I'd found it, first, and then you were gone." She leaned forward. "Did you find my name in the rock shelter near the mammoth? Or my shoes?"

"I've never dug up a mammoth."

"But I saw—Oh!" A tiny spurt of relief forced its way through her other, heavier feelings. "I bet you haven't done it yet. I would have come back later, if I'd gone then!"

Mike waved. "Dr. Durham! Come here! You'll freak!"

The urgency of his voice was like a lasso thrown across the site to rope everyone in. Dr. Durham ran, Esther running after her, Delia getting a head start on both of them.

"I don't believe it," whispered Dr. Durham, staring into the trench.

Brown hunks that might be rock or bark; a round shape, too smooth for rock, still half-buried; thin bones. The half-circle of her bracelet, arcing out of the dirt, cleaned off with spit to show the dried-out stars inside.

"Tekinit," Esther whispered, and started crying again.

FORTY-TWO

*E*sther, in the backseat of the pickup with her mouth shut tight over grief, faced Delia, who smiled at her.

"I can't believe it," said Mike. "It looked so perfect. A skull, bits of bark for carbon dating, undisturbed soil—and then—plastic! It was like the winning lottery ticket burning up in my hand."

"I know," said Dr. Durham, driving, "oh, how I know! But it's worse than that. Think! Who would bury a little girl out here? This is a murder."

Esther clenched her fists and teeth, still feeling the tightness of Dr. Durham's hand around her arm. *Don't you say a word*, the archaeologist had hissed. *Not if you want to go home.* The grad students talked and talked. Esther couldn't tell what upset them more, thinking that they'd dug up a murder, or thinking that what had looked like an ancient burial had turned out to be only a few years old.

She wasn't sure what upset *her* more—that Dr. Durham wouldn't let her explain, or that they had dug up Tekinit's grave as if it were any old archaeological site. The hollow tree must have fallen, and protected Tekinit's bones till they fossilized. It seemed wrong. She was supposed to be dirt by now.

They pulled up at the Hill Breeze Motor Lodge. "Mike," said Dr. Durham, "you found it, so you deal with the police."

"Shoot," said Mike. "We should have called on the cell!"

"We should have," said Dr. Durham. "But our heads weren't in the right place. First Esther, and now this!"

"They'll want to talk to her, too," said Delia.

"I don't want her bothered till she's cleaned up and had a decent meal."

Mike picked up the phone. Dr. Durham hustled Esther into a dingy, too-cool motel room.

As soon as the door closed, Esther burst out with: "What do you mean, if I talk I can't go home? You can't keep me!"

"I can't, but the police can." Dr. Durham sank onto the edge of a saggy double bed. "Come here and let me explain."

Esther approached, but didn't sit down.

"I don't know," said Dr. Durham, slowly, "how that bracelet got into the ground, or where you've been."

"I *told* you!" protested Esther. "I'm not a liar!"

"I don't think you are," said Dr. Durham. "But what you say is impossible, all the same."

"But it's true!"

"Prove it. Show me one of these shimmery areas. Let me walk through it."

"I can't! I don't know how they work." She crossed her arms. "But that doesn't make me a liar!"

"No," agreed Dr. Durham. "But if you can't prove that you went back in time, people will look for other explanations."

"But I can prove it. That was Tekinit's grave. When Mike found her, I'd already said Tekinit had my bracelet!"

"Maybe you're trying to cover up knowledge about how the body and the bracelet got there."

"I wouldn't do that!"

"But it's easier to believe that you would than it is to believe you went back to the days of the mammoth."

Esther was tired of crying. And there was something wrong about Dr. Durham's reaction. Esther was not only saying unbelievable things, she wasn't saying them coherently—but Dr. Durham understood her. Maybe—"What did the old lady look like, in your dreams?"

Dr. Durham looked past her. "What—what old lady?"

"Pezha. The one who told you I wasn't in the stars anymore. The one who told you the Pleistocene and Holocene touched." Dr. Durham didn't answer, but Esther saw that she'd guessed right. "What did you mean, the Pleistocene and Holocene are the same?"

"The Holocene is a handy way to refer to the time since the Ice Age ended. If the Ice Age isn't ended—if we're just in a warm period inside it—then it isn't a real age on its own. You must have read that in one of your books." She said all this rapidly and flatly, not looking at Esther.

"What about Jul?" Esther pressed. "A lame old man with a long nose? Or is he not lame in the dream-place?"

"I've dreamed about him my whole life." Dr. Durham hugged herself. "Not evidence."

"You must have seen Ahrva and me. You looked straight at us. And last night, you dreamed of us. Me and Tekinit. You said you wished—"

"—I'd got there sooner," she whispered. "*Dreams aren't evidence.* And today—working in the hot sun, bending over and straightening up all the time, I got dizzy. My sight was confused. What I saw—what I thought I might have seen—doesn't prove anything to me, much less anyone else."

"Then tell me what would!"

Dr. Durham spread her hands. "We can't test the hypothesis that you went back in time, to prove it one way or another. If we can't test a hypothesis, it's irrelevant. We'll never *know.*"

"What if you find the mammoth where I say it is?" asked Esther. "What if you find my sneakers, or my name in the rock shelter? What if you find the hearths where I say they were?"

"What if I don't?" asked Dr. Durham. "Lots of hearths don't leave a trace a hundred years later, much less eleven thousand. Not finding it won't prove anything; and finding it might have been a lucky guess. I admit, if I ever run across a mammoth near a rock shelter with the name 'Esther' carved in it, I'll have to think real hard. But if I go around believing in time travel, I'll never have a chance to dig a mammoth, because no one will hire me to dig. Could you lead me to that mammoth?"

"I'm . . . not sure."

"I don't know what you've been through, and I sure don't want to make things worse. When you disappeared, I was— criminy! You'd never have been running around in those hills if you hadn't been attracted by the dig. So whatever happened to you, it was my fault."

"Oh, it was not," said Esther. "But this *stinks.* Mama and Dad and Danny will probably think I'm crazy. And it's not right to not talk about the group, as if they'd never been here!"

"Well," said Dr. Durham, "I couldn't publish what you say, but I could record you. Maybe I'll think of a way to test your story. And I"—she touched Esther's skin blouse—"I *want* to hear. But you should clean up and have some supper first. I don't want your mother to see you like this."

Esther had a long shower, scrubbing until her hair squeaked and her skin was raw and the water ran cold. The dirt on the soles of her feet had sunk deep into the cracks of her skin, and she finally gave up on trying to clean them. Her tired, grief-stricken brain kept turning over the facts, desperate for the evidence that would make Dr. Durham, at least, understand the truth. Had Jul really been visiting Dr. Durham's dreams her whole life? Had he caused all this, created the time gates himself?

This is all his fault.

Not fair. Maybe he'd made the gates, or held them open, or something; but Esther had chosen to walk through.

When she came out, Dr. Durham said, "The police were here. I persuaded them to look at the site with Mike and Delia first. I don't want them talking to you without your parents. But I want you to think hard about what you want to tell them. Here, these clothes should fit you if we belt them tight."

The T-shirt and shorts looked beautifully clean and soft, but Esther hesitated to touch them. "Um—I have bugs. I washed as hard as I could, but I doubt I got all of them."

"I know, but you can't go to dinner in a towel," said Dr. Durham, glancing at the chair where Esther had piled her clothes. What if she had extinct bugs in her hair and seams? Esther wondered. Could you tell an American camel from a modern camel by the skin? Maybe there *were* ways to test the time travel hypothesis!

Dressed in too-big clothes and bedroom slippers, Esther crossed the parking lot to the diner behind Dr. Durham. As soon as she walked through the glass door, into air-conditioning and the smell of hot fat, Esther's neglected stomach roared to life. She ordered chicken-fried steak, green salad with ranch dressing, applesauce, mashed potatoes, green beans, Texas toast, peach pie, and milk, then had seconds on everything, making the waitress—a woman who seemed too tall, too fat, and too pale—stare. Compared to the amount of mammoth meat she could eat in a sitting, this wasn't so much. But this food wouldn't spoil, or be stolen by scavengers. She made herself stop at seconds.

Back in the room, Esther sat on the shaky bed. Dr. Durham plugged in a tape recorder. "You don't *have* to tell me anything," she said. "Once it's on tape, you may not be able to control who hears it."

"If I don't talk about it, nobody can prove it."

Dr. Durham pressed the record button and told the microphone the date, the place, and their names. Passing the microphone to Esther, she said: "Tell me your story."

Esther talked, as the world beyond the room grew dimmer, as her parents drove through the Hill Country, as the air conditioner hummed. Dr. Durham asked about being yana, about clothes, strans, the Valley. She marked a map with question marks and circles. Her eyes would light up, her voice would get eager, and then she would remember not to believe.

She brought out a box of bagged stone tools, asking Esther to identify them. Some were arrowheads—"We didn't have arrows," Esther said. "But this was from a stran, and this was for chopping, and this"—her heart fluttered as she pulled out a broken butterscotch-colored flint—"I think...This is *my* stran! See how it's lopsided? I couldn't get it even."

"That's a Plainview point," said Dr. Durham. "Just like Clovis, but without the channel flake."

"I'd have broken it if I'd tried to do that," said Esther. The tape clicked off, out of space. "Eleven thousand years ago. I made this. I know it sounds crazy, but it's true."

"I wish it could be," said Dr. Durham, flipping the tape.

"You're part of it, you know," said Esther. "Three doors through time, and you were digging near all of them. It's something to do with dreams, with Jul walking through dreams looking for the answer to what killed the megafauna—and you, and me, trying to see into the past so hard, and—it could have happened to you."

Dr. Durham shook her head, watching herself snap the lid of the tape compartment closed, as if she might do it wrong.

"I wish it had!" Esther burst out. "I was so *useless*! Everybody said I had wazicat—power—but I didn't."

Dr. Durham's hand hovered over the record button. "I couldn't eat a grasshopper."

Esther rubbed her full belly. "Sure you could! Tekinit used to crunch them up raw."

"You talk about everybody else as if they were still here," said Dr. Durham. "Tekinit you talk about in the past tense."

"I told you. She died. This morning. I mean—"

The air conditioner roared under her silence.

"You mean, they're all dead," said Dr. Durham, gently. "Death stinks. But you can adjust. That's your power. You adapted to a strange place with strange people, without losing who you were; and now, you'll adapt to home. No matter how hard we are on you."

"But I could never *do* anything for them!"

"You found the mammoth," said Dr. Durham. "You taught them the Heimlich maneuver. You took the curse off of your friends. And you make them sound real to me. I can't afford to believe, but—that's all we can do for the dead. Remember them, and understand them, as well as we can."

Esther looked at all that was left of the group—stone tools, bagged and labeled, spread across a chenille bedspread; the rattle from her hair; the camel blouse made by yana women. "Maybe Ahrva's great-great-grandchildren invented the arrow," she said. "Maybe Kiraka found a new way to hunt bison."

"Maybe Ahrva's two-hundred-times great-granddaughter married someone named Aragones."

For the first time that day, Esther felt right. They had lived; and she was alive; and someday, her two-hundred-times great-grandchildren would live, hardly wondering about her.

It was fair.

➤ AUTHOR'S NOTE

➤ SO HOW MUCH DID I MAKE UP?

The shining perfect Paleo-Indian story that appeared full-blown in my head several years ago would have been written based on a topographical map of the Balcones Escarpment as it was in the Pleistocene. I would have hiked every inch of the modern terrain myself, carrying bags of rocks and wearing an odometer. The book's weather would have precisely reflected the late Pleistocene changes in the area. Every plant and animal mentioned would have been one that is present in the fossil record, and every interesting extinct animal would have had a part in the plot. The language would have been back-engineered from existing American languages.

Sorry, I couldn't write the shining perfect story that was in my head.

I'm not a geologist, a meteorologist, a linguist, an archaeologist, or much of a hiker. Even if I had been, much of this data isn't available; or at least, I couldn't find it. I have read books, scholarly journals, and site reports; visited archaeological sites; talked to archaeologists; read more books, journals, and site reports; sent out queries on the Internet; and read more books, journals, and site reports. I could have read, visited, queried, and talked for another seven years, and still not quite had everything I wanted. Sometimes, you have to decide to run with what you've got, or stand still forevermore.

Those of you who already know something about the earliest Americans will have noticed that this novel avoids the biggest questions: When did they get here and how did they arrive?

Humans came to America in waves, mostly from Asia, at various times during the last thirty thousand years or less. The traditional view has been that they walked over the Bering Land Bridge into what's now Alaska during maximum glaciation, then walked south between the glaciers when they started to melt about thirteen thousand years ago. However, we know that people colonized Australia with boats forty thousand years ago, and artifacts have been found in South America dating to about the time the "ice-free corridor" would have been just opening up, so it's probable that the first Americans followed the coastline around the glaciers in small boats, making landfall in places that are underwater today. Genetic evidence even suggests that they might have been here before the ice came; but archaeological evidence for that is scanty. Someone could be dredging up a site, right now, that will reveal some new and startling fact that will change all our ideas about the peopling of the Americas.

So I dodged the question. My story takes place at the end of the Pleistocene. Even those who think humans are very recent additions to the Americas allow about five hundred years before my story takes place. Do you know anything about what your ancestors were doing five hundred years ago? I sure don't!

For the purposes of my story, it doesn't matter where Uduban's group's ancestors came from. They didn't know themselves.

Which brings us to the other question I dodged: Why did the megafauna (big animals) go extinct?

Was it because the climate and vegetation changed? That makes sense, because in modern times destruction of habitat is usually the single most important factor when a species becomes endangered. Except—every animal that went extinct at the end of the Ice Age had survived more than one major climate change before. Something was different this time, but what?

Was it because these animals, having evolved in the absence of people, were not afraid of humans and were too easy to hunt, so that the Clovis people accidentally hunted them to death? That makes sense, because we know people are responsible for many extinctions today, and some of the biggest animals to survive (grizzly bears and elk) came from Asia. Except—agriculture, industrialization, and population density are what make us so dangerous to other species today. At the end of the Ice Age, humans were just another animal in the landscape. Sure, there's evidence of them killing entire bison herds by running them off of cliffs, but the bison, which were hunted intensively, changed their form instead of going extinct; while the tiny pronghorn *capromeryx*, which may never have been hunted at all, went extinct with the big animals. We know of cases of hunter-gatherer populations hunting animals, such as the giant moa bird of New Zealand, to extinction, but those were small populations of animals confined to islands, not large, diverse populations of animals spread across continents. The overkill theory has major problems.

Did some widespread and virulent disease arise, spreading from species to species—possibly one that evolved in Asia, so that the invasive species were immune and the native species were not? Certainly this is possible. Good luck proving it! And why would such a disease destroy so many big animals and so few small ones?

The more I find out about the megafaunal extinction, the less sense it makes; which must mean there's still something we're missing. Why did the long-legged Dagget's eagle go extinct, but not the golden eagle that was about the same size? Why did the short-faced bear, the cheetah, and the lion, creatures adapted for running down prey in the open, die out when the prairies were expanding and the woods were shrinking? Why did flamingos die out in Oregon but not in Florida? If large animals were more vulnerable to the extinction factor, why did a small jay and a tiny pronghorn die out, when the condor and a larger pronghorn survived?

Nobody knows today, and I'd be surprised if anyone did back then. So I left my Clovis people puzzling over it like the rest of us, and got on with the story.

Some questions I couldn't dodge. You may have heard rumors that the oldest human bones found in America belonged to a white person, but this is a distortion of the facts. *You can't tell skin or hair or eye color from looking at bones.*

The concept of "race" is a modern one which exaggerates the importance of trivial characteristics. The existing evidence suggests to me that modern "races" didn't exist yet at the end of the Pleistocene. For all we know, the first human being to come to North America had black skin, green eyes, and red hair.

Documentation exists of a few blond-headed "Indians" (specifically in the Mandan tribe); maybe they were descended from blond Ice Age Asians, or maybe they were descended from medieval Europeans who "discovered" America long before Columbus arrived and left unsatisfactory written records of the fact.

We don't know. Only the modern history of intolerance based on surface features makes us care. The "racial" features that show in bones—length of face in proportion to width, size of jaw and nose, depth of skull—aren't ones that a modern American child like Esther is used to noticing. I gave Uduban's group brownish skin and black hair because we know that most of the Americans who were here when modern record-keeping began had brownish skin and black hair. It makes sense to assume that most of their ancestors looked more or less similar; and since I want to believe that my Clovis people had modern descendants and could be Esther's ancestors, I made them look like her.

My major concern was the lifeway of the Clovis people, the day-to-day details of what they did, how they acted, how they thought. If I did not show this in great detail, the story was pointless—and the only thing we know for certain about the Clovis is that they left few traces on the land. A point here, a pile of butchered bones there, a hand-dug well in New Mexico, a few bone tools. No burials. No heaps of garbage. No hearths that were returned to year after year after year. Something about the way the Clovis people lived caused this dearth of archaeological sites, and I had to decide what it was and show it in operation in order to portray them convincingly.

Do you know why the sign at the national park asks you to "Take nothing but pictures, leave nothing but footprints"? Yes, the rangers want the park to stay nice for the next batch of tourists; but they also don't want the bears, mountain lions, wolves, coyotes, and other predators eating your garbage and associating people with food. If predators associate people with food, they eat people.

Clovis people had no park rangers, no tranquilizer guns or high-powered rifles or pepper spray or even camper-trailers. Wouldn't they be a thousand times more careful than the most conscientious modern camper?

That's how I wrote this story. First, I found out every fact I could about Clovis people. When I ran out of Clovis data, I looked at the much more abundant data on human and animal behavior in historic times, and reasoned backward. I asked myself, *What do people want? What do they need? What problems do they have to solve? What logical, normal human behavior results in the sorts of traces Clovis people left behind?* Thus, most of the story is educated guesses.

When in doubt, I decided in favor of my story. It's possible that Clovis people only hunted mammoths once a year, or once a lifetime, maybe as an initiation ritual when a boy became a man. But I knew that modern readers would be dissatisfied if the mammoths weren't prominently featured; so Uduban's group hunts mammoths routinely. I knew that the weather changed dramatically at the end of the Ice Age (ironically, as modern humans are finding out, global warming means colder winters as well as hotter summers), but I don't know for a fact that the famous Texas "blue norther" didn't occur before then. I just thought the event would be more dramatic if Esther was the only one who could anticipate it.

Most hunter-gatherer bands contain about thirty people. My groups are smaller so I didn't have to cope with as many characters. Hunter-gatherers tend to come together with other groups once or twice a year when a particular resource is abundant. Usually this is a plant resource, but I wanted a big mammoth hunt, which required a big mammoth herd. Modern animals make huge herds when a food resource is abundant; so I invented "mammoth reed." Accuracy is good, but the story comes first.

Clovis points are named after the town of Clovis, New Mexico, where these distinctive tools were found with mammoth bones on a seasonal creek called Blackwater Draw. Since that important find in 1932, Clovis artifacts have turned up all over North America. Is it logical to assume that the Clovis people in Texas lived the same way as the Clovis people in Georgia, New Mexico, Chihuahua, Pennsylvania, and California? It would surprise me if all of my educated guesses turned out to be true about one group of Clovis people; but maybe the clothes I put on Ahrva were worn by expert fishermen in Connecticut. Maybe the people of the Balcones Escarpment carried skin tents around, but the people of the Mississippi Valley built brush shelters. Maybe I'm wrong about where and how different groups came together, but I'm right about how they decorated their clothes. Maybe some of the words I invented (sometimes based on animal sounds, sometimes on modern words, sometimes on staring into space until a sound formed between my ears) are sort of approximately similar to Clovis words, but Ahrva really meant "the icicles that form on the end of your nose in winter."

Or maybe I'm entirely wrong. Maybe Clovis people divided into only two cultures—a High Plains big-game hunting culture and a culture that covered huge amounts of territory in birch-bark canoes along the river networks. Maybe mammoths were hunted with nets and trip lines as well as spears, once in a lifetime. I picked a model and ran with it. Other interpretations of the data could be turned into other stories. I hope they are. I'd like to read some.

The most important things about humans are biodegradable, but universal. All human societies tell stories, sing songs, and create art. All human societies strive to understand the world and their own place in it. All human beings need to eat and sleep, protect themselves from the weather, and learn how to cope with the society they live in. People everywhere, at every time, are vulnerable to disease and physical dangers, whether dire wolves or drunk drivers, and give health care a high priority. In every time and place, most people get along as best they can, trying to survive as pleasantly as possible.

What am I good at? What am I good *for*? Who do I love? Who loves me? How should I behave?

Those are the questions that all people have to answer for themselves, in every age, under every circumstance.

Those are the questions that make stories.

A complete list of the books, articles, and sites I consulted would go on for pages and not be useful anyway, because a lot of my reading was done in obscure journals only available in universities. Some of the books I consulted frequently, which might be in public libraries, are listed below, followed by some sample websites.

BOOKS

Boldurian, Anthony T., and John L. Cotter. *Clovis Revisited: New Perspectives on Paleoindian Adaptations from Blackwater Draw, New Mexico.* University Museum Monograph No. 103, 1999. This should not be the first book you read, since the authors are writing primarily for other paleontologists, but all the pictures of artifacts, particularly of different attempts to figure out how a "stran" went together, along-side discussions of what the surviving tools tell us about how people lived, were extremely helpful to me.

Fagan, Brian M. *The Great Journey: The Peopling of Ancient America*, New York: Thames and Hudson, Inc., 1987. This book explains the "Overkill Hypothesis" in detail, but does not have the benefit of some intriguing archaeology done in the 1990s. I have not seen a more recent edition.

Hester, Thomas R. *Digging into South Texas Prehistory: A Guide for Amateur Archaeologists.* San Antonio: Corona Publishing Company, 1980. The contributions of amateur archaeologists to our knowledge of Paleo-Indians are incalculable. If you want to dig, find this book.

Johnson, Eileen, ed. *Lubbock Lake: Late Quaternary Studies on the Southern High Plains.* Texas A&M University Press, 1987. A massive site report, only for the very serious.

Kelly, Robert L. *The Foraging Spectrum: Diversity in Hunter-Gatherer Lifeways.* Smithsonian Institute Press, 1995. Everything I wanted to know about hunter-gatherers, but was wearing myself out trying to distill from hundreds of specific reports. Thanks to Chad Ryan Thomas on the world-building list for recommending this.

Kindscher, Kelly. *Edible Wild Plants of the Prairie.* University Press of Kansas, 1987.

Kindscher, Kelly. *Medicinal Wild Plants of the Prairie.* University Press of Kansas, 1992. Only two of the many field guides on plants and animals that I kept stacked on my desk and referred to continually.

Koppel, Tom. *Lost World: Rewriting the History of the First Americans.* New York: Atria Books, 2003. A friend of mine who works at a certain prestigious magazine sent me the review copy that the publisher had sent to the magazine . . . after I was substantially done with my story. Fortunately, this is about the peopling of the Americas, a topic I deliberately avoided in the story. If you want to write a Paleo-Indian book set in Alaska, Canada, or the Pacific Northwest, this is a good starting point.

Kurten, Bjorn. *Before the Indians.* New York: Columbia University Press, 1988. An illustrated overview of the flora and fauna of the North American continent in the long millennia before humans arrived. This is the book that started me on this road, and the one Esther is reading at breakfast in Chapter Two.

Lauber, Patricia. *Who Came First? New Clues to Prehistoric Americans.* Washington, D.C.: National Geographic, 2003. Intended for fifth through eighth grades, this overview of early American archaeology has color pictures and discusses the complex issues involved in nice, bite-sized chunks.

Lister, Adrian, and Paul Bahn. *Mammoths.* Alexandria, Virginia: Time-Life Books, 1994/Marshall Books, 2000. This book is mostly concerned with woolly mammoths and not the Columbian mammoths that Esther encountered, because we have more information on woolly mammoths than on most Ice Age mammals, but it's a good starting point.

Moss, Cynthia. *Elephant Memories: Thirteen Years in the Life of an Elephant Family.* William Morrow and Co., Inc., 1988. Nobody knows how mammoths behaved, but modern African elephants are well studied, and often used to extrapolate mammoth behavior.

Pielou, E. C. *After the Ice Age: The Return of Life to Glaciated North America.* The University of Chicago Press, 1991. Mostly about Canada and the northern States, but with wide-ranging implications for what animals lived where.

WEBSITES

Center for the Study of the First Americans at Texas A&M University: *http://www.centerfirstamericans.com/*

Eastern New Mexico University, presently responsible for the Blackwater Draw site:
http://www.enmu.edu/academics/excellence/museums/blackwater-draw/site/index.shtml

A Web exhibit concerning the Midwest in the Ice Age: *http://museum.state.il.us/exhibits/larson/content.html*

Megafauna: A List of Remarkable Prehistoric Mammals—a quick reference for how things looked: *http://www.kokogiak.com/megafauna/*

The Lubbock Lake Site, one of the most important in the United States, is open to the public and has a lovely interpretive center. Good nature walk, too.
http://www.depts.ttu.edu/museumttu/lll/about.html

➤ ACKNOWLEDGMENTS

Long lists of names are meaningless to the reader and poor recompense for the patience and generosity of the individuals who help an author with massive research projects like this one. All the same, I have to thank:

- Joanna Dickenson, Site Curator at Blackwater Draw, who gave up most of a day of her valuable time to me, and didn't turn a hair when I broke her atlatl;

- Matt Hillsman, Curator of the Blackwater Draw Museum (which is shaped like a Clovis point with an impact fracture), without whom I might never have made it to the site;

- My bosses at Eckmann, Groll, Inc., who didn't fire me when I insisted I had to cut my work hours to research this book;

- Bennetta Schmidt, who advised me on geology by e-mail and then vanished;

- Cynthia Leitich-Smith, who read Version 1;

- My husband, Damon Griffin, who not only read Version 2, but listened to me talk obsessively about the Pleistocene for months on end; and

- Susan Van Metre, who wouldn't take "But it's not finished!" for an answer.

These people have prevented me from making huge mistakes that would have haunted me forever. The mistakes that remain exist solely due to my brain's incapacity to hold, comprehend, and correlate all the data I needed in order to write this story.

Ahrva: Sky. Eleven-year old who befriends Esther. Tekinit and Kiraka's big sister, Podan and Silika's daughter.

Aiee: Exclamation of approval.

Apuk: Cattail tops, gathered in summer. Silika's little sister.

Bedabat: *Panthera atrox*, American lion. Leader of one of the groups.

Bzzna: Hornet. Geshwaw and Silika's cousin who joins the group with his wife Shimatash.

Chipay: Mulberries.

Chul: Red wolf. Nudawah's nephew.

Dul: Dire wolf. Cousin of Uduban and Podan, husband of Mingwah, father of Otala.

Ehdanwah: Turtle. Matriarch of the group, mother of Podan and Uduban, aunt of Dul and Kitotul.

Emni: Water. Washaw and Skedat's big sister, Shusskt and Kitotul's daughter.

Eskway: The core of a young cattail shoot, gathered in spring.

Geshwaw: Leopard frog. Silika's brother.

Gronkha: *Cironis maltha,* an extinct stork that passes through central Texas in the summer 'cause I say it does.

Harat: Jaguar.

Helad: Cardinal.

Hunumand: Great horned owl. Cousin of the man Kitotul's father killed.

Jul: Gray wolf. Nudawah's father, a senior man, dream-walker, and retired hunter; the oldest man in all the known groups.

Khenupadna: Good-bye (walk in sunshine).

Kiraka: Toad. New baby born to Silika during the course of the story.

Kitotul: Coyote. Shusskt's husband, Ehdanwah's nephew, father to Emni, Skedat, and Washaw.

Kordak: Daggett's eagle. *Wetmoregyps daggetti,* a bird with a body the size of a golden eagle and long legs. Extinct. Similar to modern great black hawk. Geshwaw and Yahaywah's oldest child.

Kru: Sorry.

Mingwah: Grapes. Wife of Dul, mother of Otala.

Neerup: Bullfrog.

Nepi: The period during which the group sleeps.

Nuaah: Resigned compliance, the equivalent of "oh, all right."

Nudawah: Terrapin. Wife of Uduban, mother of Telabat.

Nuga: Prairie turnips.

Numb-berries: Chokecherries.

Oheitika: Skilled in hunting and high in prestige.

Oong-KA-choonk: Territorial call of the American bittern, aka thunderpumper. This is a shy bird with excellent disguise skill, so Esther never actually sees one.

Oosha: Snow.

Otala: Gayfeather. Mingwah and Dul's daughter.

Petwa: Bison.

Pezha: Mint.

Pfft: Food.

Podan: Black bear. Ehdanwah's youngest son, Ahrva and Tekinit's father, Silika's husband.

Raak: Ice.

Raak-han: Hail.

Sa: A skeptical, reproving sound, something like "oh, yeah."

Scrunsh: Scrunch. The group's best pronunciation of name Esther gives them for her hair scrunch.

Shimatash: Bluebonnet. Wife of Bzzna.

Shuha: Drat.

Shuss: Shoes. The group's best pronunciation of name Esther gives them for her sneakers.

Shusskt: Plum. Mother of Emni, Skedat, and Washaw, wife of Kitotul.

Silika: Strawberries. Wife of Podan, mother of Ahrva, Tekinit, and Kiraka.

Skedat: Panther, mountain lion, cougar, whatever you want to call this big cat. Shusskt and Kitotul's son, Emni and Washaw's brother.

Stickyflower: Curly-top gumweed.

Stran: A stone point fastened to a wooden or bone handle, short for men (spear foreshafts), long for women (digging sticks), even shorter to use as a knife. The Swiss Army knife of the group.

Sulip: Mountain mint. Its dried leaves make a hot drink consumed as we might drink tea or hot chocolate, to get comfortable on cold, wet days.

Sulira: Gooseberries.

Tekinit: Finch. Five-year old sister of Ahrva and Kiraka, daughter of Podan and Silika.

Telabat: Scimitar cat. Nudawah and Uduban's sole surviving son.

Telapa: Mammoth.

Thune: Spear shaft.

Tilat: Grasshopper.

Tookam: Wimp, nerd, weenie.

Tsik: Bunch of nut trees.

Uduban: *Arctorus simus*, short-faced, long-legged bear. Oldest son of Ehdanwah, husband of Nudawah, father of Telabat.

Wahay: Witch hazel. The leaves and bark can be made into an ointment that is good for muscle ailments, such as Podan's sprain. Name of Yahaywah and Geshwaw's second child.

Washaw: Rose hips. Younger daughter of Kitotul and Shusskt, little sister to Emni and Skedat.

Wasitay: Firefly. Mother of Silika.

Wazicat: Magic, power, luck.

Weh: Good, okay, yes.

Wesk: Sinew.

Yahaywah: Sweet grass. Podan's sister, Silika's friend.

Yana: Menstruation. Yana women are crackling with life-making magic, and considered dangerous for the men to get too close to.

Zulotul: Cattail root, gathered year round.

*P*eni R. Griffin says, "To research this book I read, visited archaeological sites, and pestered archaeologists with questions until I could look down through a page and see the Pleistocene on the other side." Two of Ms. Griffin's previous books have been nominated for Edgar Awards, one was named a finalist for the Golden Spur Award of the Western Writers of America, and one, *The Ghost Sitter,* won the William Allen White Award. Ms. Griffin lives with her husband and two cats in San Antonio, Texas. Her Web site is *www.txdirect.net/~griffin.*

The text of this book is set in Figural Book. Typeface designer
Michael Gills created the Figural typeface family in 1992, for
the Letraset Corporation under the guidance of Colin Brignall,
Art Director.

Keep reading! If you liked this book, check out these other titles.

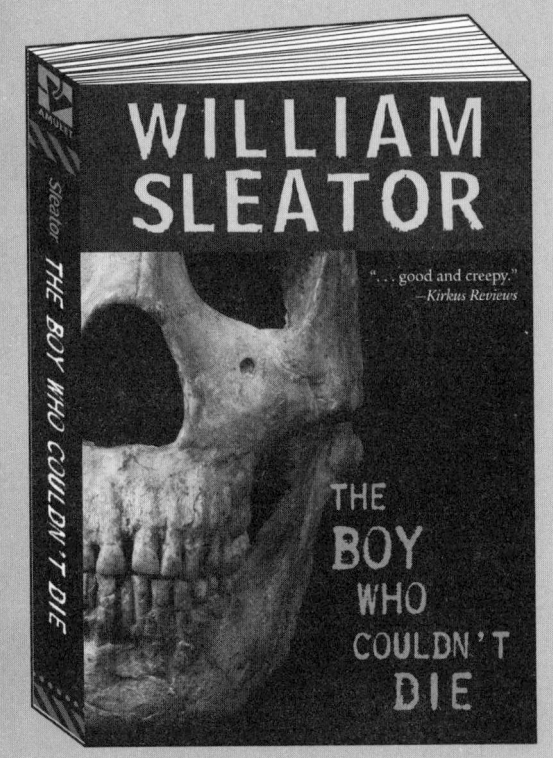